I0524904

HOLE
A SMALL TOWN HORROR NOVEL

MATTHEW DOGGETT

FIVE BROTHERS PUBLISHING

CONTENTS

A NOTE FROM THE AUTHOR

My name is Matt and I wrote the book you're about to read. I also wrote a bunch of short horror stories. And you can get five of them for free by signing up for my email list at MatthewDog gettAuthor.com/Horror

I only email a couple of times a month and give a bunch of awesome perks to my subscribers. Hope to see you in cyberspace!

Now, on with the story.

1904

Henry Hickman stopped just outside the cave entrance, peering into the darkness, breathing heavily. A breeze stirred the leaves and pine needles adorning the trees around the cave. He paid no mind to the chirping birds or the distant bark of a dog. The dappled sun was warm on the back of his neck, but he shivered at the thought of the task ahead.

Hickman's arms were loaded with sticks of dynamite, and he had a tin can full of blasting caps in the pocket of his trousers. A box of matches sat snugly in the breast pocket of his flannel shirt. He let out an involuntary whimper as he forced himself to continue, stepping into the cool cavern.

Hustling deep into the cave, Hickman passed the lanterns he'd set on the ground or on rock shelves in preparation for the day's work. But as he came to the last lantern in line, he shifted the loose dynamite in his arms and leaned down to grab the lantern off the ground. A single stick of dynamite tumbled from his arm and fell into one of the many small crevices here at the back of the cave, disappearing into the impenetrable darkness.

He didn't pay it much mind. There was nothing he could do about it, anyway. And he figured he still had plenty of dynamite to do the job.

Hickman slowed as he approached the wide chasm he'd uncovered the day before. As he stepped to the edge, he held the lantern out and peered down. "Our Father, who art in heaven," he muttered through cracked lips. "Hallowed be thy name."

Leaning further and crouching slightly, he stared into the gloom. He thought he could see the *thing*, shrouded in darkness, the light barely reaching it. "Thy kingdom come, thy will be done, on earth as it is in heaven."

As the light touched it, Hickman jerked back from the hole. Skipping toward the end of the Lord's Prayer, he said, "Lead us not into temptation, but deliver us from evil."

Several feet back from the edge of the ragged hole in the cave floor, he got to his knees, dropping the sticks of dynamite to the rough, rocky ground. He pulled the can of blasting caps out of his pocket and opened it up, grabbing one of the simple devices. Each cap was composed of a fuse and a metal cylinder with mercury fulminate and potassium chlorate inside. When the fuse burned down to the cylinder, it would cause a small explosion, which would then ignite the dynamite. He stuck the metal cylinder into the end of one stick of dynamite.

Then he repeated the process with two more caps and two more sticks.

He put all three sticks in the same hole at the side of the tunnel. Then shoved two more sticks next to them, confident they would explode even without blasting caps.

"Deliver us from evil," he said, fumbling the box of matches out of his pocket. He pulled a match out and held it against the strike pad. "Deliver us from evil."

His hands shook so badly, and he was breathing so heavily, he accidentally snuffed the first match out. But the second one flared. Hickman shut his mouth to breathe through his nose as he brought the flame up to the fuses, which he had positioned so their ends were close together.

Angry orange sparks shot out from two of the fuses as he touched the match to them. He dropped the match and the entire box and turned to run, tripping over the lantern he'd set on the floor.

He scrambled up, moving quicker than he ever had in his life.

As he reached the mouth of the cave, the dynamite exploded, shaking the earth as if God himself had made it so.

Hickman jumped down onto the ground and covered his head, but there was no need. The only thing that came out of the cave was a wave of dusty air.

Hickman got to his feet and looked at the cave mouth.

He would never go in there again. In fact, he planned to seal it. Maybe with barbed wire. He didn't want his kids going in there. He didn't want *anyone* going in there.

Hickman knew without even a moment of contemplation that he wouldn't tell anyone what he'd seen in there. Not even his wife.

No one would believe him.

He hardly believed it himself.

PRESENT DAY

A fine mist peppered the kitchen window with moisture as the man held the grimy water glass under the kitchen tap. The rushing whirr of the water as it filled the glass seemed loud in the cavernous kitchen. It *was* loud. *Everything* was loud.

The man turned off the tap and lifted the glass toward his lips. It was dark outside, and the man had only flipped one of the three switches that turned on the different sets of kitchen lights. As a result, he was backlit in the picture window's reflection, a shock of white hair sticking up from his pale head. Only his outline was visible, the rest of him—the core of him—cloaked in darkness.

He could see the little black and blue squares on his long-sleeved shirt. He could barely see the liver spots on the back of his hand. He looked into the dark oval that was his face, but he couldn't see his eyes.

The glass in his right hand hadn't been cleaned in several days. Its interior was coated with a dark haze that made the water inside look dirty. He put the cool rim to his lips and drank deeply.

His Adam's apple bounced underneath loose, gray-stubble-coated flesh as he swallowed, the sound almost as loud in the large kitchen as the filling of the glass had been.

When the last of the water was in his mouth, he pulled the glass away and swallowed, pulling in a breath like a man who's just come close to drowning.

He swallowed again, although there was no need.

He swallowed again.

And again.

He set the glass down on the tile countertop with a shaking hand.

And he swallowed once more.

The man leaned over the sink and tried to collect his thoughts. It wasn't easy.

He remembered the girl. She'd just shown up—how long ago now? He couldn't remember.

She'd just shown up, standing on his porch. She hadn't even knocked. He wasn't sure how he'd known she was there. But when he opened the door, she was looking up at him with her wide hazel eyes. And she'd presented her hand.

The man looked back into the window, at the center of his face. This time he thought he could see something there, in the darkness. But he didn't recognize it.

He swallowed and then cleared his throat.

Then he turned and walked out of the kitchen, his steps close, the soles of his shoes barely leaving the floor. He passed through the mudroom without turning the light on, moving past the cold drier and the dry washer. Past the deep single-basin sink he used to wash his hands when they got particularly dirty from working outdoors or in the shop. Past the cabinets with wooden doors hiding cleaning supplies and detergent and candles and flashlights and batteries.

He opened the door to the garage and stepped inside. The automatic light came on, providing dim illumination to the space. His two vehicles hunkered silently, sleepily. He moved to his workbench and selected a hacksaw from the pegboard there.

Hacksaw in his right hand, he moved back into the house, through the mudroom, past the kitchen, and out the back door. The mist settled on his skin like a thousand tiny gnats. Trees—mostly pine—dotted the landscape, standing like massive witnesses against the night, looking down at him from on high. There was a beaten dirt path that meandered thirty yards to his workshop. The comforting orange lights were still on, shining through the moisture-laden windows.

He headed toward his workshop but took a detour into the woods after ten yards, stopping at the woodpile and grabbing the ax from where it stuck out of a log. He made his way back to the path with his little shuffling steps. If someone had happened to see him, they would've seen a stooped old man with the weight of experience on his shoulders. They would've seen a man carrying an ax and a hacksaw into a workshop. They would've seen his eyes alight with something much older and more destructive than fear. And if they had been close, they would've seen the man swallowing constantly.

But there was no one to see the man as he disappeared into the workshop behind his house on his eighty-acre property. The only other person in the vicinity was the girl. And she was already in the workshop.

The man used the ax first. He got through most of the muscle and tough tendon with the tool. Then he moved on to the hacksaw. He worked with a feverish intensity, heart thudding arrhythmically in his chest.

And the whole time, he couldn't stop swallowing.

When he emerged from the workshop nearly an hour after he went in, he was splashed in blood. It was on his face, his hands, and all over his clothes.

And it dripped from the severed limb he carried in his right hand.

He moved past his workshop and out into the forest, carrying only the limb.

It was a leg.

And it had once belonged to a teenage girl.

CHAPTER 1

S eth Granger felt ill.

But it wasn't all bad. He'd just gorged himself on a bunch of unhealthy snacks and candy from Camp Stillwater's overpriced store. He sat on the ground, back propped against a log and his feet about a foot from the fire pit. His fellow campers sat around the fire, many of them in similar states of repose, hands clutching overstuffed bellies.

Not everyone was feeling the same. Jake Sullivan, directly across the fire from Seth, was telling a joke to Elijah Ryan. Elijah was only half listening as he eyed Tricia Ulgard, who sat at the next fire over.

The kid they all called Buster but whose real name Seth didn't know had a soda in one hand and was on his fifth or sixth belch in a row. Cries of disgust arose from girls at the nearest campfires, save Emma and Ashley, who sat near Buster, engrossed in a whispered conversation. Finally, one of the male camp counselors called over, saying, "Buster! What did I tell you?"

"Sorry!" Buster belched, then fell to laughing.

There were five fire pits in the area between the boys' and girls' cabins. And tonight was the last night they'd use them. Until next summer. Seth had been coming to church camp every summer since he was twelve. Next year, he'd be seventeen when he came back. After that, he'd have to come as a counselor if he came at all.

And every year he'd come here, the last night of camp was always a somber affair for him. It didn't keep him from having fun. But knowing that tomorrow night he'd be back home produced a sense of melancholy that settled on him like a scratchy wool blanket. And when he thought about how a little less than a month later he'd be back in school, that blanket turned into a straitjacket.

But he did miss his mom. And his dog Dallas.

In all his previous years coming to church camp, Seth had successfully managed to focus more on the camp aspect and less on the church. Granted, it wasn't like other church camps some of his friends had attended. That made things easier. There were only a few hours a day of worship, not counting the fifteen-minute session right before dinner when everyone was tired from all the activities, stomachs growling as the smell of the cafeteria food taunted them. They truly were a captive audience, jammed into the cafeteria in the evenings.

After Seth's first summer at Camp Stillwater, he'd been describing all the fun he'd had to his friend Westin. When he was done, he couldn't help but notice the look on his friend's face. Like the boy had smelled something bad.

"Man," Westin said, "my church camp doesn't have swimming or archery or an obstacle course. It was so *boring*. What a gyp!"

Seth felt for Westin. Even the two hours of worship every day stretched his ability to sit still and focus while the summer wind stirred the trees outside, whispering in his ear of all the fun he could be having.

In all those previous years, Seth had taken the worship lessons as a matter of course. It wasn't so this year. As far as he'd been concerned, he didn't need to learn more about God. He knew that God and he were on solid footing. They understood each other. After all, Seth's life was pretty good. God was looking out for him. Or that's what he told himself. It was easier than facing the truth.

He prayed before he went to bed at night, even though he did so out of a sense of duty and habit rather than any kind of real faith in the Big Man Upstairs. But for a boy still years from adulthood, there wasn't much of a difference. Besides, it seemed to be working.

It was all a way for Seth to maintain his view of his little world. One in which his father loved him, and his parents loved each other, and they would always be kind to one another. But when cracks started showing in his life two years ago, it had become harder and harder to ignore the bad and focus on the good. Suddenly, there was more bad in his life than good. And it had been getting steadily worse.

Things had come to a head not long before Seth left for church camp this summer. And as a result, he was paying more attention during the worship sessions. But not because he wanted to get closer to God—to really develop a relationship with Him—but because he had begun to see God as a cruel joke. A fairy tale for adults. A way to defer the fear of mortality with childish thoughts of an afterlife if you just followed ten rules while you were alive.

Although he couldn't truly articulate it, he had an urge to dismantle the concept of faith like breaking a leg off a chair. Because without faith, the whole religion thing fell apart. And he wanted to watch it fall apart like his own life was falling apart. The cracks in his life were so big he felt like he was being swallowed up by them. When he was at his angriest—when his youthful exuberance came out as rage—he wanted that darkness to swallow him up. He wanted there to be no God. He just wanted oblivion.

Someone tapped his shoulder, and Seth dragged his gaze from the hypnotic fire, looking to his right. Darius Lovett, his best friend at camp this year, held out half a Snickers bar. "You want this?"

Seth waved it off. "No way, man. I can't do it."

"I'll take it!" Buster shouted from across the campfire, jumping up and nearly falling in the fire as he scrambled over.

Darius handed the treat over. "Thanks, Darius!" Buster said.

"Don't thank me. Thank him." Darius hooked a thumb in Seth's direction.

"Yeah, right," Buster said through a mouthful of Snickers. "Thanks, Granger."

"Sure," Seth said. But buying the guys treats hadn't been entirely altruistic on his part.

The summer camp had the kids' parents load up their store cards at the beginning of summer, but you couldn't get the money refunded. So any kids who had money left over as the last days approached—which wasn't many—went hog-wild on sodas and Pixie Stix and miniature donuts and any other sugar-laced treats you could think of.

It was quite the racket. Especially since you could get the same junk at a grocery store for a fraction of the price. It didn't seem right to Seth. He didn't know what happened to any money that was left over on the cards, but it sure didn't roll over to the next year.

He had started the summer off with fifty dollars on his card, even though he'd told his mother he didn't need it. They got three meals a day in the cafeteria, after all. But his mother had insisted.

And earlier today, he'd still had forty dollars on the card. So he treated his cabinmates to a shopping spree of sorts. It had won him slaps on the back and grins of sugary delight from the guys before they fell into their sweets-induced stupors.

That was nice, but it wasn't why he'd done it.

He knew his mother would ask about the fifty at some point after she picked him up. And he wanted to be able to tell her he'd spent it all. Because if he didn't, his mom would think it was money wasted. And he wouldn't lie to her.

He'd only lied to her three times in his life. And he was determined to keep that number from growing. Over the last two years, he'd seen the effect his father's constant lies had on her. And he didn't want to add to her pain. So this way, he could tell her he'd spent it all and it wouldn't be a lie. He just wouldn't tell her he hadn't spent it all on himself.

"You good, man?" Darius asked.

"I'm good," Seth said. "Just . . . last day of camp, you know?"

Darius nodded wisely. He was a new face this year. And, as luck would have it, he'd been assigned to the same cabin as Seth—Oak Grove. He was one of three Black kids at camp this year. Most everyone else was white.

Not that Seth cared. But he'd got the feeling that Darius hadn't really felt comfortable when camp had first started. He didn't know if it had anything to do with being surrounded by white people or if it was just new-kid shyness. Either way, Seth and Darius had gotten along like gangbusters from the get-go, and after the first week, Darius had opened up and started having fun. Now, that fun was coming to an end. And Seth would certainly miss his new friend.

A dog barked from the woods at the edge of the campfire area. Seth looked that way. It sounded just like Dallas. As far as Seth knew, there were no dogs at the camp. He hadn't seen any. Of course, he knew Dallas wouldn't be out there. She was safely at home with his mom. But still, it sounded just like her.

Seth turned back to the fire, but the dog barked again. On a whim, he got up. "I'll be back," he told Darius.

"If I move, I might puke," Darius said.

Seth walked off toward the woods, but one of the counselors called after him. "Grange!? Where you going?"

"Uh, back to my cabin to grab something," Seth said, changing direction to head for the boys' cabins.

"Don't be long!"

"I won't," Seth answered. When he made it to the cabin, he slipped around the back and hurried into the woods. This was against the rules at night, which made Seth nervous. It also gave him a little thrill to be breaking a rule. It was something he hadn't done much of in his young life. But something compelled him to go into the woods. Sure, the familiar dog bark was part of it, but it was far from the whole reason. He'd been dealing with a swirl of conflicting and powerful emotions all year. And those emotions had driven him to do some strange things. Uncharacteristic things.

Like nearly getting into a fight with Lester Perd on the dock while waiting in line for the diving board. Lester had cut in front of Seth. Normally one to avoid confrontation, Seth surprised himself when he shoved Lester off the dock and into the water. He'd been ready to punch the kid in the face if he tried to get back up and start something, but the moment had been defused when all the kids behind them in line laughed like it was just some horseplay. Then one of the camp counselors yelled at them to knock it off.

Lester got in line at the back, and Seth was left shaking, wondering why he felt so *angry*. It wasn't like him at all. Just as it wasn't like him to sneak off into the woods. But here he was.

Of course, he suspected the root cause of these odd behaviors. The cause was two-fold. One, he was a teenager with hormones thrashing around inside him. And two, his dad was a no-good drunk whom his mom had kicked out of the house the week before Seth left for camp.

He figured it was enough to make any teenager crazy. But that didn't make things any better. He still had to deal with these feelings somehow. And the last thing he wanted was to do something really stupid. But he just couldn't control himself sometimes. It was like he was losing his willpower. And that was the scariest thing of all. It made him feel like he was going crazy. Like he no longer knew himself.

Maybe that was part of growing up, too. If so, he hoped it would pass quickly.

There was another bark from up ahead, and a blur of white-and-black fur flashed through the darkness. Dallas was black and white. Of course, so were many other dogs. Still, he changed direction, moving toward where he thought the dog was going.

Now far enough away from the camp, he whistled and called out to the dog. "Here pooch. Come here."

The only answer was a distant bark. He kept moving.

And he came to a cave in a rock bluff. Strange. In all his hikes over this property, over all the years, he'd never seen a cave like this one. The mouth was big enough for him to walk inside if he ducked just a little. There were other caves in the area, but most of them had entrances much smaller than this one. And the campers were expressly forbidden from going inside them. They'd even said something on the first day of camp about the record rainfall and the fact that the caves would likely be full of water. Extremely dangerous, they'd said. Do not go inside them. Another rule.

But Seth didn't really *want* to go inside, even if he felt like he *should*. No, this was a rule he had no intention of breaking.

As he turned to leave, the dog barked from inside the cavern. *Man, did that sound like Dallas.*

He turned back to the cave. Why did he feel such a pull to go in there? Why did it feel *important*?

He didn't have his phone on him, but he had a small flashlight in his pocket. Every camper was supposed to carry one, so they didn't trip over rocks or roots on their way back to their cabins after they put out the fires. He clicked his on and shone it inside the cave.

Something told Seth that this couldn't be one of those times where his emotions took over, propelling him over a line he normally wouldn't cross. The decision had to come from him. From the him that he knew, not this other strange him that seemed to take over his mind and body in increasingly frequent instances.

There was only silence from inside the cave. He looked over his shoulder toward the camp he could no longer see. Toward the campers he could no longer hear. And he wondered just what the heck he was doing out here. He suddenly felt like he was in a dream that was tilting toward the land of nightmares.

But still, something inside told him it was important that he go in there. *Why?*

Gotta go in to find out.

Seth Granger faced forward and stepped into the cave.

He moved along the relatively flat surface, ducking low here and there or climbing over the occasional pile of fallen rocks. The flashlight beam picked out his path. The cave grew cold enough that goose-bumps prickled his skin. Still, he forced himself forward.

Until he came to a sheer drop.

He stopped at the edge of the drop and looked down into the pool of water below, shining his light down. The surface of the crystal-clear water was about fifteen feet down. He could see that the rock formation the pool sat in was roughly funnel-shaped, the craggy tan-colored rock tapering down to a black hole where the light couldn't penetrate some thirty feet below.

There was no path down unless he wanted to climb. But it did look like the cave continued on the other side. There was another tunnel just a few feet off the water on the opposite side.

Seth flinched as he saw movement in that tunnel mouth.

A black-and-white dog walked up to the edge of the pool and looked at Seth. It was a similar breed to Dallas, looking like a husky mix, but he could tell it wasn't her. One of Dallas's eyes was ice blue, while the other was so brown it was almost black. This dog had two dark-brown eyes. Although it did look a lot like Dallas in every other way.

The dog looked up at Seth for a moment before barking once. It was a friendly bark, as far as Seth could tell. Then he caught sight of movement down in the pool of water, and he shifted his gaze.

A dark cloud of liquid was moving up out of the hole at the bottom of the rock funnel. As the column of liquid cloud split into several smaller, tentacle-like columns, Seth saw that it was a deep red. The tentacles spread and twisted like they were alive, reaching up toward Seth, looking like they would burst through the water's surface and race up to pull him into the dark underwater hole.

The dog started barking louder and more frequently. And as it continued to bark at him, the tone seemed to grow more savage. As the half-dozen blood-red tentacles reached the surface of the pool, the dog was snarling and snapping, eyes fixed on Seth. The tentacles didn't break the surface, though. The red liquid staining the water spread across the surface, obscuring the inner reaches of the pool.

Seth's heart thundered in his chest. He felt *really* sick. Sick with fright and confusion.

The dog's barking reached fever pitch. Seth wanted to slam his hands over his ears, but he couldn't bring himself to move.

Then something popped to the surface of the polluted water. It was a severed arm, floating like a macabre pool toy.

The ground under his feet crumbled, and Seth fell, grabbing at the rocks. Now he screamed. He screamed louder than the dog's frenzied barking. He screamed as loud as he could, scrambling for purchase and finding none.

He hit the water—

—And jerked awake next to the campfire.

Everyone was staring at him. Not just everyone at his campfire, but everyone all around. He could see camp counselors and kids who were standing to look over. And he realized he must've been screaming in real life. Still, the relief he felt at not being in that cave, in the water, took the sting out of his embarrassment.

"You alright, Grange?" Darius asked. "Nightmare?"

"Nightmare," Seth said, sitting up. Everyone was still staring at him.

"What's the matter?" Darius shouted. "You guys never had a nightmare before?"

That seemed to snap everyone out of it. And they all went back to what they were doing.

"Thanks," Seth said.

"No worries. It's about time for bed, anyway."

Darius was right. Not five minutes later, several of the counselors showed up with large five-gallon jugs of lake water to put out the fires. Everyone cleaned up their messes and made sure the fires were out. Then they all headed back to their cabins.

As Seth followed Darius and the other boys up the creaky wooden stairs to Oak Grove, he heard a dog bark out in the woods.

It sounded just like Dallas.

CHAPTER 2

T he trickling sound of the little woodland stream provided Seth Granger with something to focus on as he waited at the edge of the gravel parking lot. It was an unconscious form of meditation he'd taken up as naturally as he'd taken to worrying at the age of fourteen. And now, as he leaned against the brownish-red bark of a large pine tree, his unconscious mind sought to ease his anxiety by focusing his thoughts on the sound of water.

It wasn't like his mother to be late.

Maybe five or ten minutes, if something extremely disruptive had happened. Something that just couldn't be avoided.

But it was going on half an hour now.

It wasn't like her. Not her, the woman who, whether she knew it or not, had developed a way of withholding love or affection as a punishment for tardiness. Seth didn't think she meant to do it. Not on purpose. He thought it was a reaction to Seth's father being constantly late when he was in his cups. And although Seth had never even had a sip of alcohol in his life, he was a teenager, and teenagers are often late for things. Time management is not a strong suit of the young.

But his mother was almost never late.

Something's wrong, Seth thought.

That morning, he'd still been gripped by a tremendous sense of melancholy. Camp was over. Summer was coming to a close. He wished, in the way only teenage boys can, that he could stay at Camp Stillwater with the other boys and girls for just a little longer. A week. Maybe two. Certainly no longer than a month.

Yes, he missed Dallas. But in Seth's mind, Dallas was smarter than most of the adults he knew. And in his fantasy world where summer got to stretch out into the foreseeable future, he thought Dallas would understand. Somehow, his dog would know, and she would be just fine with waiting a little longer for her human to come home.

But now, as the minutes ticked by and his mother remained a no-show, Seth forgot all about the silly fantasies of that morning.

The trickle of water momentarily forgotten, he levered himself off the tree as a station wagon turned into the camp entrance some two hundred yards away. The afternoon sunlight slanting through the forest canopy made it hard to tell what color the car was. He could tell it was a Volvo, but was it a dark blue one? With little specks of sparkly silver in the paint? Did it have damage to the front right fender—damage Seth had caused himself the third time he'd borrowed it?

It hadn't been much. A scraping of the black plastic bumper against the concrete base of a light pole in the grocery store parking lot. He hadn't tried to hide it. And his mom even laughed at how worried he'd been about the damage. She'd always been good like that. With some things, anyway.

When his dad had seen it . . . well, that was a whole other story.

Seth's heart plunged into his stomach as the Volvo moved through a bright patch of sunlight. It was maroon, not dark blue. And it didn't have any damage to the front right fender.

Something's wrong.

One of the younger kids—Seth didn't know his name—ran out from behind a tree on the other side of the parking lot, waving at the vehicle.

The Volvo pulled over and the kid's parents got out. They hugged, and the dad stepped behind the trees and appeared a moment later with the kid's bags. The kid talked excitedly about his time at camp, probably all jacked up on sugar from commissary snacks.

Where is she? Seth wondered.

"Hey, Grange," a familiar voice said from behind him. He turned to see Darius plopping his bags down on the ground near Seth's own. They'd traded numbers and social media handles, but Seth thought Darius had already caught a ride home, like most of the other kids. Apparently not.

"Hey, Dare," Seth said. The two boys slapped hands in a complex greeting they'd spent hours perfecting over the summer.

"Your ride late?" Darius said after the unique handshake was finished.

"I guess. My mom's not usually late, though. And she hasn't called me."

"You called her yet?"

Seth nodded. She hadn't picked up.

"Well, my mom's coming right now. I can ask if we can give you a ride?"

Seth shook his head. They'd already established that Seth's hometown was an hour past the town of Victorville, where Darius lived. It would make for a two-hour round trip for Darius and his mother. "She'll be here," Seth said, glancing at the entrance.

Not for the first time that morning, he thought about the strange nightmare he'd had. Suddenly, the sound of the stream was like the buzz of insects in his ears.

One of the camp counselors in charge of seeing kids off stepped over to talk to the parents in the maroon Volvo.

"She'll be here," Seth said again, whispering the words like a mantra.

But, somewhere deep down, Seth knew she wouldn't show up.

He knew that something was very wrong.

***

Seth called his mother one more time as Mrs. Lovett pulled into the parking lot in her black Range Rover.

No answer.

Darius grabbed his bags and walked them over to the newly parked SUV. His mother got out and popped the back hatch. "I'm so sorry, baby," she said to her son. "There was some kind of accident on the 60. Traffic was stopped for a good twenty minutes."

"This is unacceptable, Mom," Darius joked with his mother. "Don't let it happen again." Seth looked up from his phone and smiled, seeing Darius give his mom a big hug.

"Talk to your mother like that!" Mrs. Lovett said, putting her son in a headlock even though she had to stand on her tiptoes to get her arm around his neck.

Looking back down at his phone, Seth hovered his thumb over the little phone symbol next to the word *Dad*. He took a deep breath, then swiped the application away and pocketed his phone. "Actually, Darius, Mrs. Lovett, if it's not too much trouble, could I get a ride to Victorville with you?"

"This is Seth Granger, Mom," Darius said. "Remember I told you about him?"

Mrs. Lovett nodded, looking at Seth. She wore her dark red hair straight and parted on the left side. Her pantsuit was dark grey and looked expensive. Seth thought her black blouse was made of silk.

"I remember," she said. "Where do you need to go?"

"Just anywhere in Victorville. I'm sure by the time we get there, I'll be able to get ahold of my mom."

Mrs. Lovett and her son exchanged a look, passing information wordlessly. Seth could guess it was a "Do I need to worry about this kid?" look, but he wasn't sure.

"Of course I'll give you a ride," Mrs. Lovett said.

"Thanks," Seth said, smiling weakly.

Something's wrong, he thought as he moved to grab his bags.

As he loaded the bags into the back of the SUV, the last thing on Seth's mind was the soothing sound of the small creek nearby. But the water continued to flow steadily, quite the change from the slow trickle of previous years. It had been an unusually rainy summer all over the eastern portion of the state.

Once everything was loaded up, Darius got in the front seat and Seth got in the back. Mrs. Lovett, who told him to call her Jessa, took her place behind the steering wheel. The tires of the luxury SUV crunched over the gravel in the parking lot as Jessa backed up. The shadows cast by the tree branches in the slanted afternoon sunlight slid over the vehicle like dark, spidery hands grasping for the vehicle's occupants.

CHAPTER 3

"How about the bus station?" Seth asked.

"Uh-uh, no way," Jessa said, looking at him in the rearview mirror. "I'm taking you home."

"Yeah, man. It's not that far out of the way," Darius said.

"It's an hour each way!" Seth said. "I can take a bus. I've done it before. They run three times a day."

He still hadn't been able to get in touch with his mother. He found that his palms were moist, and his heart was beating a little faster than normal. The truth was, he wanted to get home as fast as possible to figure out what happened to her. But he'd had politeness beat into his brain over the years. In his mind, making Jessa and Darius drive two hours out of their way just for him was about as rude as you could get.

He hadn't tried his dad—not after making the decision back at Camp Stillwater. And neither of his two travel companions asked him about a father. They probably assumed he was out of the picture. Seth had certainly never told Darius anything about him. Out of sight, out of mind during summer camp. It was a reprieve from his old man. And a much needed one.

"We're going to pull over and discuss this," Jessa said. "Last thing I need is a fender bender."

They were in Victorville, approaching the downtown area featuring mom-and-pop boutique stores interspersed with a number of nationwide franchises.

As Jessa put the right blinker on to pull into a small shopping center parking lot, Seth's phone buzzed in his hand. A sigh of relief escaped him as he saw the single three-letter word on his phone screen.

"Mom?" he said, answering. In the front, Jessa looked at him in the rearview mirror while Darius leaned toward the center console.

"Seth," his mom said, sounding strange. "I'm sorry I'm not there yet. Something has come up."

"Are you okay?" Seth asked.

"Yes," she said, flatly. Seth waited for her to go on, but she didn't. She sounded dazed.

"What's wrong?" he asked. "Where are you?"

"I'm still at home," she said. "I've sent Mr. Winchell to pick you up. He left about forty-five minutes ago."

Mr. Winchell? Seth thought. *Why him?* Winchell lived on their street, about a quarter mile away. He worked for the utility company. Outwardly, he was a nice enough guy, but Seth's mom had always called him a busybody. And it was true. The man had ratted Seth out more than once for being out past curfew when he was younger. He was the self-proclaimed head of the neighborhood watch. There were several other options on his mother's roster when it came to calling in a favor such as this one. He wondered what would've caused her to seek Winchell's help.

"Um, okay," he said. "But my friend Darius's mom has taken me as far as Victorville. Do you think he could pick me up here?"

There was no reply. Only his mother's breathing.

Finally, after nearly ten seconds, Seth spoke again. "Mom? Did you hear me?"

"Yes. Yes, I'm sorry. I'll call him and tell him. Where are you going to be?"

Seth looked out the window. "Outside of Food Giant." He paused. "Mom? What's wrong?"

"I'll tell you everything when you get home," she said. "Keep an eye out for Mr. Winchell. He's probably just outside of town now."

"Okay, but—"

His mother clicked off without saying goodbye.

As he brought his phone down from his ear, Seth realized that it wasn't just his propensity for worry that had him all riled up. Unlike many other times in the last couple of years when his anxieties got away from him, this time, there was something *wrong*.

"Someone's coming to pick you up?" Darius asked, half-turned in his seat.

"Yeah," Seth said, staring down at the phone in his hand. "Yeah, thank you."

***

Mr. Winchell's white Chevy Silverado pulled into the Food Giant parking lot twelve minutes after Seth hung up with his distraught mother.

"That's him," Seth said, opening his door and stepping out.

Darius and his mother both got out of the vehicle while Seth stepped over and waved his arms to get Winchell's attention. Winchell spotted them and steered over. He pulled into a nearby spot, leaving an empty spot between them. He shut off the truck and got out.

Knowing Winchell, Seth figured they'd be in this parking lot for a good fifteen minutes while the man talked Mrs. Lovett's ear off.

Winchell had thinning black hair and a body shaped like a parking cone on stick legs. He was in his early fifties and had been divorced for as long as Seth could remember. Still, he usually had a closed-mouth smile ready for everyone he came across. The smile had always struck Seth as genuine, if a little sad. But as the man got out of his truck and approached Mrs. Lovett with a hand held out, there was no smile. His normally bright eyes were somehow dark. He wore faded jeans, thick white tennis shoes, and a rumpled yellow polo shirt.

"Thank you for looking after Seth," he said, his emotionless inflection suggesting a lack of gratitude.

"Not a problem," Jessa said, shaking the man's hand.

"How are you, Seth?" Winchell asked, retrieving his hand from the woman.

"Fine," Seth said, tracking around to the back of the SUV to get his bags.

Darius met him there. "You know this guy, right?" he whispered.

"Yeah, I know him," Seth said, his thoughts on his mom's voice. She'd sounded so . . . different.

"Friend of the family or something?"

"Kind of, I guess," Seth said, hefting his backpack up onto his shoulder.

"Okay," Darius said. "Well, hit me up when you're home."

"I will," Seth said, performing the handshake the two teenagers had come up with during their time at camp.

As he walked toward the Chevy, Seth found it odd that Mr. Winchell was already back in his truck, waiting. Mrs. Lovett—Jessa—stood next to the SUV, looking at Seth with concern. He tossed his bags in the back of the truck and then came back over to shake the woman's hand.

"Thanks for the ride," he said. "I appreciate it."

"Nice to meet you, Seth," she said, smiling wanly. Then, a little quieter, "You know him well?"

"Well enough," Seth said. "I'll be okay. Thanks again."

He waved goodbye to the mother and son, then got into the front of the truck with Mr. Winchell.

The man started the truck and pulled forward through the empty space ahead. They turned onto the road toward Seven Springs. Seth expected Winchell to start up a conversation, as he'd always done before. But the man was silent. It was as if Seth wasn't even there. He just stared out the windshield, hands at ten and two. Finally, Seth was done waiting. Done being polite.

"Do you know what's wrong with my mom?" he asked.

Winchell's head swiveled to face him. Half of his left eye was black. Like there was a curtain of black liquid going across it from left to right. Seth sucked in a breath and leaned away from the man. But then Winchell blinked, and the blackness was gone.

"All in good time, son," Winchell said, looking at Seth blankly. It had been several long seconds since the man had looked at the road, but he was keeping the vehicle in the middle of the lane, and the nearest car was a good way ahead. Still, as the seconds continued to pass, Seth grew worried.

"Okay," the teenager said. "Okay, that's okay."

Winchell swung his head back and looked out the windshield. "We're going to have to make a stop first," he said. "It'll be real quick, and everything will be good after. You'll understand then."

"Oh," Seth said, "okay. What's the stop?"

"You'll see," Winchell said, turning back to him. And this time he did smile. But it wasn't a smile Seth had seen before. This one was full of brown teeth and blackened gums. It was a sick smile. From a sick man.

CHAPTER 4

"I'm tellin' you, something's going on with the people in this town," Russell Jobson said from his spot at the front window. He was peering out between the open blinds at the quiet street.

"You always say that," Sammy Jobson said from the kitchen. "Every time we come back from summer vacation, you say the same thing." Her voice was interspersed with the clink of a butter knife against a glass jar.

Russell's stomach growled. He wondered when lunch would be ready. "No," he said. "I always say that these people are weird. I don't always say there's something going on with them. There's a difference."

"There is?" Sammy said.

"Something about being away from here for two months just makes me realize how strange these people are, I guess," Russell said, ignoring his wife's question.

The two of them had only been living in Seven Springs for five years, having moved from Atlanta when two teaching jobs opened up at the high school. It was the only place they found that had two teaching positions and at a salary that was slightly above average for those who had no experience. Plus, the low cost of living had been attractive.

The first year had been bumpy for the newly married couple, as it is for most brand-new teachers. But the second year was slightly better, and the next even better. They'd finally hit their stride last year. When school started next month, it would be the start of their sixth year in the town, and their sixth year teaching.

"What's going on out there?" Sammy asked, bringing two loaded plates into the living room to set them on the coffee table.

Russell turned around, smiling at the sandwiches, and then at his wife. Her wavy brown hair had natural blonde highlights thanks to all their time out in the sun this summer. As she bent down to put the plates on the coffee table, Russell got a glimpse down her sundress. Suddenly, he knew what he wanted to do with the rest of the afternoon. Or at least an hour or so of it.

Sammy straightened up, seeing the look on her husband's face. She propped her hands on her hips but couldn't hide her smile. "Like what you see?"

Russell nodded with exaggerated motion.

"Well, eat up, mister. You'll need the energy."

Russell smiled and moved away from the window to the couch. He sat down and grabbed the remote for the smart television.

"Seriously though, why do you say something's going on with the people?" Sammy said, sitting down.

"I don't know," Russell replied. "They're just actin' weird."

"How do you mean?"

"Well," Russell said, leaning back on the couch and forgetting about the television for the moment. "Lyle was doing something in his old broke-down garage. I never even seen him open that thing since we've been here. All of a sudden, he's pulling stuff out of it like he thinks there's gold buried in there."

Sammy had taken a bite of her sandwich, but she made approving sounds as she chewed, wiping a bit of mayonnaise away from the corner of her lip with a pinky.

"And Mrs. Stein?" Russell continued. "She was just standing on her lawn in a pale green, uh, under-thingy. What do you call those?"

"You mean a slip?" Sammy said. "Or a nightgown?"

"What's the difference?"

"Well, I guess a nightgown isn't really supposed to be seen, whereas a slip is like an undergarment, but it's meant to be seen."

Russell mulled that over for a moment before saying, "How do you know if it's supposed to be seen or not? I mean, how can you tell intent? What if she just walked out of the house like that, forgetting herself for a minute?"

Sammy smiled at her husband. It was a look that told him he was in the middle of one of the idiosyncrasies that Sammy thought were so cute. He hadn't been trying to do it, but anytime he could make her smile was a good time, in his book. "Since we know Mrs. Stein well enough, I think we can surmise that she didn't intend for it to be seen if it was anything close to looking like an undergarment."

Russell nodded in agreement. "Good point, babe," he said, giving her an exaggerated wink. "Anyway, she was just standing out there at the bottom of the hill, looking at her lawn like it was the most interesting thing in the world. I stopped and watched her for a good thirty seconds, and she didn't move. I wonder if she's okay."

"And you got this all from one little trip to the mailbox?"

"That's what I'm saying. It's like they're getting weirder. Other times we've come back, I've only seen one of them being weird at a time. Never two at once!"

"Maybe at the end of next summer, you'll see three neighbors being weird. Then we might have to move."

Russell smiled. His stomach growled. "What do you want to

watch?" he asked, getting back to the task at hand.

In the end, they settled on an episode of a British baking show that they both liked.

About halfway through his sandwich, Russell caught movement out of the corner of his eye. He looked out the window and saw Mrs. Stein walking stiffly past their house on the cracked and uneven sidewalk. He only got a glimpse of her face because she turned to veer across the street. But he could've sworn that her mouth was hanging open. And that she'd been swallowing, the fleshy wrinkles of her neck working with the muscle movements.

He watched her until she was out of sight. And when he went back to his sandwich and the baking show, he had one final thought before forgetting about it. *Looks like she's goin' over to Lyle's house.*

CHAPTER 5

M r. Winchell turned off the highway several miles before Seven Springs. It was a narrow dirt road that Seth had never been down before. He couldn't recall ever even seeing the road. Leafy branches hung down over it, creating a tunnel of foliage. Some branches scraped the top of the truck as they passed through, moving into and out of splotches of waning sunlight.

"What's back here?" Seth asked, trying not to sound scared.

"Our stop," Winchell said.

It did nothing to calm Seth's nerves. He had a terrible feeling about all this. Just yesterday, he'd been studying Bible verses, swimming in Stillwater Lake, and laughing with Darius and the other guys about fart jokes and the way Jerry-Joe Ryan scared Tommy Delong so bad he dropped his ice cream sandwich in the dirt on the way back to the cabin.

Now something was wrong with his mom, and Mr. Winchell was acting strange. The awful smile kept coming up in Seth's mind. It had looked as if Winchell had been sucking on charcoal all day. He couldn't think of anything else that would turn a man's teeth and gums black and brown. The last time he'd seen the man was before going off to camp, and his mouth had been normal then, Seth was sure of it.

The trees thinned out, and then they were driving through a clearing. Up ahead, encompassed by a semicircle of trees, was an abandoned house. It was one story, gray with age, and leaning heavily to the right. The porch awning had collapsed, covering the front of the structure, making it look like it was asleep. Or dead.

Winchell stopped the truck about fifteen yards from an ancient stone well out in front of the house. He put it in park and then turned in his seat to face Seth, who was pressed up against his door, as far away as he could get. Seth's right hand rested on the armrest, his fingers inches from the door release.

"Well, Seth," he said in his new strangely emotionless voice. "I hate to tell you this, but your mom asked me to, son. There's no good way to say it, so I'll just come out and say it. Your dad's dead, Seth."

The teenager took a deep breath, letting the words sink in. He tried them on for size in his mind. *My dad's dead. My father is dead. I have no dad.* He expected the hurt and the panic and the despair to come, but it didn't. And he was suddenly worried that there was something wrong with him. Shouldn't he feel something now? Something other than this . . . what was it . . . relief? No, not relief. That would be a terrible thing to feel. *No one feels relieved when their dad dies. Do they?*

"How did he die?" Seth asked after a few moments.

Mr. Winchell was still looking in his direction, but it seemed like the man's eyes had drifted, and he was now looking out the window. The look of consternation the man had donned was still in place, but it seemed more like a mask than a real expression of emotion.

Seth waited, but the man said nothing. It was as if he hadn't heard the question.

"Mr. Winchell?"

Still nothing. Seth turned and followed the man's gaze, but saw nothing of interest out the window. Just a clearing overgrown with wild grass and bordered by trees. As he was turning his head back, Winchell grabbed him at the base of his neck. Seth let out a cry of surprise at the sudden touch. And when he turned to look back into the man's eyes, he saw that the entire left eye was black, like oil had spread over it.

Seth scrambled, opening the door and trying to jump out. But he was buckled in. He looked down from Winchell's face and unclipped his seatbelt.

"Where you goin', Seth?" the man asked, gripping Seth's shoulder. "I'm sorry to be the bearer of bad news, but that's the way it goes sometimes."

Seth looked back up to see that the eye was back to normal. "What's wrong with your eye?" he cried.

Winchell frowned, then turned his head to look in the rearview mirror. Of course, he saw nothing wrong. "What are you talkin' about, son?" he asked. "I think we should get you home now."

"Yes," Seth said. "Fine. Please. Take me home."

Winchell looked at him expectantly.

Seth realized he still had his door open. He reached out and closed it. But this time, he left his seatbelt unfastened.

Winchell took his hand back and put the truck in reverse. As they were driving back out through the tunnel of foliage, he spoke again. "Sorry to be the one. Just, your mom said she couldn't do it."

"How did he die?" Seth ventured again.

"Terrible thing," Winchell said. "Terrible. He was murdered."

CHAPTER 6

The town of Seven Springs had a police department that was ten strong. Two of those ten were detectives. And neither one had the luxury of specialization. They worked the gamut from property crime to murder—the latter of which was a rarity in the town.

Detective Oliver Bessum was the one working Tim Granger's case. He'd moved to Seven Springs nine years earlier after a man he'd arrested got out on bail and came to his house with a thousand rounds of ammunition and a semi-auto rifle with a bump stock that essentially made it fully automatic. The perp had parked his truck in front of Bessum's house and proceeded to fire the weapon through windows, doors, and walls.

Both Bessum's wife and son were home at the time, along with Bessum himself. His son—who'd been fourteen at the time—got away unscathed. His wife, however, had been shot in the leg. She survived, but she still walked with a limp.

Bessum had left her bleeding on the bedroom floor to get outside and flank the asshole. He'd killed him outright, emptying his seventeen-round magazine into the man.

His wife never forgave him for leaving her alone in the bedroom, scared and injured and crying. She'd taken their son, and he hadn't put up much of a fight. He was just happy they'd both walked away from it. For his part, he'd suffered only minor injuries. Flesh wounds, really.

After the divorce, he decided to leave Philadelphia and head somewhere quieter. He ended up in Seven Springs. It was close enough to Philly that he got to see his son several times a year.

Now he was pushing fifty and had long since found that small-town life was very much to his liking. Or at least it had been until weird shit started happening all over town.

And Tim Granger's murder was just one of these strange happenings.

A week ago, Bessum had been called at home in the middle of the night. One of the uniformed patrol officers had been sitting behind a billboard at the edge of town and down the street from Maggie's Brewhouse when a man he'd never recognized walked past carrying a severed human arm.

The officer, a guy named Paul Tulards, had described it to Bessum later. "Hand to God," Tulards said. "He just walked by like it was the most natural thing in the world to do. He even looked at me—looked right through the windshield and our eyes met—and his expression didn't change. Not one iota. And you know there's that streetlight right above the billboard, so there was enough light there for me to see him see me. But he just kept on walking, like he went for a stroll every night with some poor bastard's severed arm."

Needless to say, Tulards had stopped the man and arrested him. The guy said nothing at all during the arrest. He didn't even acknowledge that he understood the Miranda warning. And when Bessum had arrived on scene, the guy was still tight-lipped. Had been ever since. It was clear looking at and smelling the guy that he was homeless. So the first thing Bessum did was head down to the nearby creek where the homeless had been known to camp from time to time. It was a stone's throw from an active rail line and down enough from the road that you couldn't see it well just driving by.

After getting down the treacherous slope to the area next to the creek, the detective pulled out his pistol and looked around with his flashlight. It was the kind of thing you were supposed to do with a partner, but he didn't want to pull Tulards away from the perp. Last thing they needed was the guy to somehow get out of the cruiser while they were both gone and run off into the night. So he went down himself, hoping he wouldn't run into an accomplice. He could only see so far into the dark trees around the creek with his flashlight, so he called out, warning anyone out there to come out or risk getting shot. No one came out.

Bessum hadn't gone far when he found a raggedy blue-and-gray tent on the opposite side of the creek. After crossing the narrow stream, he approached it carefully, checking the ground with his flashlight. About ten yards from the tent's entrance, he saw the hatchet. It was lying on the ground, covered in drying blood.

The tent flap was unzipped and hanging open, so the detective was still a good five yards away when he shone the light inside and found a man's severed head staring back at him, purple tongue sticking out, eyes looking strangely unconcerned. He'd seen his fair share of dead bodies, and people who died violently often left a terrified look on their faces when they shook off their mortal coil. But not this one.

Figuring he'd find the rest of the guy's body—a guy he thought he recognized but couldn't be sure yet—Bessum searched the surrounding area. But he found no body. He found no other limbs, either. There was only the head and the arm. The right arm, to be precise.

It was odd.

And when he searched again after the sun came up, he still couldn't find the rest of the body. The perp, a man named Hector Reynolds, wasn't forthcoming with information. He was a regular statue, staring at Bessum during their little interviews but saying nothing.

Now, seven days after arresting the guy, it was starting to look like they'd never find the rest of Tim Granger's body. (Bessum thought, upon first seeing the head, that it belonged to deadbeat alcoholic and violent drunk Tim Granger. He'd been right.) It was also starting to look like Reynolds would be going to a facility for the criminally insane instead of prison. It was all the same to Bessum, as long as the guy was off the streets.

But the case plagued him. Where had the rest of the body gone? And when would Reynolds and Granger have come into contact with each other?

There had also been a couple of missing person reports filed in the last two weeks. And, as if to add fuel to the fire, people around town were just acting *weird*. Case in point, Bessum was talking to the source of one of the missing person reports, a woman named Janelle Silver, mother to Kate Silver, who had disappeared less than forty-eight hours ago.

"And what was she wearing?" Bessum asked as they sat in the woman's kitchen. Dishes were piled up in the sink. A cat was meowing incessantly near the empty food dish in the corner. The place smelled like the cat litter box, wherever it was, hadn't been cleaned in about a week. And when Bessum had walked into the kitchen, led by Mrs. Silver, one of the stovetop burners was on, glowing bright orange. There was nothing nearby—not pots, pans, or kettles. The woman didn't seem to notice when he turned it off.

"I already told the officer all this stuff," she said. She was a severe-looking woman with a hooknose and stringy white hair that looked as coarse as the threads in a steel scrub sponge. Her white t-shirt was stained at the armpits and around the collar, and her sweatpants weren't much better.

"Yes," Bessum said. "But it's common practice to do a second interview. Sometimes people remember things. Going over it again helps. So, what was she wearing?"

Janelle Silver groaned and reached for her pack of cigarettes on the kitchen table amid the empty water glasses, junk food wrappers, and smashed cigarette butts that spilled from the overworked ashtray. While she was lighting up, Bessum pointed toward the cat. "You have any food?" he asked. "She looks hungry."

"Huh?" Silver said, turning to look over her shoulder as she exhaled a column of smoke. "My goddamn daughter's cat," she said, standing up and sending a waft of body odor in Bessum's direction. "That's why you need to find her. I can't stay on top of everything that needs done 'round the house without her." As she spoke, Silver grabbed a bag of dry cat food from a kitchen cabinet and dumped a good portion into the feline's bowl, spilling about half of what she poured onto the dirty linoleum floor. When she was done, she brought the bag of cat food back with her, setting it on the table and displacing various pieces of detritus, sending them spilling to the floor.

Bessum had no idea what the place had looked like before Kate Silver had gone missing, but he didn't figure the mess here for only forty-eight hours in the making. In his estimation, this mess had taken much longer to generate. How much longer, he wasn't sure. He cleared his throat and asked again, "What was your daughter wearing the last time you saw her?"

"She had on a short-sleeve pink-and-black flannel shirt," Silver said. "You know, the kind the hipster kids wear these days?"

"What else?"

"Black skinny jeans with holes in the knees. They were so worn they were more gray than anythin', really. And she had them black-and-white lace-up tennis shoes on. You know the ones."

Bessum nodded, writing this all down even though it matched what he'd read from the patrol officer's report. It gave him something to do and helped cement aspects of the case into his mind. "And did she leave with any clothes that you know of? I mean, any other clothes or supplies, like she was going on a trip?"

Silver sucked on her cigarette, shaking her head. "No. Her backpack is here. So's all her clothes, far as I know. She didn't have that many to begin with, you know? Times been tough."

"What about her purse or wallet?"

Again, Silver shook her head. "Her little clutch is still in her room. Only things she took with her was them clothes she was wearing and her phone."

"And you don't have any idea where she'd go?"

"I've called all her friends and that. They don't know where she is, neither. Ain't seen her, they say."

Bessum had already talked to several of her friends. In fact, he'd already run down every lead he could think of, which was why he was now back at the house, searching for something else to go on. "You mind if I look at her room, Mrs. Silver?" he asked.

"Have at it," she said, waving a hand toward the hallway out of the kitchen. But something came into her eyes, then. Something that kept Bessum from standing up and heading to the room. He waited while a look like recognition came into the woman's face.

She gazed over Bessum's shoulder, eyes fixed on nothing at all. "You know," she said, her voice low, "sometimes I think I know where she went." She paused, and Bessum waited, not moving a muscle. Some-thing—call it a cop's instinct—told him this was important. And after a few long moments, she spoke again. "Sometimes, I *know* where she is. It's like I can *see* her . . . or . . . feel her. Like she's on the ridge yonder, or down in the valley by Battle Creek, or just sitting in the dark in an old woodshed on the outskirts of town. But then the moment passes. Everythin' gets all . . . jumbled up again. All noisy." Silver smiled, and her eyes focused again as they moved back to Bessum's face. He waited, thinking she was going to say something else, but she didn't. And then her smile faded, and she got impatient. "What're you starin' at me for?" she said. "I thought you were gonna look in her room."

It was Bessum's turn to smile. "Right," he said. "Yes, ma'am." He stood up and headed down the hallway, but the eerie feeling that had settled on him when Silver started talking softly didn't dissipate like he thought it would. It stayed with him as he went over her words again and again.

Something inside—that cop's instinct, maybe—told him that something very strange was happening in this town.

And what he found in Kate Silver's room only solidified the notion.

CHAPTER 7

Seth Granger opened the truck door and jumped out before Mr. Winchell came to a complete stop in front of his house. As he stepped onto the front lawn, he paused, looking up at the two-story craftsman. The shades were all drawn, which was uncommon when the sun was still shining. The place looked shut up, like a mausoleum.

For one awful moment, Seth thought something had happened to the best friend he'd ever had. He stood frozen in the lush summer grass, his ears straining to hear the sound he was looking for, the sign that would at least make this difficult time bearable. But there was nothing. Not for a long moment.

Then a deep bark sounded from inside the house. Seth smiled. *Dallas.* He ran up the stairs and turned the doorknob, but the door was locked. The door was never locked. *I guess if a member of your family gets murdered, you start locking your door,* he thought. Then Dallas was scratching at the inside of the door, barking to be let out.

"Okay, hold on," Seth's mother's voice said from inside. The door opened and Dallas bounded out and jumped up on Seth, her tail whapping the doorjamb and her pink tongue lolling in excitement.

"Hey, girl," Seth said, bending down to pet the black-and-white dog. Dallas was a lab husky mix, with the husky winning out, making her look more like a black-and-white wolf than a dog. One of her eyes was dark brown and the other was pale blue, giving her a unique look. She licked Seth's face, paws on his thighs, body shaking with excitement.

Seth got down on his knees and stuck his head out toward her. At first, he thought she wouldn't do it. But then Dallas seemed to remember. She reached her own head up, placing the bottom of her jaw on the top of Seth's head. She went still, controlling her excitement as they shared their special greeting. It was their version of a hug, and they'd been doing it since Dallas joined their family when Seth was ten.

The moment passed, and Seth got up off his knees. Dallas was once again shaking with delight. For a moment, seeing the dog made him forget about the terrible news and Mr. Winchell's strange behavior.

"Good girl," Seth said to Dallas. Then he turned to his mother, who was standing in the doorway. She'd been watching the exchange with a small, sad smile tugging at the corners of her mouth. Now, she looked into Seth's eyes with a blankness that momentarily shocked the teenager; it was a look he'd never seen on her face. Or anyone's, really. But he pushed the uneasy feeling aside and bent down to hug the woman who'd brought him into the world. "I'm sorry, Mom," he whispered into her ear. It felt as if she'd gotten smaller in the last few months. She certainly seemed to have more gray in her dark-brown hair.

His mother let him go and stepped back, looking over his shoulder and giving a wave to Mr. Winchell. She dropped her hand, but her gaze remained fixed past Seth. The moment dragged on. Finally, Seth turned and looked at Mr. Winchell, who stood at the bottom of the porch steps, staring back at Seth's mother.

Dallas stood between the teenager and Winchell. Although the dog's hackles weren't raised, her posture was one Seth recognized. She was staring intently at the man, as if trying to decide whether he was a threat.

The sense of doom that had been undulating inside Seth since earlier that afternoon came back to the surface as he looked between his mother and Mr. Winchell. It was as if they were the only two people in the world. But it wasn't a loving gaze between them. There was some kind of communication going on, but Seth couldn't tell what it was. It certainly wasn't love. If anything, it was the opposite.

He had no idea how long it had been going on when he finally got the courage to speak. Absently bending down to stroke Dallas's head, Seth said, "Mom?"

She didn't respond.

Turning his head to Mr. Winchell, Seth was surprised to see that the man was now peering at *him*. A flash of black clouded Winchell's eyes as quick as a blink, then the man smiled, tilting his head. "Well, I better be going."

Seth nodded blankly.

"Come on inside, Seth," his mother said. He turned to see that she looked like herself again, although stressed and saddened.

"Yeah," he said, "I'm coming. Just need to get my bags." He got Dallas inside with his mother, noting an unpleasant smell emanating from within the house. Previous trips, when he'd been away from the house for days or weeks, Seth would come back in and smile at the familiar smell of home. But this time was different. There was something foul in the air. Like a sewer line had backed up.

He shut the door and quickly snatched his two bags out of the truck bed before hurrying back into the house. As he shut the door, the sound of Winchell's truck heading down the road faded away.

Dallas stood nearby, grinning and wagging her tail. Seth set his bags by the stairs and got on his knees to play with the dog. "Why are all the shades drawn, Mom?" he called out, hearing that his mom was in the kitchen.

"Huh? Oh, I guess I just didn't feel like seeing sunshine today," she said.

Seth nodded. That made sense. Scratching Dallas, he looked around the house. The normally tidy interior was cluttered with dishes, clothes, water glasses, and coffee mugs. It looked as if they had been accumulating for at least a month.

He sniffed, still smelling that malodorous stench. Seth thought Dallas had left him a smelly surprise, but a quick look around the house told him that wasn't the case. And it wasn't overpowering, like dog poop in an enclosed space. This was more subtle. And it seemed to be everywhere in the house. It didn't get stronger near the bathrooms or weaker in the bedrooms. It was everywhere.

Seth stood and walked into the kitchen, finding his mother at the sink, staring out one of the only windows in the house that wasn't obscured by shades. She was looking out at the old standalone garage at the back of the property. It was rusty red, its two leaning doors meeting off-kilter in the middle. The familiar weather-beaten chain and padlock securing the two doors together seemed, for many years now, to be the personification of his father. Tim Granger had always been locked away from Seth. And, in recent years, his mother, too. Like the padlock on the garage, Tim was the only one that held the keys. The only one that could let his wife and son in. But he rarely did.

After years of being locked out like this, Seth had begun to feel about his father like he did about the old garage. He just wanted to tear it down and get a new one. One that wasn't locked all the time, seeming to hide all the secrets Tim Granger possessed. One that Seth was welcome inside. Welcome to help with whatever project was going on in there.

But now that his dad was gone, those thoughts seemed callous and wretched. As he stood there behind his mother, looking at the old garage, he began to wonder if his halfhearted hopes for a new father—a better one—had played a part in his death.

He wrapped his mother in a hug from behind. And he kept his arms around her even as the tears dripped off her face and onto his arms.

CHAPTER 8

Seth took his bags up to his room and found Dallas cowering under his bed, which was totally out of character for the dog.

"What's wrong, girl?" Seth said, getting down on his hands and knees. Dallas looked up at him, shame and joy seeming to fight on her face. "Why are you acting so strange? Do you want to go for a walk?"

That little word got Dallas out from under the bed, tail wagging raucously.

Seth smiled. "Okay," he said. "Let's go." The two walked down the stairs together. Seth had left his mother in the kitchen, but now she was nowhere to be found on the first floor. He hadn't heard her go upstairs, but that was where she had to be.

"Mom, I'm taking Dallas for a walk," Seth called up the stairs, assuming his mom was in her room. She didn't answer, but after a moment he heard her moving around up there. *Strange.*

He got Dallas's leash hooked up and, with the roll of small poop bags in his pocket, they were out the back door. Dallas usually liked to sniff around the backyard first before they went to check out the wide world of fascinating smells in the neighborhood.

Dallas led Seth down the stairs and into the grassy backyard. The sweet smell of the blossoming Greenspire Linden tree in the yard quickly filled Seth's nostrils, not quite replacing the low-key foul smell from inside the house. Dallas made quick work of sniffing around the backyard before leading Seth out to the street.

His house was near the crest of a gently sloping hill, and it was their habit to walk to the top of the hill. Boy and dog walked up and looked around. Seth's vision caught on the tops of some trees over beyond the High Valley Methodist Church.

The church backed up to the woods, but something had changed there. Like someone had gone in and chopped down a group of trees beyond the church. But that didn't seem likely. There was no road leading back there. Seth had played in those woods after church his entire childhood, and it wasn't an ideal place to collect lumber.

A whine from Dallas caught his attention. Seth looked down at his dog, who was staring across the street. He followed Dallas's gaze, his heart lurching in his chest at the ghostly figure he saw there, gazing at him. It took him a moment to realize that it was Mrs. Faulk, standing on her porch in an off-white nightgown.

Dallas whined again, still looking at her. Seth raised his hand in greeting, but Mrs. Faulk didn't make a move. She just stared at him.

"Are you okay?" Seth asked, thinking of all the times his dad had grumbled about the "kookie old couple up the street."

Mrs. Faulk still said nothing. Although Seth's heart had calmed considerably after first seeing her, the unwavering gaze she held on him was fast making his cardiovascular system ramp up again.

He looked left and right to make sure there wasn't any traffic, then he crossed over despite his uneasy feeling. He thought maybe she was having a stroke or something. He wondered where her husband was.

"Mrs. Faulk? Are you alright?"

Her eyes followed him as he moved toward her, but she gave no answer. Like his mother, Mrs. Faulk looked considerably older than when he had last seen her. Seth had no idea how old she really was, but her wrinkles seemed to have multiplied. Her skin seemed washed out, and her stoop more pronounced.

"Let's get you back inside," Seth said, moving toward her but stopping when the leash went taut. He looked over his shoulder to see Dallas hunkering down, refusing to get any closer to the woman. There was a low whine coming from her, and her eyes were frightened, fixed on Mrs. Faulk.

"Come on, Dallas," Seth coaxed, pulling gently on the leash.

Dallas wasn't having it.

There was a speed limit sign nearby, so Seth led Dallas over to it; the dog had no problem moving further away from the woman. Seth secured her leash there and turned around to see Mrs. Faulk standing right behind him. Her hands came up, freezing cold as they clasped Seth's head. Her yellow-tinged eyes were wide, her papery skin lined with dark veins just under the surface.

"Heeeeellll," she said in barely a whisper, her hands squeezing Seth's head, her breath foul. Seth grabbed her wrists and tried to pry her hands off, but her strength was immense. "Heeeellllllllp."

Seth heard a growl and felt something bump the side of his leg. A moment later, Mrs. Faulk let him go. All the intensity was suddenly gone from her face. Both she and Seth looked down to see that Dallas had bitten her just below the hem of her nightgown. The dog had had just enough play in the leash to strain past Seth and take a chunk out of the side of her calf.

The blood was a dark red—almost black. And it was strange that a single bite could take a chunk out of her like that. The small bit of flesh was lying in the grass next to Seth's feet. Dallas was licking her chops fervently, like she was trying to get a terrible taste out of her mouth.

Other than dropping her hands and looking down, Mrs. Faulk

showed no signs that she'd even felt the bite. Seth looked up at her face, shocked at what had happened, but she was already turning around, walking with her uneasy gait toward her porch.

"I'm sorry," Seth said, following her. "Do you want me to call an ambulance? Maybe I'll get your husband. Dallas doesn't usually bite. I don't know what got into her."

She just kept walking, not saying anything.

"Mrs. Faulk? Do you . . ." Seth trailed off, unsure what to do. He quickly decided to find Mr. Faulk, so he ran ahead of the old woman, moved up the porch steps, and knocked on the door. "Mr. Faulk? Are you in there? There's been an accident."

Seth heard nothing, but there was that familiar miasma, clearly coming from inside the house. It was just like the mysterious smell in his own home.

Opening the door, Seth leaned inside and called for Mr. Faulk again, but there was no answer. Behind him, Mrs. Faulk was shuffling forward at the top of the steps. Seth moved out of the way so she could pass, which she did without a word.

She glanced at Seth once she was inside, one hand on the door. Seth couldn't meet her emotionless gaze for long, and his eyes flicked down to the wound on her leg. As she went to close the door, Seth noticed several flies already around the wound, shifting position, beating their wings, and rubbing their front legs together. By the time she closed the door, there were a dozen flies at the oozing bite.

Seth backed off the porch in a daze, suddenly aware of the utter silence around the neighborhood. There were no radios playing, no lawnmowers humming in the distance, no children hollering and laughing as they played. There wasn't even the hum of a faraway car engine.

Moments after he became aware of this, a dog barked in the distance. And then another. And another. Soon, the whole neighborhood was filled with the sound of frenzied barking. Dallas even joined in, barking and howling at the sky as the clatter continued.

Then, as abruptly as it started, it stopped. The neighborhood was silent again.

He turned and started walking distractedly back to Dallas, still tied to the sign. He didn't see a single car moving down any of the streets visible from the hilltop. Nor anyone walking or biking or skateboarding along. *Where is everyone?*

A deep and intangible fright burgeoned inside Seth, expanding like oil from a wrecked tanker spilling into the ocean. The sun would go down soon, and the very idea of darkness descending made him want to scream, although he didn't understand why. Just that something terrible had happened while he was away. And it wasn't over. It was *still* happening.

Seth untied the leash from the speed limit sign and ran home with Dallas, seeking a comfort in his childhood home that was no longer to be found. His home, like the town, had changed in ways Seth couldn't begin to comprehend.

CHAPTER 9

Detective Oliver Bessum sat in his car outside the Silver house, flipping through the diary he'd found in Kate Silver's bedroom. The patrol officer had missed it on the first sweep of the room because it had been hidden. Even Bessum had only happened upon it as quickly as he had by chance.

He'd been inspecting an old water bottle with mold or something growing inside. He'd picked it up from the dresser in the girl's room, not because he thought it had something to do with the case, but because he didn't understand how people could live like that. When he went to put the crusty bottle down, he knocked a small framed picture of Kate and a friend onto the floor. It was when he bent down to retrieve the picture from the narrow gap between the foot of the bed and the side of the dresser that he saw the diary. There was just a sliver of it visible, sticking out from behind the dresser.

He stood up with both items, placing the picture in its place and inspecting the diary before opening it up. The first three-quarters of it were filled with writing, but toward the back, Bessum saw there were some drawings. He stopped at one and studied it, a frown creasing his face.

It was a crude drawing of a smiling human done in pencil—he

wasn't sure whether it was supposed to be a male or a female. Maybe neither. But the human wasn't intact. All the limbs were drawn severed, each one in a different corner of the page. The smiling head was still attached. The small dot-eyes stared up at Bessum from the page.

"Find anythin'?" Janelle Silver asked from behind him, making him jump.

He snapped the diary closed, recovered quickly, then held it up. "Mind if I take this?"

The woman had barely looked at it. She waved a hand. "Never seen it before. Do what you want with it. Just find my daughter."

Now, sitting in his car mere minutes after the interaction, Bessum took his time with the diary. He counted twenty-two drawings in the back of the book, all of people with their arms and legs separated from their bodies. Some of them even had their heads separated. And it wasn't like the lines were straight at the separation points. They were jagged, squiggly. Like they'd been chopped off.

But one thing never changed across all the pictures. The crudely drawn humans were always smiling.

Bessum flipped to the last written entry in the diary. It was dated July 10th. Nearly a month ago now. There was only one thing that stuck out to the detective in the entry. It was a name. Grady. There was only one Grady in Seven Springs that was of an age to be traveling in the same circles as Kate Silver, and that was Grady Drummond.

Judging from the way she wrote about him, the two were involved. To be sure, Bessum didn't like the idea of going down to the Drummond property. It wasn't technically within the town limits. That made it the purview of the county sheriff's department. But the Drummonds did their business in Seven Springs—what little of it there was—and that meant Bessum knew who they were. In fact, he probably knew them better than most other citizens who actually lived in town. And not because they were a sociable bunch.

Sighing, Bessum set the diary in the seat next to him and started up the old Crown Vic's engine. He pulled away from the curb and headed out of the neighborhood. He turned off Lily Pad Lane and onto Fisher Creek Road, deciding that cutting through the neighborhood would be slightly quicker than going down to Center Street.

As he was coming up on the Jobson place, he slowed and leaned forward to peer out the windshield. He knew Russell and Sammy often liked to sit out on their porch during the evening when the weather was good, and it was good today. It was something a lot of people did in this town, but most of them were old. Russell and Sammy were both old souls, to be sure, but they were about twenty years younger than him.

Sure enough, he saw them sitting together, swinging on the porch swing Russell had installed shortly after they bought the house. Russell saw him and waved. Sammy smiled, which always got Bessum to smile. She had a book in her right hand, her finger holding her place.

Bessum pulled over to the curb and stopped, rolling down the passenger window. "Welcome back!" he called. "How was the vacation?"

"It was great!" Sammy said as Russell stood up and strolled over on his long legs. Bessum and Russell had met at the local watering hole one Saturday night nearly five years ago. They'd played several games of pool and got along like gangbusters without so much as a strained thought or uncomfortable silence between them. They'd been good friends ever since.

"How's it going, Ollie?" Russell said, his curly hair catching the descending sun, making it look more blond than it actually was.

"It's going," Bessum said, not wanting to sour his friend's homecoming with news about missing or murdered people. They'd hear about it soon enough, he was sure. "How's it feel to be back?"

Russell shrugged like he was about to give a generic answer. Then his face grew serious. "Actually, it's been kinda weird," he said.

"How's that?"

"Well, I don't know, really. Just a couple of neighbors acting out of character. Matter of fact, I haven't even seen Mrs. Stein since earlier. And she's almost always sitting on her porch the same time Sam and I are. I guess I should go check on her. That's the neighborly thing to do."

Bessum nodded. "Well, just wanted to say hi," he said. "I'm sure Mrs. Stein is okay, but if you can't find her, call it in. We've had a couple of missing person calls lately."

This got Russell's attention. "Really? Who?"

"Kate Silver, for one," Bessum said.

"Oh, no," Russell said. "She's one of my students."

"I know it."

"Well, I hope you find her. You know she's involved with that Drummond kid, right? The youngest one?"

Bessum nodded. "Where I'm headed now."

The two men looked at each other for a moment, silently commiserating. "Well, see you at Maggie's Saturday?"

"See you then," Bessum said.

Russell stood up from the window and Bessum drove off down the road. He looked in his rearview mirror and saw Russell standing on the sidewalk, looking down the hill toward Mrs. Stein's house.

CHAPTER 10

"Babe?" Russell said from the sidewalk.

Sammy looked up from her Stephen King novel. She was still sitting on the porch swing, gently swaying. "Yes, dear?" she said in her you've-interrupted-my-reading-time tone.

"I'm gonna walk down to Mrs. Stein's house. Be back in a minute."

"Sounds good," she said. "I'll be here."

Sticking his hands in his pockets, Russell started down toward the old lady's house in the only way he could, given the weather and the setting sun and the mood he was in: he sauntered. Mrs. Stein's house was only three houses down, but he took his time, walking with loose joints and a jaunt in his step. He kicked a dandelion, busting the white puffball apart and sending the little seeds sailing on the soft breeze.

When he came to Mrs. Stein's house, he stood and looked at the spot in the grass where he'd seen the lady standing earlier, as if it would give him some sort of clue as to where she was. He really didn't think anything was wrong. He was just being what Sammy called a Nosy Nelson. He figured the lady was inside her house, being as crabby as ever. She really wasn't a pleasant woman most of the time, but Russell didn't mind. She reminded him of his mother's mother. She wasn't pleasant, either, and he loved her just the same.

Getting no help from the patch of Kentucky bluegrass, he lifted his gaze to the house. The small white bungalow was narrow, longer than it was wide. It was white with faded black trim, and the whole thing needed a good paint job. The porch, normally occupied at this time of day, was empty.

As Russell walked down the walkway toward the house, he looked up toward Sammy, who was engrossed in her book. Then he glanced over his shoulder, toward Lyle's house. He saw no movement there.

On the porch, he glanced at the rocking chair Mrs. Stein favored, seeing a collection of dog-eared Sudoku books stacked on a little table between the rocker and a threadbare fold-up lawn chair that looked like it was from the 1950s.

Russell poked at the nearer chair, watching it rock on its runners. Then, as an awful feeling swept up his spine and into his brain, he reached out and stopped the chair from moving. It was too much like the ghost of Mrs. Stein was sitting right there, rocking away in the chair. He chastised himself for being silly. Mrs. Stein was still alive. And he was about to prove it right this minute.

Russell reached out and opened the flimsy screen door, sticking his bony knee out to keep it open while he knocked on the slightly less flimsy wooden door. He waited, listening for movement from inside the house. But there was none. So he knocked again.

Nothing.

"Mrs. Stein?" he called out. "You home?"

Birds chirped in the trees. Insects trilled. The house sat silent, and, it seemed to Russell, brooding. He looked at the rocking chair. Then, without thinking too much about it, he tried the doorknob. It turned. The door opened.

And the smell hit him.

He thought for sure it was the smell of a dead body. He'd never smelled a dead body, but his imagination was as good as anyone else's. He pictured a bloated, discolored version of Mrs. Stein lying in her bed. But then reality came back to him, which only increased the mystery more. He'd seen her earlier, so there was no way that the stink was coming from her. Even if she had gone straight home and dropped dead minutes after he saw her out his living room window, the time in between wasn't anywhere near long enough to generate a smell of this odorous magnitude.

So what was generating it?

He swallowed and gagged as he looked around the darkening living room. He opened his mouth to breathe and soon regretted it because he could *taste* the smell. Which meant little particles of stink were settling on his tongue. He gagged again.

"Mrs. Stein—ghh," he managed. "Are you in there?"

The words *probable cause* floated into his mind, as though he were a cop doing a . . . what did they call them? A wellness check? That sounded right. He was going to need someone to do a wellness check on *him* if he stayed in here for too long.

As his eyes adjusted to the low interior light, he saw that the place was a mess. There were dirty mugs and glasses everywhere, along with some plates and food wrappers. A couple of tin cans stood open, spoons or forks sticking out of them.

"Hello?" he called, moving farther in. He brought his left hand up, cupping it over nose and mouth. It didn't help.

The kitchen was next in line, and it wasn't much better off than the living room. It seemed as though every conceivable dish in the place was out of the cabinets and on any available flat surface. They all had food remnants in them, and the glasses were coated with grime.

Something was wrong with Mrs. Stein, all right. She'd had a stroke or was suffering from Alzheimer's or something like that. What Russell couldn't understand was why no one had seen this place and done something about it. Mrs. Stein had a daughter who lived across town, and she came over with the grandkids every so often. The lady also had regular company. Other old ladies would come over and talk or play cards or watch Family Feud or whatever old ladies did when they got together in their little gangs.

How had anyone allowed it to get this bad?

The stench seemed to be worse in the kitchen, but there was no readily apparent reason why. Russell figured he was just getting closer to the smell, which was surely in one of the back rooms. He moved down the hallway flanking the kitchen and came to a bathroom. Grimy sink and toilet and bathtub basins. No dead bodies. He moved on.

There were two bedrooms at the back of the house, and neither one of them held anything that would account for the smell. And now that he was on this side of the house, the stench had lessened slightly.

It was coming from the kitchen.

The woman didn't have any pets that he knew of, so he couldn't imagine what it would be. As he stepped back into the kitchen, he flipped the light switch on, looking at the array of cabinets low and high. Stepping over to the sink, he opened the small window above the fixture and stuck his nose against the dusty screen, breathing deeply and readying himself for the search.

He figured it was more likely to be low than high, and he was already standing in front of the sink, so he crouched and grabbed the small cabinet door handles. He opened them and immediately stood up to throw up into the sink, his vomit splashing over the dishes piled there.

It was definitely coming from under the sink. He hadn't actually seen anything—just a hole in the bottom of the cabinet—but the pungent reek had put him over the edge. He pressed his face against the screen again, breathing in through his nose and out through his mouth. When his stomach had settled, he took a deep breath in and then crouched again to inspect the area under the sink.

There was a hole in the wood that looked like a ragged expansion of the one for the sink drainpipe. It was about a foot and a half in diameter, and all the cleaning supplies and the other normal under-sink stuff had been pushed aside. The wood looked wet, and there seemed to be some kind of black mold growing on it. The stuff was everywhere.

Swallowing, Russell eased himself forward, sticking his head into the cabinet so he could look down into the dark hole. The smell was definitely coming from down there.

He got his head situated over the hole, but it was too dark at the bottom. He couldn't see anything but vague shapes. Still, he could tell that the hole was more than a foot deep. He didn't know if the house had a slab foundation, but if it did, the hole likely went right down to it.

As he reached for his pocket to grab his phone, he thought he saw movement down in the hole. He paused, squinting, trying to see.

Yes, something was moving down there. Insects, he thought.

He pulled his phone out and hit the button on the side as he brought it out over the hole.

A mass of writhing insects about the size of a basketball sat at the bottom of the hole, surrounded by that strange black mold. Russell's eyes went wide, and he flinched away from the gruesome sight, slamming his head into the S-trap for the sink drain. This vibrated the pipe that the writhing mass was pressed up against, and a cloud of flies erupted from the thing, buzzing angrily, and sounding to Russell's ears like a chainsaw coming at his head.

Russell cried out as dozens of flies swarmed up, battering his face. As he frantically pulled his head back out from under the sink, he could've sworn that he saw the fleshy red mass that the flies were sitting on *move*. Not just a twitch, but a real, deliberate movement. Like it was alive. But the reality of this wouldn't hit home until later, when he'd had a chance to reflect on it. At the moment, sheer panic was dictating his actions.

He threw himself away from the sink as the houseflies dispersed throughout the kitchen with a maddening buzz. He dropped his phone as he scrambled to his feet and booked it toward the front door, slamming out of the house and into the front yard, hyperventilating as he went.

CHAPTER 11

Sammy was just getting to a good part in her Stephen King book. She wasn't even to the halfway point, but something was about to happen to Terrence Maitland. Something bad, probably. It was all so deliciously mysterious. But she was pulled out of the fictional world as she heard her husband scream from down the street.

She knew it was him. There was no doubt about it. But she'd never heard him scream like that before. For one crazy moment, before all the horrible possibilities ran through her mind like a group of shoppers slamming through a box store's doors on Black Friday, she realized she'd never heard Russell scream before *at all*.

She stood from the porch swing, taking a moment to save her spot in the book with her bookmark. Something told her to stay calm, and that meant saving her spot in the book, like she normally would. It wouldn't do to go throwing her book around and freaking out in the process. That wouldn't help anything. She set the book down gently on the porch railing and moved with purpose down the stairs, stepping out to look down the road.

Russell was sprinting toward her, up the low hill. He was running, so that was good. His leg hadn't been broken. His arms looked fine. There was no blood that she could see. But his eyes. His eyes scared her, perhaps more than they should've.

She walked toward her husband, that same instinct that had told her to save the spot in her book now telling her to *walk, keep calm, take things as they come*. Something her mother loved to say came to mind: "The calmer you are, the stronger you'll be, Sammy." And it was important to be calm as a teacher. Especially in the era of mass school shootings, where any day could bring a life-or-death situation.

"Russell," she said as he approached. She said it calmly and was surprised when some of that crazy look in her husband's eyes faded. He slowed as he came to her, but he was still breathing hard from the running. "Something's wrong," he said between gasps. "Something's down there."

Sammy nodded, taking her husband's hands. "Okay," she said. "Do we need to call the police? An ambulance?"

This seemed to stump Russell. He turned his head and looked back down at Mrs. Stein's house. "Police, I think. I don't know."

"Did you see Mrs. Stein?" she asked.

"No," Russell said. His breathing was approaching normal. "No, I didn't see her. There's something under her sink. Something . . . like a . . . I don't know. A dead animal. It was covered in flies and other bugs—all kinds of bugs. I've never seen anything like it. I think it . . ." He trailed off, eyes still fixed on the house.

"You think it what?"

He shook his head. "I thought it moved, like it was still alive or something. But it was probably just the bugs on it moving. That was probably it."

"Okay," Sammy said. "Let's go sit and discuss this."

"Her house, Sammy . . . it's a wreck. She was always so neat and clean. Something's really wrong. We need to find her."

"I'll call the police and report her missing. And tell them that they should probably check out her house."

Russell nodded, but then something occurred to him, and he turned to look over at Lyle's house. It was getting dark now, but they still had another few minutes before the streetlights came on. It certainly wasn't light enough to be milling around in a house with the lights off, so it was a bit strange that Lyle's house was completely dark—and his old Chevy truck was parked in his driveway. She'd never known him to go on evening walks, but people could change.

"I thought I saw Mrs. Stein heading over toward Lyle's house earlier, when we were eating the sandwiches," Russell said. "Let me check there first, see if he's seen her."

Sammy was glad to see that the Russell she knew was back. Hearing him scream and then seeing the look in his eyes had frightened her more than she realized at the time. Now that she was calming down, too, she realized she was shaking, and that she had a slight touch of nausea. "Okay," she said. "I'll go with you."

A car was coming down the street, headlights on, so the couple waited. Russell stared across the road, but Sammy raised her hand and waved as Mrs. Meyers drove past in her little sedan. There was no response. Mrs. Meyers didn't even glance at them. Sammy shrugged it off with one thought: *Russell was right, everyone* is *acting weird.*

They walked across the road in the gloaming, holding hands. Directly across from their house was a modest cottage that had belonged to a nice African American family, the Garners. But they had moved six months ago now, and some investment company had swooped in and bought the house, turning it into an Airbnb. It didn't seem to be doing so well, as far as Sammy could tell.

The next house up the street was Lyle's. It was a single story, with a narrow, screened-in porch. Like most of the houses on the street, it was longer than it was wide. Lyle took excellent care of his lawn and flower beds, but this seemed to come at the expense of his house, which needed a coat of fresh powder-blue paint. Shingles were missing off the roof, and the windows all had spiderwebs on the outside.

Russell led the way, pulling on Sammy's left hand like a dog going after something that smelled too good to be ignored. They passed the front door before she started digging her heels into the ground. "Where are you going?" she asked.

"He took a bunch of stuff out of his garage," Russell said. "Look." He pointed between the nose of Lyle's parked Chevy and the corner of the house. Sure enough, there was a bunch of junk piled in the driveway in front of the standalone garage that hunkered behind and to the left of the house.

"So what? Is Mrs. Stein there?"

This seemed to bring Russell back to the task at hand. "Right," he said, letting Sammy pull him toward the front door.

Lyle—she wasn't sure if that was his first name or his last name—was a crotchety old man. Afraid to go onto the porch, the Jobsons stood on the two concrete steps in front of the outer porch door. Russell knocked on the door, which rattled in its frame, clearly unlocked. "Lyle, you home?" he called.

There was no answer. The house seemed perfectly still.

"Ah, dash this," Russell said, extracting his hand from Sammy's grip and opening the screen door, forcing Sammy to get off her step so he could open it all the way. He stormed across the narrow porch to the front door and knocked on it loud enough to wake the dead. "Lyle, you home?" he called again.

The house seemed to double down, getting even quieter, if that was possible.

"He's not home," Russell said, marching back and shoving open the porch door. Without hesitating, he moved toward the driveway.

"What are you doing?" Sammy asked, following him.

"I just want to check something."

He moved through the gap between truck and house, and Sammy followed. She had to step carefully so as not to trip over rusty paint cans, old oil jugs, broken mower parts, and water-damaged boxes of who-knows-what. She glanced up at one of the windows, sure she'd seen movement, but there was nothing there. Although she might not have been able to see someone even if they were standing on the other side of the glass. It was too dark in the house, and the sun wasn't much more than an afterthought on the horizon.

Russell stopped in front of the garage, which was of the old style, featuring two doors that opened up outward on hinges with wheels at the bottom corners. He grabbed at the new-looking chain and padlock securing the doors together.

"What are you thinking, Russell?" Sammy asked. "Why are you so interested in his garage?"

"I don't know," Russell said in a flat voice, looking down at the key-operated lock in his left hand. He dropped the lock and stepped over toward the pedestrian door to the right of the vehicle door. But before he could touch the knob, the scream of unoiled hinges cut the night air. They both turned toward the sound, watching as Lyle stepped out through the back door, holding a double-barrel shotgun, which he pointed at Russell.

"Get off my property," he said, pronouncing "get" as "git."

Russell smiled at first, thinking it a joke, but then reality dawned on him, and his face fell. For her part, Sammy knew something wasn't right. She couldn't quite place what, but she thought maybe it was something in his voice. Or the way he held himself. Or the fact that he'd been sitting inside a house with no lights on. He had never been a friendly man by any means, but he'd also never been downright hostile. Russell had made him laugh a couple of times over the years, and they always brought him a Christmas card and some homemade hot chocolate mix during the holidays. But as he pointed the shotgun at Russell, she knew he wasn't himself.

"Okay," Russell said. "I'm sorry, Lyle. I shouldn't have come back here without your permission. We were just looking for Mrs. Stein. Have you seen her?"

"No, I ain't seen her!" the old man said. "Now get off my property."

"Okay," Russell said again, holding his hands out from his sides as he moved back the way they'd come.

"Are you okay, Lyle?" Sammy asked.

The old man turned toward her, jaw suddenly moving as if he was chewing something. He swallowed twice, loud enough for her to hear, before answering. "I'm fine. Just fine."

"Well," she said, "if you need anything, just let us know."

They worked their way down the driveway and back across the street. When they were on their own porch, they both turned and looked at Lyle's house. It was still dark. And they hadn't heard the scream of the back door's hinges again.

"I think he's still standing out there on his back stoop," Sammy said.

"I think so, too."

"What the heck do you think's going on with him?" she asked.

"I don't know," Russell said. "But I think it's time to call the police."

CHAPTER 12

The Drummond house was located off a narrow and bumpy paved road just southwest of Seven Springs. The area consisted of thick trees and rolling hills crisscrossed with dirt roads and game trails. The mostly untouched land was dotted with rocky outcroppings and the occasional cave entrance.

The house itself was several miles from Highway 40, which meant it was several miles from any major developments. But it hadn't always been so. Back during prohibition, the area had been used by bootleggers for setting up stills to manufacture moonshine.

There were still several families living out in the woods in what amounted to little more than shacks. And as Bessum drove down the narrow Yellow Creek Road, he passed several structures that had been abandoned sometime in the middle of the 20th century. They looked like carcasses, with their doors and windows gone, empty black sockets seeming to stare accusingly at passersby. Mother Nature was slowly reclaiming them, and she would likely be allowed to finish the job; the terrain was too remote and too hilly for major construction.

It had only been about ten minutes since Bessum had left Russell standing on Fisher Creek Road, looking down at Mrs. Stein's house. He hoped to God the old woman wasn't missing. There weren't enough cops to go around with the sudden influx of strange happenings in the town.

As Bessum turned onto the Drummond driveway, he was sorely tempted to turn around and wait until the next day. There weren't more than fifteen minutes of daylight left, and the thick forest canopy made it prematurely dark. But time was of the essence, and he had a job to do. If he was lucky, young Kate was holed up with Grady Drummond, and he could get her home this very night. But he wasn't feeling lucky. Not a bit.

The Crown Vic passed the rusted-out skeleton of an old El Camino off to the right of the dirt driveway. On the left was a collection of three riding lawnmowers, all in various stages of disrepair. Nearby was a small earth mover that looked like it might actually still work. Next to it was a pile of dirt with weeds sprouting out of it. There was at least one bathtub, two toilets, and a kitchen sink in the trees around the house. And as he got closer to the structure, the detritus increased. There was trash everywhere. Bike parts, car parts, motorcycle parts, trailer parts, and discarded five-gallon buckets. Empty jugs of all kinds littered the yard; those that had once contained milk, oil, antifreeze, and industrial lubricants. Gardening tools were everywhere, most of them rusty.

The house itself was a Frankensteined structure that sprawled out in all directions. The original structure had probably been built over a hundred years ago, and the family had just made the odd repair here and there, doing the bare minimum to keep it from falling in on them. But as time went on and new children were spawned, they had to expand the house. Unfortunately, none of them seemed to know much about construction.

When they could, they tried to barter for repairs from professional carpenters or handymen in town. Bessum knew of at least two men who were still awaiting payment from the Drummonds for repairs they'd done. When they'd burned all those bridges, they tried to do the work themselves. There were two blue tarps strapped over an addition on the right side of the house as Bessum drove up. The addition on the left side of the house was leaning badly and looked as if a poorly made treehouse had been yanked from a tree and hastily nailed to the structure.

He noted the presence of the two operational trucks the Drummonds owned. One was a blue Ford from the nineties, the other a Chevy from the early aughts. Bessum breathed a resigned sigh as he put the Crown Vic in park behind the Chevy and shut off the engine. He'd been half hoping that old Edmund Drummond would be off somewhere doing whatever the hell it was he did all day. No such luck.

As he stepped out of the vehicle, he swept back his suit jacket with his right hand and felt the pistol at his hip. It was a Glock 17, the very same one he'd been carrying since his days as a detective in Philadelphia. He put his portable radio into his left outside jacket pocket. After looking around at the darkening woods, Bessum ducked back into his car and came out with a black Maglite flashlight, another holdover from his days in Pennsylvania. The heft of the full-size flashlight in his hand made him feel a little better as he shut his door and walked around the back of the car toward the front of the house.

"Mr. Drummond!" he called out as he walked. Every other time he'd come up here, there'd been one or two members of the Drummond clan either working on some piece of equipment outside the house or fixing a meal inside. Right now he saw no one, which was odd, given that both their vehicles were here.

"Anybody home?" he called. There was no answer. Not even any movement.

Stepping carefully onto the rickety deck, he moved to the front door. He peered through a narrow crack in the curtains, but there were no lights on inside the house. He couldn't see anything but a narrow strip of the dark entryway. Using the butt of the flashlight, he knocked on the door. When he heard no movement from inside, he stepped off the porch and started around the house, glancing at the windows as he went. All the front windows had shades drawn, but as he got around to the back, he could see that the curtains were parted over one of the rear windows.

The window in question was next to the back door, and as Bessum made his way up to it, dodging around all the junk piled in the backyard, he saw splotches of red on the two wooden back stairs. He stopped, turning his attention toward them. The click of the flashlight seemed loud in the eerily silent woods. Training the beam on the stairs, he confirmed it. Blood. And it wasn't just a few little spots. It was a trail. He turned, following the evidence with the flashlight beam out into the yard directly away from the house. The spots of blood got smaller as they went further from the house.

Bessum turned back around and hurried to the window, shining his light in. He was looking at a crowded dining room table just inside the window. He moved the flashlight, shining it down past the table, toward the floor.

More blood. A puddle of it in the kitchen. What he couldn't see was where it had come from. There was a wall blocking his view. All he could see was a sliver of a puddle of red on the floor. He moved back over to the door, mindful not to step in the blood, and tried the knob with his left hand. It was unlocked. He pushed the door open and shined the light inside. "Oh, Jesus," he said, reaching for the radio in his left jacket pocket.

Lynn Drummond, the matriarch of the family, was sprawled face-up on the kitchen floor. Her limbs had been chopped off at the elbows and knees with a meat cleaver that lay nearby, stained in her blood. Her eyes were open, her face blank. The lines that had already been entrenching themselves on her face in life were doubly pronounced in death.

From where he was, he couldn't see the severed limbs. He had a pretty good feeling they would be missing.

He brought the radio up and held down the transmit button. "This is unit five requesting assistance for a 10-39 at 127 Yellow Creek Road," he said. "Again, 10-39 at 127 Yellow Creek Road. Suspects still on the loose."

"Uh, okay, copy that unit five," Sharice back at the station said.

"I'm on my way, Bessum," a man's voice said over the radio. It was Paul Tulards, the same guy who'd discovered Tim Granger's similar murder a week ago.

"Anyone else who isn't busy, we're probably going to need your help over here," Bessum said, looking over his shoulder into the woods. There was very little light left, but Bessum was determined to use it. He closed the back door and stepped into the yard, pointing his flashlight beam down at the ground.

He followed the blood for about thirty yards before he lost it in the dark dirt, fallen leaves, and branches. Clicking off his flashlight, he walked out into the woods, letting his eyes adjust. He told himself he wouldn't go far—just over the next hill. After all, he needed to wait for backup. The Drummonds had about as many guns as the whole of the Seven Springs Police Department.

But when Oliver Bessum got to the top of the hill, he saw something that all his years as a police officer couldn't have prepared him for.

CHAPTER 13

The remaining members of the Drummond family were in a clearing about fifty yards from where Bessum stood at the top of a hill. The clearing was slightly down from where the detective stood, and the last remnants of the day's sunlight, slight as they were, gave him a view of the scene.

Grady Drummond, the youngest of the brood, thrashed on the ground, muffled cries barely escaping his mouth. His father, Edmund, pinned the boy on his back with one hand on his chest. In his other hand, he held what could only be his wife's severed leg. And he was shoving the edge of the foot into the teenager's mouth. As he did this, the man was muttering and cursing, his words so jumbled and guttural that Bessum could not understand them.

The other severed appendages were scattered nearby in the clearing, as though dropped there in haste. Both feet were bare, prompting Bessum to remember that every time he'd ever seen Lynn Drummond on her property, she'd been walking around barefoot.

The other three Drummond kids stood around, watching blankly. There was Albert Drummond, the oldest, standing nearby with a Remington 700 hunting rifle held absently in his hands. He stared out from under his mop of dark hair as though he were watching a couple of dogs fight over a bone.

Keith Drummond, the seventeen-year-old, had his back to Bessum, but his posture and stance gave the detective no indication that he was the least bit concerned about what was happening in front of him.

Then the other offspring, Janie Drummond, sat on a fallen tree nearby, jean-clad legs spread, and her elbows propped on her knees as she watched her dad try to force-feed her brother a piece of her mother.

Mother of God, what is going on in this place? Bessum asked himself, swallowing a lump in his throat.

Edmund let loose a cry of anguish as he tossed the severed lower leg aside and slapped his son across the face, the sound of both the cry and the slap seeming to linger among the trees. Still holding his son down, the man extended his right hand toward nineteen-year-old Albert. "Give me the gun," he said, gruff voice choked with emotion.

Albert's eyes shifted to his father, but he made no move to hand him the weapon.

Bessum stared, shocked into inaction as his mind struggled to comprehend the scene. Nothing about this made sense.

Edmund growled and lurched up, stepping over and snatching the rifle away from Albert, who gave it up without resistance. The man had it up to his shoulder and pointed at his son when Bessum's paralysis finally broke. "Edmund!" he called.

All the heads in the clearing snapped up to look at the cop, who suddenly felt very alone.

"No!" Edmund yelled, whipping the rifle up to aim it at Bessum. Oliver wasted no time, throwing himself back the way he'd come just as a crack from the rifle snapped through the woods. The bullet hit a tree near where Bessum had just been. He pulled out his Glock as he ran back toward the house. With his left hand, he retrieved his radio.

"Shot's fired," he said. "Shots fired at 127 Yellow Creek Road. Officer needs assistance."

"I'm almost there," Tulards said, voice tight. "Two minutes. Hang in there."

"Copy that, unit five," Chief Medina said. "On my way. So is everyone else. Because if they don't, they won't have a job tomorrow."

Bessum kept running until he came to the house. He hadn't heard another gunshot, and he didn't know if the Drummonds were following him or not, but he wasn't about to stop and find out. He rounded the ramshackle house and threw himself into the car, sticking his pistol under his thigh as he fired up the engine and shifted into reverse. He hit the gas and guided the car down the driveway about thirty yards before pulling over to the side and stopping the car.

He left it running as he opened his door, popping the trunk before jumping out, pistol in hand. At the trunk, he leaned in and opened a gun case, retrieving a Colt AR-15 rifle.

Behind him, he could hear a siren getting closer. Lights bounced off the trees and the trash as Tulards zoomed up and came to a sliding halt with his car next to Bessum's, both now effectively blocking the driveway.

"Where they at?" the patrol officer said, jumping out of his car and keeping his head down as he went to his trunk to get his own AR-15.

"They were in the woods about two hundred yards behind the house," Bessum said.

"How many shooters?"

"Just one. But . . . I don't know. Something weird is happening."

"What do you mean?"

"I don't know," Bessum said.

There was silence as they peered over their cars toward the house. Tulards had turned his flashing lights off, but he'd turned his spotlight on as he got out of the car. It was pointed up at the structure.

"How many weapons?"

"Only one that I saw," Bessum said. "A Remington 700 with a scope."

"Well, shit. What should we do? You think we can talk to him?"

"I certainly hope so because he had his kids with him."

"Shit."

"Yeah." Bessum raised his rover to his mouth and said, "Chief, let's get someone over on Blue Sky Road. If they make their way on foot, they'll come out over there. Have someone drive up and down, keeping an eye out for them."

"You hear that, Wesley?" Chief Medina asked. "That's all you."

"Copy that," Ann Wesley replied over the radio. "Be there in two minutes."

"So what exactly did you see?" Tulards asked as he scanned the woods for movement. "Something like what we found last week?"

"Why do you ask that?" Bessum said.

Tulards was silent for several long moments, seeming to gather his thoughts. "I've just been noticing some strange behavior in this town over the last week or so. People are acting awfully odd if you ask me."

"How's that?"

"Well, I got a wellness check a few days ago for Ginny Abraham. Apparently old Nash walked her to church on Sunday as he always does, but she wouldn't go inside. Said she was feeling strange and needed to go lie down."

"Yeah?" Bessum said.

"Well, Nash, being the gentleman he is, walked her back up the hill to her home. And he made her promise to call him the next day. Well, she never called. And Nash went up to Augusta to see his grandkids on Monday. He tried calling her on Tuesday, and she didn't pick up.

So I get the wellness check."

Bessum put up a hand to stop Tulards and then pointed into the woods to the right of the house. Both men looked that way. Something moved out in the trees.

"It's a rabbit," Tulards said.

As soon as the patrol officer said it, Bessum saw that he was right. Still, they were silent for about a minute as they scanned the entire area.

"Well, what happened?" Bessum finally asked. "If you found her dead, I would've heard about it, I'm sure."

"No, she ain't dead. But she was acting awful odd, like I said. I been to her house before, you know? She's not the cleanest lady in the world, but she keeps her place pretty tidy. But when I went in there, there was junk all over the place."

Bessum thought about the Silver house. It was a mess. "How was she acting?"

"Yeah, that's the other thing," Tulards said. "She seemed zoned out. Like she was taking too much of some kinda wacky medicine for mood disorders or something. She just kinda stared blankly at me when she opened the door. I had to ask if I could come in, and that's strange for her. You know."

"Yeah, I know," Bessum said.

Headlights cut up the road behind them, and they looked back to see Chief Medina's truck heading up the driveway.

"So what do you think's going on?" Bessum asked.

"I don't know," Tulards said. "But it ain't good. I *do* know that."

Chief Holden Medina, a small, stout man of Hispanic heritage, jumped out of his truck and moved up to them with his massive revolver held in one thick-fingered hand. "Any movement?"

"Just a rabbit," Bessum said.

Another cruiser rolled up behind them, and then another behind that one.

The two men ran up, armed with their rifles, and took position next to Tulards. They all looked toward the house.

Nothing happened for several long moments, but none of the men spoke. It was as if they could sense what was coming.

"Movement!" Tulards said. "Second window from the left."

The window shattered in time with the muzzle flash as someone fired on them from inside the dark house.

***

Bullets punched into Tulards's squad car, thumping into metal and cracking through glass. The five officers gathered behind the two cars knelt as the barrage continued. Bessum quickly lost count of the shots, but he was certain that it was only one gun doing the firing. For now.

There was a break in the firing, and all five officers stood and unloaded on the house, aiming for the window from which the first shots had come.

"Cease fire!" Medina yelled after dozens of shots had been fired. "Stop firing!"

They all stopped, kneeling again and looking wild-eyed at each other.

"Jesus H. Christ," Medina said, shaking his head in bewilderment, even though he fired all six shots from his revolver before apparently coming to his senses. He cupped his hands around his mouth. "Edmund, you still alive up there?"

There was no answer. Then again, Bessum wasn't sure he would've heard an answer at all unless Edmund Drummond had been standing right next to him. His ears were ringing from all the shots.

"Any of the kids up there?" Medina asked Bessum.

"They were all gathered a couple hundred yards behind the house when I saw them. All but Lynn, who I saw dead in the house, arms and legs chopped off."

Medina stared at him for a second, dark eyes seemingly black in the poor lighting behind the two vehicles. "Chopped off? Again?"

Bessum nodded.

"Jesus H. Christ," Medina said again. Then he yelled toward the house once more. "Any of you kids up there? You come out with your hands up and we won't shoot you!"

No answer.

"All right. Let's go on up there."

"How do you want to do it?" Bessum asked.

"Well, I guess we'll take your unmarked because this one's toast," Medina said, gesturing at the bullet-riddled squad car. "You drive it on up and we'll follow behind. You see shots, just stop and get your head down."

"Fine," Bessum said. He got into the front seat, setting his rifle down next to him and pulling out his pistol after putting the vehicle in gear. He checked his rearview mirror, seeing that everyone but the rookie, Mitchell, was behind the unmarked. Apparently, Medina had told him to stay put for a good vantage point.

Bessum eased on the gas and guided the cruiser up the gentle hill toward the house. He pointed his pistol out the windshield just in case he had to shoot through the glass. He turned the car and stopped in the driveway, positioning the vehicle so they could use it for cover if they needed to.

Medina shouted once more, and once more received no answer. They all gathered on the driver's side of the car and discussed the entry plan. Once that was done, Bessum popped the trunk and Tulards retrieved a sledgehammer from the space.

They ran to the house in a line, checking the near window before waiting for Tulards to do his work with the sledgehammer. It took the man four swings, but he finally got the door open, stepping out of the way and letting Medina, Bessum, and Brenner rush inside.

They quickly cleared the house, finding Lynn Drummond just as Bessum had seen her. They found Edmund Bessum in the front room where the first shots had originated. He had a bullet hole in his head, two in his chest, and one in his arm. He was clearly dead. Had probably been hit within the first couple of seconds of return fire. There was no one else in the house.

"Dammit all to hell," Medina said, looking at Lynn in the kitchen. "I guess I'm calling up the county guys again. Second time in a week."

"We need to find the kids," Bessum said. "Let me take Tulards and head out into the woods."

"They'll come around," Medina said. "You said Edmund's the one who shot at you, right? He's probably the one who did this."

"I'm not so sure," Bessum said. "And Chief, her arms and legs are not here. They had them out in the woods. Like they were bringing them out there for a purpose."

Medina swallowed, looking up at his detective. "You think the kids might still have them?"

"I think they might, yeah."

"Jumpin' Jesus. All right. Take Tulards and see what you can see. But be careful, for God's sake."

CHAPTER 14

Sammy had called the police while Russell paced in the living room, staring out across the street at Lyle's house. Knowing that the 911 operator was based out of town, she skipped the middleman and called the police station directly. Sharice had answered and waited patiently for Sammy to explain the situation. Then she said she'd send someone out just as soon as she could, but that it might not be for a while because there was an emergency elsewhere and it was all hands on deck.

That was nearly twenty minutes ago now. Russell had been pacing the whole time, saying how Lyle's house was still dark every two minutes until it had driven Sammy half crazy.

"Let's just go back down there. Maybe she came back," Sammy said now. It was better than sitting here on the couch watching her husband work himself up into more and more of a frenzy. Having a shotgun pointed at him had done something, Sammy knew. It had riled him more than he wanted to admit. She could tell it was bothering him because it was the one part of the evening's excitement that Russell hadn't mentioned in all his ranting and pacing.

He stopped pacing and stared at Sammy for a moment. "Yeah, okay," he said. "Maybe you're right. Maybe she's back. Wouldn't that be something? Just a misunderstanding. But it still wouldn't explain the state of her house. Or that *thing* I saw under her sink."

That was something else, Sammy thought. She wanted to get a look under the sink. There had to be some reasonable explanation for it. Maybe a hurt animal had crawled under there or something. Whatever it was, she was curious.

They got up and headed out into the night. Sammy made a mental note to bring the novel back inside when they came home; she'd left it on the porch railing. Lyle's house was still dark, and so was Mrs. Stein's, as far as she could tell.

But as they got closer, she saw a lighted window about halfway down the side of the house. Near the kitchen.

"Were there any lights on when you went inside?" she asked Russell as they moved down the sidewalk. The night was alive with the sounds of summer insects. She thought she even heard some bats swooping around above the streetlights, snatching their dinner out of the air.

Russell considered her question. "I think I turned on the kitchen light."

Sammy nodded. They paused as they came to the walkway that led to Mrs. Stein's house. Russell reached out and grabbed her hand before they walked up to the porch.

There was no answer when they knocked on the door. No answer when they called out her name. Russell had slammed the door in his rush out of the house, and he was the one to reach out and turn the handle now.

As the door opened, Sammy recoiled from the smell. "Oh God," she said.

"Yeah," he said. "It's about ten times worse in the kitchen."

Letting her hand go, Russell stepped inside and slapped at the wall for a light switch. He found one, and the previously shadowy living room came to light in all its cluttered glory. "Wow, you weren't kidding," Sammy said, looking at the mess.

They moved through the living room and to the kitchen. Russell moved warily toward the still-open sink cabinets, reaching down to retrieve his phone from the floor. The stench was worse here, but it wasn't as bad as Russell had made it out to be. He pointed to the cabinet. "It could be an animal or something," he said. "So be careful. Or, better yet, how about we find a mirror to use. I'm sure she's got a hand mirror around here somewhere."

Sammy knew when her husband needed to do something—needed to be useful. "Yeah, okay," she said. "Wouldn't hurt to check the rest of the house now, anyway."

They moved out of the kitchen together, checking out the two bedrooms at the back of the house. There was no sign of Mrs. Stein or anyone else. Russell found a mirror in the master bathroom and brought it out. They went back to the kitchen, and Russell handed the mirror to Sammy. But he didn't let it go when she grabbed it.

"Do you want me to do it?" he asked.

Sammy smiled. "That would defeat the purpose, wouldn't it, honey-baby?" she said, ribbing him just a little. "I want to see for myself, remember?"

Russell smiled weakly. "Right," he said, releasing the mirror.

Sammy took it and knelt in front of the sink, pulling her phone out of her pocket and turning the flashlight function on. She stretched the mirror out in her left hand and got it over the hole. With her right hand, she extended the phone and shone the light down into the hole.

And she saw nothing. Nothing other than a hole that went down into the crawlspace under the house. She worked the mirror and the light around, getting a better look at the space. Then she set the mirror aside and moved her head in to look down directly.

Bless him, Russell kept his mouth shut while she did this, even though he was surely freaking out.

"Well, babe," she said finally. "I don't see anything. It must've been a hurt animal that crawled further under the house or something."

"Let me see," Russell said, getting down on his knees next to Sammy. She handed him the phone as she moved out of the way. He peered down into the hole for a few long moments before coming back out.

"Yeah, whatever it was is gone."

They sat on the kitchen floor for a moment, neither of them saying a word. They just looked at each other. Sometimes, for them, that was enough to communicate what would otherwise have to be said in a few sentences.

Russell got to his feet first and then helped Sammy up. She grabbed the mirror and asked Russell to put it back where he'd found it. While he went to do that, she wandered back into the master bedroom for one last look around.

Later, when she had a chance to think about what happened next, she would tell Russell that she didn't know what possessed her to go to the window. It wasn't really a conscious decision. It was just one of those things.

While Russell was in the bathroom, she moved around the bed and parted the curtains over the back window. And there was Mrs. Stein in her green slip, about ten yards from the window. She had her back to Sammy, but her head was craned around, almost uncomfortably so, to peer at her own house. The way her arms were situated, Sammy surmised that she was holding something in front of her. Something Sammy couldn't see, but it was surely big enough to require both hands to hold it.

The two women stared at each other for a long moment. There was something about the look on Mrs. Stein's face that froze Sammy, like she was one of her painfully introverted students called up to give a report in front of the whole class. The old woman's eyes were dark, she realized. They weren't just dark from the lack of light in the backyard. No, Sammy had seen Mrs. Stein plenty of times in limited light. The woman had pale green eyes that were brighter than freshly mowed Bermuda grass. But not now. Now they were dark. Clouded over with darkness, Sammy thought.

Mrs. Stein turned her head back into its neutral position and then ran—really ran—toward the woods backing her house. Sammy couldn't remember a time she'd ever seen the woman move so fast. But even though she was rushing out into the darkness, she was moving awkwardly, thanks to whatever she held in her arms.

Her paralysis finally broke, and Sammy yelled, "Mrs. Stein! Where are you going?"

She didn't answer, didn't even turn. Soon, Sammy lost sight of the old woman.

Sammy whipped away from the window, running directly into Russell. "Did you see her?" he asked.

"She's running into the woods!"

Sammy broke away from her husband and bolted out the door. Russell followed closely, asking rapid-fire questions about what she'd seen.

Sammy finally slowed as she approached the edge of the woods. Russell was breathing heavily—more from excitement than from exertion. "What did you see? Did she see you? What happened?"

"She saw me, all right," Sammy said, peering into the woods. "Something's wrong with her, Russ."

"How do you mean? Like dementia?"

"I don't know," Sammy said. *Her eyes*, she thought.

"Well, I suppose we should go try to find her."

"Should we?" Sammy asked, not so sure.

"Of course. What if something happens to her out there?"

"What if she doesn't want to be found?"

"Why wouldn't she want to be found?" Russell asked, now looking at his wife closely.

She gave no answer. Instead, she asked another question. "What if she *wants* us to go out there?"

CHAPTER 15

The sound of the back door opening in the still, late-summer night was unmistakable. Even from his room upstairs and on the opposite side of the house, Seth had no problem hearing it. He lay sprawled on his bed, waiting for a text back from either of his two best friends. Dallas lay on the floor nearby. The dog raised her head and looked toward the cracked bedroom door just as Seth did the same thing.

Had things been different—had his alcoholic father not been murdered and his normally warm and affectionate mother not been acting extremely strange—Seth wouldn't have given the sound a second thought. But as it was, his thoughts went to possible reasons for his mother to be going out the back door. Seth himself had taken out the full-to-overflowing kitchen trash after making dinner, so that wasn't a possibility. Dallas was up here, so it wasn't as though she was opening the back door to let the dog go out.

He listened hard, holding his breath as he set his phone aside. And he heard the faint rattle of chains. The garage.

Seth swung his feet off the bed and hurried out into the hall. He took a left, going down toward the window at the end of the hall that overlooked the driveway. As he approached the window, he slowed.

Angling himself so that he wouldn't be seen easily, he peered out the window and toward the garage.

His mother, having unlocked the padlock that secured the chain, pulled one of the two sagging doors open just enough to slip inside. From his angle, Seth couldn't see what she was doing in there, but she didn't turn on the light and she didn't have a flashlight with her. She was inside for less than thirty seconds before she slipped back out again and moved out of Seth's line of sight. He moved into the hallway bathroom and leaned over the toilet to peer out the small window, bringing the backyard and half of the garage into view. His mother appeared from behind the garage with an item wrapped in a black trash bag. Whatever was in the bag was about two and a half feet long and maybe five or six inches in diameter, although it was hard to tell because she carried it with one end tucked between arm and body.

She slipped into the garage again. Seth thought for a moment that it was a present for him, although his birthday wasn't for another couple of months. Still, it seemed the only logical explanation. But he knew where his mother hid the presents, and it wasn't in the garage. Besides, he was far past the age where snooping for presents was a worry.

His stomach rumbled with discontentment, and he had a sudden urge to pee. A crushing feeling settled on him, close to sending him into a spiral of panic. It was the feeling that he was living with a stranger. This woman down in the garage didn't seem like his mom. Not really.

He swallowed hard, choking back a sob. Something nudged his thigh, and he looked down to see Dallas peering up at him with her different-colored eyes. He reached down and scratched behind her ears, stepping back from the pit of panic as he did so.

His mother came out of the garage without the bag-wrapped item and went about closing the door. She fastened the chain and locked it, pocketing the key.

Seth expected her to come back into the house, but she didn't. She turned to walk down the driveway between the house and the Volvo station wagon parked there. And as he pulled himself away from the window for fear of being seen, he noticed something. The knees of his mother's jeans had little circles of dirt on them. She'd been on her knees in the garage. The floor in there was dirt, not concrete, and she'd done something with that item that involved getting on her knees.

But this curiosity was soon replaced by a stronger, more immediate one. Where was she going? And why didn't she tell him she was leaving?

Maybe she's checking the mail, he thought. His mother went in that direction, but Seth soon lost her from view. Still, he waited. It was clear she wasn't checking the mail. She would've been back already.

In a split-second decision sitting on a foundation of momentary courage, Seth decided to follow her. He had to see where she was going.

He needed to figure out what was wrong with the only parent he had left.

***

Dallas had whined when Seth told her to sit tight in the house. She had been sitting at the back door, shifting her weight between her two front paws, and looking at him with an expression that was about more than just being left inside. He felt bad about leaving her, as he always did. But it was necessary.

Now, as he crept down the hill, keeping his mother in sight some sixty yards away, he went over every strange interaction with her since arriving home mere hours earlier.

Their interactions had been stilted, to say the least. Previously, their conversations had always been open and flowing and natural. Today, they'd been anything but.

Seth had volunteered to cook dinner not only because his mother seemed to be in no condition to do so, but also because their normal dinnertime was ten minutes away and she still hadn't started, despite telling him that she'd handle it earlier that afternoon. He'd made Hamburger Helper with microwaved potatoes and canned green beans heated on the stovetop.

During the meal, which had taken place at the already cluttered dining room table, Seth did his best to keep the conversation away from the subject of his father's death. He talked about camp, even though she hadn't asked. He told her about Darius Lovett and his mother. And about all the friends he'd made last year who'd come back this year. And about all the activities they'd done. Even though he wasn't into the religious aspects of church camp, he told her about those, too.

His mother simply smiled and nodded and said, "That's nice." She barely touched her food.

When he'd fed Dallas that night, the dog scarfed down the food like she hadn't been fed in days. And when he'd gone to clean up some of the dishes around the house—mostly water glasses—his mother had snapped at him, telling him to go to his room so she could think.

He went over these things again and again in his mind as he followed her down the hill.

County Spring Road, where Seth's house was located, traversed a long and gradual hill. Seth's house was near the top, where it more or less leveled out and led eventually toward the small downtown area of Seven Springs.

At the bottom of the hill, County Spring Road came to an end against a wall of trees. But just before the road ended at a dirt turn-around area with No Dumping signs posted on trees, there sat the High Valley Methodist Church.

Seth realized with no small amount of relief that his mother was headed to the church. It was only natural that his mom sought support in the arms of the Lord. She'd always been the most religious of the family.

Feeling much better about things, Seth slowed down, a column of guilt settling itself in his gut for following his mother like she was some kind of criminal. Despite this feeling, he didn't turn around. He'd come this far already, so he wanted to make sure, without a shadow of a doubt, that his mom was headed into the church.

There was a stretch of lightly wooded area between the last house on the street and the church. Seth ducked into this area and moved through the shadows so he could watch the church doors to make sure she got inside okay.

The church was a small affair, made of white-painted wood and complete with a thin steeple. It was old, which was why Seth wasn't all that surprised to see that someone was in the middle of working on it. The side he could see from his spot in the woods had boards missing and discarded in a pile at the back of the building.

As his mother approached, the front doors opened, and Mrs. Simpkins stepped out. The old widow lived across the street and three houses down from Seth and his mother. You could always count on her hobbling down the sidewalk to the church on Sunday mornings, and then hobbling back after the service.

The two women said nothing to each other. Mrs. Simpkins, dressed in a simple tunic sweater and jeans, held the door open. Once Seth's mother was up the three steps and through, she followed her inside, closing the door behind her.

Seth moved out of the woods and stood on the sidewalk, peering at the church. He still didn't understand why his mother hadn't told him she was leaving. Maybe she'd just gotten so used to him being away at summer camp that she'd simply forgotten. She was clearly traumatized and dealing with stress. He decided to cut her some slack. She would talk to him when she was ready.

As he turned around to head back home, the sound of construction came to his ears. The sound of hammering was unmistakable. Only it wasn't the kind of clean, precise hammering you hear when someone is trying to build something. It was the kind of chaotic, smash-it-all hammering you hear when someone is trying to destroy something.

He turned and looked at the small white building.

There was no mistaking it. The noise was coming from the church.

CHAPTER 16

"You know this area better than me," Bessum said to Tulards as they crouched in the woods. "Where do you think they would go? What's even out here?"

They'd crept through the dark woods as quietly as possible, using nothing but their eyes to search for the Drummond kids. There had been some debate, as they'd prepared themselves for the trek, about whether they should use their flashlights. In the end, Bessum's notion won out, and they ventured into the woods without the telltale beams piercing the night.

"Hell," Tulards said now, "there ain't nothin' out there but more woods and hills. Maybe a little cave or two. Maybe an old shack. You never know what these hill people get up to out here."

"Very comforting," Bessum said.

They'd just passed the clearing where Bessum had seen the four Drummond children and their father what seemed like an eternity ago. There'd been no sign of the kids, nor any of the limbs that had been there.

"What do you want to do?" Tulards asked. "Keep goin'?"

Bessum had to ruminate on that one. He kept flashing back to the scene of Edmund Drummond trying to force his wife's foot into his youngest son's mouth. There was something seriously wrong with these people. And being out here in the woods gave him the creeps.

Finally, he said, "Yeah, just a little further. If we don't find them in another five minutes, we'll give it up until daylight."

They rose from their crouches and continued on, not speaking. The only sounds were of crickets and night birds and their crunching footsteps.

Then they heard a distant *thunk* sound. Like a stone dropping to damp ground. They both froze, turning their heads in unison to the right, toward the sound.

It came again. *Thunk.*

They moved toward the noise without a word or a look. Both of them still had their rifles with them, and they drew them up. When Bessum had seen the clan in the woods, there had only been one rifle. But they could've made it back to the house to arm up in the time it took for backup to arrive.

For all they knew, every single one of the Drummond kids now had a gun on them.

Thunk.

It was coming from down in a divot up ahead. And it no longer sounded quite like a stone dropping into damp dirt.

Bessum hoped against hope that it wasn't what he thought it was. But his years as a cop had made him a worst-case-scenario kind of guy. And his hope mechanism wasn't all that strong anymore.

As they approached the divot, they both pulled out their flashlights and got them ready. Using hand signals, they made a plan. They would separate by about ten yards, coming on the divot that looked like a creek bed from either side in an effort to corral whoever was down there without the danger of crossfire.

They moved away from each other as the noise continued every five or six seconds. When they were about ten yards away from each other, they could still just barely see one another. Bessum held up his hand with the flashlight, raising his pinky, ring, and middle fingers. He dropped his pinky finger. Then his ring finger.

Both cops clicked on their flashlights and stepped to the edge of the divot, shining their beams down into the dry creek bed.

Grady Drummond, the youngest of the brood, froze with his right arm raised, rusty hatchet in hand. His sister's mutilated body lay before him. Both her arms and one of her legs had already been hacked off. Gripping her lone intact leg with his left hand, Grady was in the middle of cutting through the knee joint.

There was sudden movement at the edge of the illumination from the two flashlights. His mind still processing the disturbing scene, Oliver Bessum whipped his flashlight up in time to see Albert and Keith Drummond turn to run.

Their arms were full of body parts.

"Stop!" Bessum shouted.

They didn't stop.

"Tulards!" Bessum said, knowing that he wouldn't have a chance of catching the two teenagers in a footrace. Tulards didn't need to be told twice. He ran up and jumped down into the creek bed well away from Grady, who hadn't moved except to blink. As the patrol officer scrambled up the other side, Bessum returned his gaze to the two siblings, one of which appeared dead. Janie Drummond's eyes were open, but they seemed fixed on nothing. Besides, if she'd been alive and conscious, she no doubt would've been fighting or screaming or convulsing.

The sound of three sets of footfalls died away, but he could still hear Tulards shouting for the other two boys to stop running.

"Drop the hatchet," Bessum said. He needed to get down there to cuff the boy, but he wasn't about to jump down while the teenager was still mobile.

Grady, who was splashed in blood—all over his arms and his clothes and his face—looked down at his sister's body.

When he looked back up, he had a smile on his face that sent Bessum's heart beating harder than it already was. But he dropped the hatchet and sat back on his feet.

"Now get down on your belly," Bessum told him. "And put your hands on your head, fingers interlaced."

The boy did it without a sound. With his face down, there was no telling if he still wore that freaky smile.

"Don't you fuckin' move," Bessum said. He got down on his butt and then slid off the edge, down into the creek bed.

Bessum knelt with one knee on Grady's back and then set the flashlight aside. With one hand, he retrieved his handcuffs and secured the boy's wrists together.

Then he grabbed the flashlight, stood up, and stepped over to Janie Drummond's body. As he was leaning down to feel for a pulse, the girl blinked. She turned her head and looked up into Bessum's face. And she smiled.

CHAPTER 17

There had never before been a time in Seth Granger's young life in which he'd felt the need to spy on his mother. Not counting the fun games they'd played with each other when he was a child of five or six, of course.

In those days, he would sneak through the house and peer around the corner at her while she was washing up or cooking dinner or folding laundry, or performing one of the other endlessly occurring chores that facilitated a well-functioning household. Of course, she'd always known he was there. As a child, Seth thought it was because his mother—like all mothers, he assumed—had a special kind of sense when it came to their children. Like radar in one of the war movies his father liked to watch. He pictured a sweeping, green-glowing fan constantly going round and round in her head, pinging off him every few seconds.

Then, as he got older, he realized that he'd probably just been bad at sneaking. That seemed the more logical explanation in the harsh burgeoning light of the Real World.

Still, those were fun times. She would pretend not to see him for just long enough to tempt him into getting closer. Then, as soon as he was making his move, she'd turn around, catching him in the open. This always prompted him to scramble to get behind cover again, trying to be silent but unable to fight off the keening giggle that inevitably escaped him.

He thought about those times as he crept toward the back of the church, having gone around in a wide arc after ten minutes of indecision. The sounds of demolition were still coming from inside the House of God. That logical brain he'd been cultivating as he rushed headlong toward adulthood considered the noise, working it over like he would a Rubik's Cube.

Maybe they're doing some remodeling, he thought. But at nine o'clock at night? And why would his mother be participating? As far as he knew, she had no expertise in demolition, construction, or even interior design, beyond the casual decoration she did at their home, anyway. He just couldn't imagine why his mother would be there. His logic failed him.

Now that he was behind the church, he could see that almost all the wood siding had been removed from this side of the structure. It was piled up in the woods.

There were windows along the sides, but Seth hadn't yet made up his mind to risk getting that close to the church. It felt wrong somehow. And he thought about the mom radar conjured by his childish mind. For some reason, he thought that she *would* know if he got too close. That *they* would know.

Who were *they*? He had no idea. He wasn't even sure if the *she* in this equation was his mother. It looked like his mother, but. . .

There was a flash of black-and-white fur in Seth's peripheral vision off to his left. He turned his head that way, thinking of Dallas. Had she gotten out and come to find him? She'd done similar things before. But when he looked into the dark woods there, he saw no evidence of any animal. What he did see was that something was off. Although *see* wasn't quite the right word for it. It was too dark to make out any details deep in the woods there, but still, there was something strange that he couldn't quite put his finger on. Then he remembered looking down from the hill near his house while walking Dallas earlier. He recalled how he thought the trees looked different; like there was a gap in them.

Happy for the distraction from the church, he moved that way, skirting the piles of wood siding torn from the church. He moved closer, hoping to figure out this mystery. And all the while, he knew it was a form of procrastination. A curiosity that transferred the problem of *truly* spying on his mother to his subconscious, at least temporarily. The irregular but constant sounds of destruction in the church continued. It was this fact that prevented him from hearing something large coming through the woods until a nearby cracking of a branch pulled his attention away from the strange gap in the trees—now thirty yards away—and toward the sloping hill to his left.

Pulse thrumming, Seth ducked down behind a fallen tree and looked that way. He immediately spotted the dark-blurred shapes of two people coming down the hill toward him. They didn't speak, at least not that he could hear, and they used no flashlights, which was strange.

A cascade of serial killer stories rushed through his mind, sending his heart beating even faster. Somehow, he *knew* these people were up to no good. He knew that if they caught him, nothing good would come of it.

There was a loud snap, and one of the shapes fell. "Son of a bitch!" a familiar voice called. "That's it. I'm turning on my flashlight."

Another voice—a woman's voice—began to protest. But a moment later, the threat was made good. A light came on, illuminating in its backwash two of Seth's teachers, Mr. and Mrs. Jobson.

Seth stood up. "Hello? Mrs. Jobson?"

The two teachers gasped in fright, and Mr. Jobson whipped his flashlight beam toward Seth. "Son of a bitch!" he said again, earning him a slap on the arm from his wife. "You scared the bejesus out of us, Seth. What the hell are you doing out here?"

The demolition sounds from the church suddenly stopped, sending goosebumps prickling all over Seth's flesh. What he did next, he did on little more than instinct. That logical mind of his was perhaps a little overworked and tired—or maybe just not so ingrained as he thought. It was, after all, still in many ways a child's mind. And children are often more attuned to their instincts that adults.

"Shh!" Seth said, rushing toward his teachers.

"What's wrong?" Mrs. Jobson asked, looking not at all like the in-control teacher he knew from school.

"Turn off the light," Seth said as he came up to the two adults, reaching out and grabbing them by the wrists to pull them back behind a nearby indigo bush.

"What's going on?" Mr. Jobson asked, not turning off his light but allowing himself to be led behind the bush.

"Please," Seth said, "just turn it off."

"Do it," Mrs. Jobson said.

Her husband complied, and the darkness swallowed them.

Seth watched the church from over the bush. He was able to see just enough of the area in front of the building to tell as the door opened, spilling a widening shaft of light toward the road. Shadows obstructed that light as people walked out of the church. A moment later, he could see them as they rounded the corner.

Both of the Jobsons had taken their cues from him, and they made no noise.

Seth's mother wasn't there, but an old lady whose name Seth

couldn't remember was, along with Pastor Simeon and Mrs. Simp-kins.

The three of them moved beyond the back of the church and peered out into the woods in the general direction of the two teachers and their student. They stood still and kept looking out as the seconds passed. And then the minutes.

Seth tried not to move, although he felt sure that the trio near the church could see him. On either side of him, both Jobsons did the same. He expected either one of them to whisper or move or even just break cover and go talk to the other adults. But they didn't. And he wasn't sure why. All he knew was that he didn't want to move.

Since he was slightly crouched and cocked forward at the waist, his leg and back muscles started to flare after several minutes. He didn't know how much time had passed, but he was guessing a good five minutes. It was a long time to be staring off into the woods.

Finally, the two older women and the pastor turned in unison and shuffled back into the church.

As soon as the bar of light disappeared, denoting the closing of the church door, there were three sighs of relief from behind the indigo bush.

Seth shared a look with his teachers through the gloom. They were all rattled.

It was Mr. Jobson who broke the silence as he spoke to his wife. "Well, at least now we know where Mrs. Stein went."

CHAPTER 18

The county guys still hadn't shown up when Bessum and Tulards arrived back at the Drummond house with the youngest Drummond in cuffs. Tulards had given it a go, but he'd quickly lost the other two brothers, Albert and Keith, in the woods. He'd come huffing back to Bessum's side just a couple of minutes after Janie Drummond left the world for good.

By that time, Bessum had managed to get a couple of makeshift tourniquets around her bleeding stubs (he wore a paracord bracelet everywhere) but it hadn't done any good. She'd already lost too much blood. And as she died, the smile died with her.

But even now, as Bessum walked toward Chief Medina in the front yard, he couldn't get the sight of her out of his mind. He recalled the drawings he'd seen in Kate Silver's diary. Over twenty of them, each depicting a smiling person with their limbs separated from their bodies. That couldn't be a coincidence.

Then there was the fact that he'd seen Grady's name in that diary. It was what had led him to the house. But before he could further contemplate the insanity he'd just witnessed, he needed to give Medina the bad news.

"It's bad, Chief," he said even before the stocky man could get a word out. "We found Janie Drummond in the woods. She's dead."

Medina held his gaze on Grady, who hadn't said a word the whole way back. He hadn't even acknowledged that he'd understood the Miranda warning. He was no longer wearing the smile he'd given Bessum—it seemed to have died around the same time as his sister, although Bessum wasn't completely sure on that count. Instead, the teenager wore a blank look. Given the blood splashed all over him, it wasn't much better than the smile.

Finally, Medina broke his gaze and signaled for Bessum to load the kid up in one of the cruisers without bullet holes in it. Bessum's unmarked didn't have a divider between front and back, so he wasn't about to put any perp in there. He found a car, put the kid in, and then moved back over to join Medina and Tulards.

"They were carryin' severed arms and legs," Tulards was saying, filling the chief in. "They dropped a couple. I can probably show Penny where they are." Penny Wright was their one and only crime scene technician. She'd have her hands full unless the county guys showed up soon.

"Christ on a bike," Medina said, shaking his head. He looked at Bessum and said, "What do you make of all this?"

"I've never seen anything like this. We used to see some crazy stuff on the occasional full moon, but nothing like this. I don't understand it. It's like there's something in the water. I don't know."

"You think it's a serial killer? You think that young man has been doing all the killin'?" Medina asked, hooking a thumb toward Grady Drummond in the cruiser.

"It's the only thing that makes any sense, but it just doesn't seem right, you know?" Bessum said. "Unless the whole family has gone nuts at the same time and decided to start chopping people up—including their mother. I mean, why would those two boys run off with the limbs?"

"There are stories about things like that happening 'round these parts," Tulards said. "Hill people going nuts, killing folks."

"What're you sayin'?" Medina asked, square hands propped on his belt.

Tulards shrugged. "Could be kind of a chicken and egg thing . . . or like a . . . what do you call it? Unconscious copycatting? I don't know what it's called."

"You're saying that maybe the lore influenced this violence in some kind of way? The town's past?" Bessum asked.

"Yeah, maybe. I mean, you hear about all kinds of strange things happening to groups of people at the same time. People getting the same ideas without no way of talking to each other about it. Could be something like that."

Bessum preferred not to think like that, but he was at a loss. So he just nodded and looked over Chief Medina's shoulder toward the cruiser that held the young Drummond boy. The teenager stared right back at him through the window, still wearing his blank expression.

Medina's cellphone rang, and he excused himself to answer it.

Bessum and Tulards stood in silence.

Sean Mitchell, the rookie whose cruiser Grady was in, had finished putting up crime scene tape. The two off-duty patrol officers had been called in. One of them was currently in the house, while the other was sitting at the mouth of the driveway, recording the comings and goings of the scene.

Meanwhile, Ann Wesley was still on Blue Sky Road, just in case the two other Drummond boys came out of the woods in that area.

"I could use a cup of coffee," Bessum said, just to be saying something. He had a bad feeling. Worse than the feeling he'd had when he'd awoken to bullets punching through the house where his wife and son were sleeping back in Philly.

"Yeah," Tulards said. "A nice strong one. From The Cherry."

Medina stepped back over, clipping his phone back to the carrying case on his belt opposite his revolver. "That was the county guys. They'll be here in a few minutes. I'm going to have Mitchell take the perp to the station. Once the guys get here, we'll have to run through everything with them. Starting with when you got here."

Bessum nodded. He knew the drill.

A few minutes later, Mitchell was backing his cruiser up to turn around. Bessum watched the vehicle. The blank-faced teenager in the back stared at Bessum through the window until the vehicle was out of sight.

CHAPTER 19

"I still think I should just go knock. See what they're up to. I mean, it's a pastor and some old ladies in a church, for chrissakes."

Seth thought it was a terrible idea, but he'd already voiced this when Russell had first broached the subject. Now here the man was, saying it for a third time.

At first, Sammy (both of them told Seth he could use their first names while not in school) had been vehemently against the idea. But Seth could see it working on her the more times he mentioned it. Now, she only said, "But what would you say?"

"Easy," Russell replied. "I'll just say that I was out for a walk, and I heard the noises. I just wanted to see what it was all about and if I could lend a helping hand."

"I'm sure at least someone in there will know that you live on the other side of the woods," Sammy said.

"I'll tell them it was a long walk."

When there was no further rebuttal from Sammy, Seth thought the issue was settled. He felt that, as the only teenager in the situation, it wasn't really up to him what either of these two adults did. He certainly couldn't stop them. And to be fair, he *did* want to see what his mother was up to in there. At the same time, he didn't want her to know that he'd been spying on her. So Russell's suggestion seemed like it could be a viable solution to his problem.

But none of this changed the fact that he still thought it was a *bad idea*.

Still, neither Russell nor Sammy sought his opinion presently, so Seth put forth no further objection. Russell stood up from where they'd been whispering behind the indigo bush and brushed his pants off.

"Wait!" Sammy said. "I want to see. Wait for us to get across the street, will you?"

Russell looked toward the church. The noise hadn't started back up again. In fact, the building was eerily quiet. "Okay," he said. "Let's go."

The three of them moved through the woods, flanking the church while giving it a wide berth. Twice Seth peered out into the woods toward the gap in the trees he could barely make out. He was still curious, but it wasn't the time. He ignored the gnawing feeling in his gut, telling himself he could always inspect the woods during the daytime, once he knew his mother was okay. But he couldn't help but wonder why he felt such a strong pull toward that area of the woods.

The land across from the church was nothing but more woods. The nearest house on that side of the road was about fifty yards off. Once Seth and Sammy had found a spot they liked directly across from the church, Russell started off at a jaunty walk, waving once in farewell.

"How is he so calm?" Seth asked. Russell and Sammy had filled the young man in on why they'd been trampling through the woods. In turn, Seth had told them what had brought him out into the dark woods. They'd all agreed that something odd was happening around town, but the two adults had done their best to assure Seth there was some kind of reasonable explanation for everything. Their presence had a calming effect on him.

But now, Sammy surprised the teenager by saying, "Oh, it's for show. He's scared. He's just putting on a brave face for you."

"For me?" Seth asked, surprised.

"It's a teacher thing," Sammy said, watching her husband cross the road. "It's like second nature at this point, I think. If we don't project confidence, we'll get eaten alive."

Seth smiled. "Makes sense, I guess. Although I personally don't much like the taste of teacher flesh."

Sammy smiled back at the rather dark joke. Then they turned to watch as Russell came up to the church doors. At first, it looked like Russell tried to open the doors, only to find them locked. Then he raised a fist and knocked three times. Nothing happened for several moments. Then the door opened.

This time, no fan of light expanded out as the door opened. There was only darkness beyond the threshold.

Russell bent forward, as if to squint and peer inside.

Several dark tendrils whipped out of the doorway and gripped Russell around the arms and torso. He screamed and jerked, trying to pull away. The tendrils yanked him inside the church. The door slammed shut.

***

Sammy's grip on Seth's arm was painful. He couldn't remember when she'd first taken hold of his arm. He had no idea how much time had passed since they'd seen . . . what? What had they just seen?

"Where'd he go?" Sammy asked, voice cracking on the last word.

"I—I don't know," was all Seth managed.

"I have to go get him," Sammy said breathlessly.

"I don't think . . ."

Sammy turned to Seth, looking at him in the darkness. She let go of his arm and looked back at the church. "Russell!" she shouted.

"Don't!" Seth said. "They'll hear you!"

Sammy paid no attention. She walked forward and screamed her husband's name again. And then she started running.

Seth started after her, knowing that if she went over there, it was over for her, just like it was over for Russell—and maybe even for Seth's mother.

His younger and longer legs enabled him to reach her when she was in the middle of the road. He grabbed her wrist and yanked, digging his heels in.

She tried to pull her arm away, releasing a screaming cry as she did. When Seth didn't let her go, she turned and slapped him across the face with her left hand. The noise multiplied among the trees and served as punctuation to Sammy's cry. Her mouth dropped open as she looked at the minor, the warring emotions twisting her face into half surprise and half frightened determination.

Then, as they stood there staring at each other, there was movement from the front of the church. The door opened, and Seth swiveled his eyes in that direction. Sammy soon followed suit.

There was still no light coming from inside the church. Despite this, it wasn't hard to recognize Russell as he stepped out onto the stoop. And it was with equal ease that Seth saw something was wrong. Russell's head seemed to hang limply, his chin on his chest. His arms looked boneless as they flapped at his sides, and his legs were bent at the knees, his toes somehow holding him up.

He looks like a puppet on a string, Seth thought, his inner voice shouting this like it would to warn him of a fire.

"Russ?" Sammy said, stepping away from Seth, who let go of her wrist.

Russell's right foot came forward, his body swaying with the movement. It wasn't a step. There was no weight put on that foot. It was an imitation of a step.

Seth suddenly felt an almost implacable urge to run away. His toes scrunched up in his shoes, and his feet vibrated with the notion. It was harder to stay put than it was to run. But he did it. Because his mother was in there. And Sammy, a teacher who he genuinely liked, was right here.

Russell's left foot came forward.

"What's wrong!?" Sammy screamed, crying again. "Talk to me, Russ." But she'd stopped moving. She was three paces ahead of Seth, at the edge of the road, about ten yards of church lawn and walkway separating her from the stoop.

Russell's head flapped back, and he seemed to jump into the air, extending his arms and legs out in an X. There was an awful ripping sound as his arms and legs kept going, tearing away from his torso. Blood splattered the stoop as it spilled out of his body. His head was the last to separate, coming off with a crunching pop. And that was when Seth saw them. The blackish tendrils—tentacles, really—that controlled each now-separate part of Russell's body.

Sammy's scream was ragged, sounding like she was ripping her vocal cords with its ferocity.

Russell's body danced above the church stoop as Seth lunged forward and grabbed Sammy, yanking her away and up the hill. She stumbled along with him for the first few yards, her head twisted over her shoulder, unable to look away. Then the tentacle holding the head extended out, zipping toward them in a taunt or a threat or both. She faced forward and ran after that.

They both ran. They ran like there was a monster chasing them.

.

CHAPTER 20

Sammy gripped Seth's hand like it was her lifeline as they bolted up the hill and away from the church. And in a way, it was. Had Seth not been there, she most certainly would have stood there at the side of the road until whatever that *thing* was did to her what it had done to Russell.

She swallowed the bile that wanted to come up her throat and tried to focus on running. The hurt she felt was so big and so heavy that it would drag her to the ground if she let it. But part of her couldn't believe what she'd just seen. It was the stuff of nightmares and horror movies. It was insane. It was not real. It *couldn't* be.

They were nearing the top of the hill when Seth stopped, looking around. Suddenly, Sammy realized that people were coming out of the homes lining the street. She thought maybe her scream had drawn them.

A man at the house nearest them stepped out his front door with a rifle in hand.

"Can you help us?" Seth asked.

The man raised the rifle and aimed it at them.

Sammy couldn't comprehend why he would do such a thing. This was just another not-real thing.

But then the man fired, and she felt the bullet pass next to her head, no more than an inch or two away. "Run!" she screamed.

And they were running again. People were stepping calmly out of more than half the houses she could see. Many of them had guns—rifles, pistols, shotguns. Their faces were blank. Like walking mannequins. The lack of any discernible emotion on their faces gave roots to the fear flailing inside Sammy. Roots that dug deep, squirming into what seemed like every fiber of her being.

Someone else took a shot at them, the bullet striking the ground near Seth's feet.

"My house!" Seth said, pointing to a two-story home at the top of the hill. Not far now.

Another gunshot sounded, and Seth screamed, falling to the ground in front of the walkway to his home.

Sammy didn't think twice. She stopped, turned around, and ran the few steps back over to Seth, who was struggling to get back up. Pulling his arm, she helped him up, and he hobbled with her across the lawn. She could hear a dog barking from inside the house.

"Around back," he said through clenched teeth.

There was another booming gunshot, and she heard what must've been birdshot hitting the front of the house just after they rounded the corner. The back door was unlocked, and as soon as they went through the door, a large black-and-white dog with one brightly colored eye greeted them with solemn interest.

Sammy got the back door locked while Seth limped through the kitchen toward the front of the house, followed by the dog. She found the light switch and turned it off. Then she peered out the back door, waiting for someone to come around and try to break in.

Why are they shooting at us? she thought, remembering Lyle with his shotgun.

Still looking out the window, she listened for Seth. She wasn't sure what he was doing, but didn't feel like leaving the back door was a good idea right now. Just two seconds later, a short and thin man with a hunting rifle stepped around the back corner of the house. Sammy dropped out of sight and looked around in the dark kitchen for something to use to defend herself.

She expected the man to shoot at the door or at least come up and try the knob. When nothing happened, Sammy raised up and peeked out the window to see the man standing there, holding the rifle like a soldier, staring at the door. She wasn't sure, but she thought his eyes were dark, like he was wearing large black contacts.

"They're just standing there," Seth said from the front of the house. He paused. "I think I need to go to the hospital."

Sammy moved away from the door and grabbed one of the three remaining knives from the knife block on the counter. She figured the other ones were somewhere in the mess that was the kitchen sink and surrounding counters.

She found Seth near the front door, peering out a window. The dog sat nearby, staring at him. The back of his calf was wet with blood under the hem of his shorts, and his sock was soaked. She moved up beside him, determined not to make a big deal out of his injury. But she knew they had to deal with it. Which was good. It gave her a goal to accomplish. Something to focus on. So she could get the image of Russell's severed head out of her mind.

There was light from the stairwell to her right, illuminating the living room. But as she moved toward Seth, the light went off, along with the air conditioner. They'd cut the power to the house.

Seth looked around. "The breaker box is outside," he said, voice dreamy.

She peered over Seth's shoulder to see three people standing on the front lawn, staring at the house. There were two women and a man, all of them with guns. She recognized one of them as Lisa Roebuck, mother to a son who'd graduated high school two years earlier. Her son, Ray, hadn't been a great student, and he hadn't been a terrible one. Middle of the road, through and through. The kind of student that teachers who'd been at it for a decade or more loved. They'd take a whole class full of middle-of-the-road students and be perfectly happy.

"What are they doing?" Seth asked, voice flat.

"I don't know," Sammy said. "But as long as they stay out there, I'm okay. We need to get your wound checked out."

"We can take my mom's car to the hospital in Victorville," Seth said. "You can drive."

"Sure. But first I need to stop the bleeding, okay? Then we'll go to the hospital." She wasn't sure they'd be going anywhere. Not with four armed nutjobs outside. She needed to call the police. But first, she wanted to get Seth's leg elevated to slow the blood loss.

"Come on," she said, gripping his shoulders. "Do you have clean towels around here?"

Seth nodded, pointing to the kitchen. "Right of the sink, last drawer down."

She got the towels and then got Seth situated on the couch, lying on his stomach so she could see the wound. She had him hang his right leg off the side and prop his left one up on the couch's arm. Once that was done, she pulled out her phone and dialed 911.

The call failed, her phone beeping twice before reverting to the dial pad.

She tried again, shaking her head and attempting to quell the terror blossoming inside.

The call failed again.

"Do you have your cellphone?" she asked Seth.

"Yes," he said, reaching awkwardly into his right front pocket and getting his phone out. He unlocked it and stared at the screen for a moment. "No service," he said. "No internet."

They were both silent for a moment. The dog stared at Seth from close by, sitting calmly on its haunches.

"What the hell is happening?!" Seth screamed.

"Shhh, it's okay. Just let me see it." Sammy took his phone and tried to call 911. It didn't work. The dog whined and inched forward, sitting again when it was closer to Seth. Sammy swallowed hard and looked into Seth's face. Tears were pouring down his cheeks.

"Nurse Sammy, at your service," she said with the best smile she could muster.

Outside, someone started screaming.

CHAPTER 21

"How's he been?" Bessum asked Sharice Burton shortly after walking into the Seven Springs Police Station.

Sharice had her headset on and her personal phone in her hand. She held up a finger. After a long moment, she looked up. "Do you have cell service?" she asked.

Bessum pulled his phone out and frowned at it. "No," he said, "I don't."

"It just dropped," Sharice said, chewing her maroon lipstick off her lip.

"Radio's still working, though, right?"

"Of course," she said, putting her phone down. "Sorry, what was your first question?"

"I asked how our prisoner has been. Have you checked on him?"

"Just once," Sharice said, shivering. "He creeps me the hell out."

Sharice was one of only a handful of Black residents in Seven Springs. She was in her late thirties and what Bessum thought of as a beautiful, full-figured woman. They'd been dating casually for several months, which Bessum still found strange because he was significantly older than her and damaged goods. Still, he wasn't about to look a gift horse in the mouth.

"Probably won't be able to get together tonight," he said. "I'll be working late."

Sharice smirked at him. "I hear everything," she said. "I already know."

Bessum smiled and raised his hands, palms out. "Just saying. Don't ever accuse me of not communicating."

Sharice was about to quip back, but she got a call over the radio, pressing one chewed-up fingernail to her earpiece.

Knowing she could be a while, Bessum waved and moved away from her little office, his smile falling off his face as he headed back to the two small holding cells near the back of the building.

Glancing through the small grated window in the steel door, he made sure the kid hadn't somehow gotten out of the cell. Given that the two cells were at ninety-degree angles to the entrance door, he couldn't see Grady Drummond without stepping into the area. He retracted the heavy latch and swung the door open.

Before he stepped inside, he paused. A strange noise came from Grady's cell. Almost like a wet flapping sound. Images of attempted suicide came immediately to mind, prompting him to rush inside and peer into the cell.

At first, his mind completely rejected what he was seeing. It was incomprehensible. Impossible. Unreal. Surely it was some sort of prank.

Grady Drummond stood in the cell next to the steel bunk, facing the cell bars. He was convulsing, his arms held out from his sides, fingers splayed. His head was thrown back to face the ceiling. And several irregular black-gray tentacles, each about the size of a roll of quarters, protruded from his stretched-open mouth. But they weren't the orderly tentacles of an octopus. They were messy and lumpy, lacking any semblance of uniformity. They featured strange dark growths that looked like some kind of mold or maybe even fine hairs, although it was hard to say for sure as they flapped wildly near the ceiling.

Grady suddenly straightened his head on loudly cracking vertebrae. The tentacles continued flapping, but now they slithered between the bars. Bessum stepped back, his eyes fixed on the teenager's red face. His jaw was stretched so far it was surely about to break, and his eyes bulged insanely.

A cringe-inducing tearing and popping sound erupted as the boy's jaw dislocated. His cheeks split at the corners of his mouth as more tentacles forced their way out. His eyeballs popped out even as a crack formed up his face. When his face split roughly in half, popping open like a dropped watermelon filled with blood, Bessum found himself again. He moved, feeling the tentacles grab at his suit jacket as he got through the doorway. He slammed the steel door and looked through the window, seeing the tentacles prodding at the grate. They wouldn't fit through. The holes were too small.

Grabbing his gun, he backed away from the holding area door. There was no training for this. No clear course of action. He simply wanted to run. To run away and not come back ever again.

"You okay?"

Bessum spun around to see Sean Mitchell in the hallway, holding a thin stack of paperwork in his hand. When he saw the look on Bessum's face and the fact that the detective had his gun out, he took a step back, face filling with fear. "What is it?"

"There's a monster," Bessum said, surprised at how calm he sounded. He wasn't calm. He wasn't even close to calm. He felt like his head was going to explode.

Mitchell smiled. "A monster, huh?" he said. "Boy, I can't wait until this 'messing with the new guy' stuff is over and done. But while I have you, maybe you can help me with this paperwork."

Bessum looked down at his gun. For one insane moment, he

thought about putting a bullet in his brain right there, with Mitchell watching. It had been a long time since he'd thought seriously about suicide—since the bad days of the divorce—but it was never far from his thoughts.

The thought of killing himself steadied his mind, putting things in perspective. He slipped his Glock 17 into his holster and said, "Come with me."

He walked down the hall and turned into the bullpen, heading straight for the water dispenser at one wall. He grabbed a paper cup and filled it with water as the upturned five-gallon jug burbled. Mitchell had stayed with him, but he was studying his colleague closely. Bessum drank the water, took a deep breath, and said, "Put that stuff down."

"Wh—why? What's wrong?"

Bessum crumpled up the paper cup and tossed it into a nearby trash can. "Just put it down, okay, Mitchell? I'm going to show you something you're not going to like, but I need you to be on the same page with me here. It's just you, me, and Sharice here now. So I'm going to need your help."

"Uh, okay," Mitchell said, setting the papers down on a nearby desk.

The detective led the way back to the hall, where he stopped fifteen feet from the steel door. The rookie cop stopped as well, waiting for an explanation. Bessum grabbed him by the shoulders and looked into his pale green eyes. "We're going to walk down to the holding area and we're going to look through the grate. You're not going to believe what you'll see, but I need you to know that it's okay to be scared. But what I want you to do is promise me you won't run. I need your help, okay? I don't think this is an isolated thing, so it's important that we keep our shit together."

Sharice popped her head out from her office down the hall, catching Bessum's attention. The detective looked at her and held up a finger. Apparently seeing the look on his face, she frowned and ducked back into her office.

Bessum turned back to Mitchell. "Do you get me?"

"Yes, sir."

"Good. Let's go."

His arm around the young man's shoulders, Bessum guided them down to the door. The tentacle things were no longer prodding at the grate, which meant they'd have to get closer.

"This isn't a prank?" Mitchell asked.

"No, this is not a prank. It's the real thing."

He guided Mitchell to the wall next to the door and told him to wait. Then he stepped up and looked through the grate. The room was sloped slightly inward to a drain in the middle of the floor between the two cells. A thick ribbon of blood flowed slowly down from the cell to the drain. But there were also blood drips on the other side of the drain because the tentacles had stretched all the way across to the bars of the adjacent cell and were wrapped around as the thing used them to try and pull the rest of its body out of the other cell.

It had managed to get Grady Drummond's crushed and dismantled head through the bars, along with one of his arms, which also looked to be broken, but it was having a hard time getting the rest of him out. Still, from the sounds, he thought it would only be a matter of time.

"What's that noise?" Mitchell asked with a disgusted face.

"Remember what I told you. This is not normal. It's okay to be scared. But it's imperative that you keep your head."

Mitchell nodded, and Bessum stepped away, motioning for the younger man to step up to the window grate.

The detective watched carefully as Mitchell stepped up and peered through. His face blanched, and he swallowed hard. "What is that?" he whispered, never taking his eyes off the thing.

"I don't know. But we're going to have to deal with it. We're going to have to kill it. And then we'll be famous for killing an alien."

It was supposed to be a joke, but it didn't seem to land very well. Mitchell turned away from the door and ran back into the bullpen. The sound of vomiting came to Bessum as he moved down the hall to repeat the process with Sharice.

Let's hope he made it to a trash can, Bessum thought.

Sharice stepped out of her office and crossed her arms. "What the hell did you do to that boy? What's going on, Oliver?"

"I need to show you something."

Sharice narrowed her eyes. "So show me."

Bessum waved her down the hallway, then stopped. "Maybe you should grab a trash can."

Having figured out where he was taking her, she moved deftly past him and looked in through the grate, getting on her toes to do so. She stared through for a long time before stepping back, eyes glazed and face ashen.

Then she bolted down the hallway and ducked into her office. Bessum shook his head as she vomited.

If the situation weren't so surreal, he might've found it funny.

He glanced through the grate again, seeing that the creature was making progress. It was compressing Grady Drummond's limbs, breaking them where needed until they could fit between the bars. Judging by the creature's behavior in the cell, he figured he had some time. It wouldn't be able to get through the steel door easily.

He marched back down to the bullpen and looked inside. Mitchell was nowhere to be seen. "Goddammit," he said, jogging through the room and to the front of the station. He shoved the door open and stepped outside, looking at the parking lot for Mitchell's Chevy Silverado. It was gone.

Then something caught his eye across the street. He peered into the shadowy darkness where a streetlight's illumination failed to penetrate the area under a tree. Three figures stood there. He could see well enough to tell that they were all facing the station. And that they were carrying rifles.

Bessum moved back into the station and locked the door.

"What the hell is going on?" Sharice said from directly behind him.

CHAPTER 22

s far as Sammy could tell, Seth hadn't been shot directly. She would've expected more damage and possibly even a broken bone if he had. She dug out what looked like part of a bullet, although she wasn't a doctor or a firearms person. But she'd seen bullets. And the piece she dug out of Seth's left calf was smaller than the ones she'd seen.

Her worry was that there was still more bullet left inside him. But she doubted it, considering the size, shape, and limited depth of the wound.

Once she had him bandaged up, she returned to the window to look out at the people still standing out there. The screaming had stopped now, and she was more than thankful for it. When it had first started, she'd gone to the window to see that a woman was in the middle of getting pulled out of her car by three people. Since the driver's side of the vehicle was facing away, Sammy couldn't tell what had happened to her when they got her on the ground, but she knew it wasn't good.

And now, as she looked out, she could see a darkly reflective stain spreading slowly down the asphalt. The woman's blood, no doubt. The car remained where it had been parked, the driver's door open, engine still running.

Maybe the woman had stopped to see what was going on. That seemed like the most likely possibility. Because if she'd been with these others, they would've had no reason to attack her like they did.

Now her mind turned to why they weren't attacking *them*. The people—if that's what they were—clearly knew Seth and Sammy were inside the house. They'd seen them go in. They'd heard Seth scream out in frustration earlier. The same thin man with the rifle was still standing guard in the backyard, near the standalone garage.

So why were they just standing out there?

She thought about Russell coming out of the church . . . and what had happened after that. The act of ripping him apart struck her as meaningful. There were far easier ways to kill a person, so it seemed to her that the horrific violence of her husband's death was a sick show, meant to stoke fear and panic. But she didn't understand *what* had done it or *why*.

"We can take my mom's car," Seth said from the couch. Now that he'd been bandaged up, he was sitting with his leg propped on a stack of throw pillows on the coffee table. The dog—Dallas, she'd learned her name was—sat curled up next to Seth, her one blue eye seeming to glow in the dim room.

"Well, we can't really get out there," Sammy said. "Not while there's a man with a gun out back. And more out front."

The look on Seth's face twisted her heart.

"Where are the keys?" she asked, thinking that locating the keys would give her time to consider their options, limited as they were.

"They should be next to the back door, on the key rack."

Sammy nodded and went to look for them. When she didn't find them hanging on the key rack, she came back to the living room. "Not there. Where else would they be?"

"Did you see a purse in there?"

"Of course," Sammy said, heading back to the kitchen. There was a purse sitting in a chair halfway pushed into the kneehole of a cluttered desk at the side of the kitchen. But she found no keys inside.

When she stepped back into the living room empty-handed, Seth shook his head. "I don't know where else they would be. She always kept a spare in her purse. I don't know why she'd take them with her."

They were both silent for a long moment. Then Seth spoke again. "There's a rifle in the garage. It's locked, but I know the keys are here. I saw them earlier. And there's also a car in there. My father's Jaguar XJ6. He spent years restoring it and when he was done, he never even took it out but for one trip, other than to drive it around the neighborhood every so often. Do you think that's right?"

The kid was in shock. And she couldn't blame him. But the fact that there was a gun and a vehicle in the garage gave her a sliver of hope. Maybe they could get out of here and get to the police station. They had to tell someone about this. Whatever was going on here would require more than just a small-town police force, but it was a start.

"Getting into the garage would be even harder than getting into your mom's car. We still have the problem of the man outside—and the others out front."

"What if we knock him out?" Seth said.

"How would we do that?"

"The bathroom window upstairs leads out onto the back awning. It's small, but either one of us could fit through. We can drop something on his head."

"We might kill him doing that."

Seth spoke his next words slowly, carefully. "Yes. I know." A tear escaped his right eye and traveled down his cheek. He didn't bother wiping it away.

Despite what she'd seen, Sammy wasn't yet ready to start killing people. Even though she knew somewhere deep down that this had everything to do with what happened to Russell, she was still trying to think like it was all some big coincidence. Like there was some logical explanation for the blank-faced people standing outside, staring. Maybe if she'd been the one shot, she'd be thinking differently.

Still, she knew they had to do something.

"Okay," she said. "Where are the keys to the garage?"

***

Seth thought back to when his mother left the house, wondering why she would've taken both sets of car keys. She'd gone out to the garage, unlocked it, and then retrieved something from behind the structure before putting it inside. When she came out a short time later, she locked up and left, bypassing her car in the driveway to walk down the hill to the church.

He pushed the thoughts aside. It didn't matter. He'd seen the keys they needed shortly after Sammy had wrapped up his leg and he'd gotten up to walk around and see how it felt. The keys to the garage were on the same keyring as the keys to the Jaguar. When his dad had been alive, the keys were almost never off his person. But now that he was dead, the keys were accessible to Seth for the first time in his life.

Earlier in the evening, when he'd been doing some cleaning before his mother snapped at him, he spotted the transparent property bag lying on his mother's small desk at one side of the kitchen. Clearly, the police had given Tim Granger's keys, wallet, and pocket change back to his mother at some point since his murder. And his mother had just put the bag on the desk to deal with later, which was not like her at all.

When he thought about what might've happened to her in that

church, he wanted nothing more than to break down and cry. So he pushed that thought out of his mind as he opened the plastic bag and got the keys out.

As he stood there with the keys in his hand, he had a sudden flash, like a premonition, which was accompanied by a feeling of heavy black dread. Nothing seemed worth it anymore. It was like he'd lost all his optimism, and he could only see the poor outcomes. The painful, violent, horrible outcomes. He couldn't even imagine ever being happy again, even if he got out of this alive with Mrs. Jobson. The possibility of suicide flittered across his mind like a diseased rat, leaving behind a trail of pestilence that seemed to stain his thinking.

Seth leaned over and took a couple of deep breaths, pulling himself back from the brink of losing it entirely. He clenched his jaw and bit back a sob, then shook his head and found that he could once again imagine a positive outcome. It was far-off and blurry, but he could see enough of it to hang onto. With some effort, he brought his mind back to the task at hand.

Sammy said that Seth should be the one to go out to the garage once the guy outside was knocked out. Her reason being that otherwise he'd have to run all the way back downstairs and outside. Given his current condition, that didn't seem like the best idea. Plus, he knew which keys were which.

The Jaguar key wasn't hard to spot. And Seth couldn't remember how many times he'd watched his dad unlock the padlock on the garage doors, asking to be let in to help with the work. But there was always some excuse. Sometimes, it was something as simple as: "I don't need you underfoot." Other times, it was: "This is man's work. You can help when you get older."

But by the time Seth got older, he'd stopped asking altogether. And his father never offered. He knew the real reason was that his father didn't want to be around him. He'd come to accept that. And when the drinking had gotten really bad, Seth wanted to be as far away from his father as possible. The feeling had become mutual.

"How are you feeling?" Sammy whispered.

Seth turned around, keys in hand, and nodded. "Okay."

"What about Dallas?"

"She can come. She won't slow us down. I promise." Seth looked down at Dallas, who sat nearby, studying the two humans.

"Okay," Sammy said. "I'm going up. Be careful."

Seth nodded.

Sammy had chosen the inner part of a slow cooker to throw at the man. It was made of heavy ceramic and seemed like the best option. Everything else seemed a little too light, too heavy, or too unwieldy for her to handle on the roof. She grabbed the black oval ceramic piece from the floor and headed upstairs.

"Ready, Dallas?" Seth asked.

Dallas tilted her head slightly in answer.

"Okay," he said, stepping over to the back door and parting the curtain just enough to see out.

His heart thumped, each rapid beat reminding him of the injury to his calf. He had the keyring in his right hand, one of the two keys to the garage padlock pressed between suddenly sweaty thumb and index finger. With his left hand, he held the curtain open.

There was something wrong, he suddenly realized. Something he wasn't thinking of. His thoughts had been such a jumbled mess all day. And it had only gotten worse since he'd seen Mr. Jobson torn apart in front of the church.

I'm missing something, he thought. *Something important.* He just couldn't think what.

There was a faint thump from upstairs. He felt certain that the short and thin man who stood outside—a man Seth knew as Mr. Wassberg—would look up. But he didn't. He stood there, still staring at the back of the house. But since it was too dark for Seth to see his eyes, he wasn't sure where exactly the man was looking. They were just dark circles under his brows, so he could've been looking directly at the window—directly at Seth—for all the teenager knew.

A flash of shiny blackness fell through the air, hitting Mr. Wassberg. It happened fast, his head jerking violently sideways as the ceramic pot broke into several pieces. Seth unlocked the door and jerked it open, limp-running down the steps and angling around the unmoving man. A grooved line on his forehead was filling with blood as Seth moved past, Dallas following closely.

He got to the garage doors and grabbed the lock. The chain rattled loudly against the worn metal handles affixed to the old wood.

The sound of footsteps came from the front of the property. The people were coming back to see what all the noise was about.

Seth jammed the key into the lock—or tried to. It wouldn't fit. He turned it around and tried again. The tip of the key slid in, but then it stopped; it was the wrong key.

Then it came to him, much too late to be of any use. The lock was new. It wasn't the same one that had been on there for years. It was a new one. The clues had been in front of his face the whole time. His mom had left with a key—he'd watched her pocket it—yet there were two keys on the keyring currently in Seth's hand. How could he be so stupid?

Dallas started barking. Seth looked over his shoulder, seeing over his mother's car a man and a woman moving down the driveway.

Shoving the keys into his pocket, he grabbed the handles of the two doors and pulled them as hard as he could. The two doors bounced off the tightened chain, and the handles seemed to hold steady.

Dallas was still barking, but now she was also snarling. She was halfway between the garage and Seth's mother's Volvo station wagon, hackles raised and head down.

Sammy came running out of the house. And as Seth gripped the lip of the left-hand door in both hands, he yelled for her to get back inside. He yanked on the door—and heard the crackle of old wood.

"Look out!" Sammy yelled.

Seth looked over his shoulder just in time to see Dallas charging at a man who'd been standing guard at the front of the house. He had his rifle up and aimed at Seth.

Seth jerked away from the doors, trying to get out of the line of fire. Dallas lunged for the man, connecting with his left wrist just as the man pulled the trigger.

The bullet punched into the door just above the left-side handle—right where Seth had been moments earlier. But then the man was on the ground, and Dallas was attacking him.

On the other side of the driveway, a woman with a pistol in her hand was closing in. Sammy ran over and threw something at the woman's face. Seth didn't see what it was until it had already careened off the woman's face and then bounced off the fence flanking the driveway, coming to rest on the concrete. It was a knife from the kitchen. And it had hit the woman in her left eye, which was now a bloody mess.

The woman still had the gun, and one working eye. She didn't seem all that fazed by the injury to her other eye. She turned the gun toward Sammy, who backed away with her hands up.

A flash of black-and-white fur darted across the Volvo's hood. Dallas slammed into the woman from the side before she could get a shot off. The two of them fell.

Seth, operating mostly on instinct now, turned back to the garage doors and yanked on the left door once again. The wood attached to the handle splintered, thanks in no small part to the gunshot damage. One more yank, and the handle came off altogether as the wood ripped apart.

"Come on!" Seth yelled, pulling the left door open. Sammy didn't need to be told twice. They both ran into the dark garage.

Seth tossed the keys onto the roof of the Jaguar, which was facing out. "You should drive," he said, heading toward the back of the dim and dusty space to grab a rifle case. He had to use his phone's flashlight to find it. But when he had it, he moved to the rear passenger's side door of the maroon-colored luxury vehicle and opened it as Sammy fired up the engine. He tossed the rifle case onto the tan-colored leather of the back seat and then shut the door.

"Dallas?" he yelled, stepping up to the front passenger door. He couldn't see her anymore. The woman she'd attacked was twitching on the ground, blood coming out of wounds in her neck. The man she'd attacked was just getting to his feet, but both his hands had been mangled. It would be impossible for him to fire his rifle, which lay at the edge of the driveway.

"Dallas!"

"We need to go. We'll pick her up out there," Sammy said.

Seth put his left leg inside the car and sat down in the seat, barely noticing the dozens of flies that came buzzing from underneath the vehicle. Before he could pull his right foot in and shut the door, a hand grabbed his ankle. He cried out in surprise, trying to pull his leg up.

"What?" Sammy said. "What's wrong?"

"Just go!"

"Shut your door," she said.

"Someone's under the car!" he yelled, peering down to see a sickly hand gripping his right ankle. "Just go!"

She hit the gas while Seth grabbed under his knee with both hands and tried to yank his foot up. But whoever had hold of him wasn't about to let go so easily. For a moment, as Sammy eased the car forward, he thought he'd be pulled out of the vehicle and run over. But just as he was about to tell her to stop, the pressure let up and he was able to pull his leg in. When he went to slam the door, it bounced off something. Looking down, he saw that the arm was still attached to him. The hand was still wrapped around his ankle.

Unsure what else to do, he pulled the whole thing inside and slammed the door. The man with the mangled hands was able to get out of the way just as the Jaguar moved into the space between his mom's Volvo and the side of the house. The driveway wasn't meant for two cars, and both side mirrors broke off, the Jaguar scraping both the side of the house and the Volvo as it went through.

"Where's Dallas?" Seth said, looking around as they came to County Spring Road. To their left, he could see several people with guns standing along the street. But no Dallas. He knew that going to look for her was a bad idea, so he clenched his jaw and said nothing.

As Sammy sped out of the driveway, Seth turned his attention to the severed arm in the footwell, still gripping his ankle.

Gunshots sounded, and both of them slumped in their seats, knowing the bullets were meant for them.

CHAPTER 23

The Benelli M4 Tactical shotgun Bessum held was one of two the department had. During his years in Seven Springs, they'd only had cause to use the pistol-grip, semi-auto shotguns a handful of times. During his first year in town, there had been a problem with meth labs, and the Benelli provided a good way to breach locked doors so they could raid the poison-manufacturing facilities.

The breaching rounds commonly used for this purpose were designed to destroy hinges or a deadbolt before the load dispersed into a powder. The idea behind these rounds was that you didn't want to kill someone accidentally on the other side of the door, as could happen with slugs or buckshot.

This was just the opposite of what Bessum wanted. Which was why he'd loaded the shotgun with six 2 ¾" shells containing double-aught buckshot. The nine pellets in each shell could do some serious damage to the human body. And he was hoping it would work just as well on the thing inside the holding room.

Last he'd checked, which was about two minutes ago now, the thing had pulled itself all the way out of the cell. When he'd glanced through the grate, he saw what looked more like a flattened human whose disparate parts were held together by thin but strong-looking strips of flesh reinforced with a mottled dark-gray-and-red muscle-like substance. It had been moving around the room in unbalanced lurches, tentacles moving frantically as it searched for a weakness it could exploit.

"Ready?" Sharice asked now. She was standing by the door, ready to unlock and open it so Bessum could step up and blast the freaky thing back to hell.

"Want to switch with me?" he asked.

Sharice smirked, momentarily hiding the stressed expression she'd been wearing.

Smiling, Bessum nodded. She pulled the heavy-duty metal lock back and yanked on the door, flattening herself against the hallway wall as Bessum moved forward.

The thing had been waiting. It launched itself out, tentacles whipping all around as it flew toward Bessum's face.

He pulled the trigger, blasting the thing out of the air. It landed with a splat, then wasted no time in rushing toward him like a giant spider with a dozen uneven legs and no discernible body.

Sharice, being the smart lady she was, had already high-tailed it down the hall. So Bessum didn't have to worry about her as he backpedaled and fired again, the gas-operated shotgun having automatically loaded another shell into the chamber for him. The second shot separated about a third of the thing from itself. The rest of it kept coming.

He fired again. And again.

Then one more time for good measure.

With only one shell left, he surveyed the mess in the hallway. Each shot but the first one had blown more of the thing apart. Now the pieces in the hallway looked less like a crushed human and more like the floor of a slaughterhouse where none of the employees knew what they were doing.

Some of the bits were still twitching as Bessum took more shells from his pockets and loaded them into the Benelli, getting it back to six.

"Is it dead?" Sharice asked from the bullpen.

"I guess," Bessum said.

The sound of a car horn honking and squealing tires had him turning and jogging up to the front to see what was going on.

He stopped next to the glass door, his back against the white-painted cinderblock wall, and peered out. He saw the headlights coming down the road before he saw the car. His eyes went wide when he noticed movement from the three figures who'd been standing in shadow across the street.

They all leveled their rifles at the oncoming car and let loose before Bessum could process it. The sound of bullets punching into glass and aluminum preceded the sight of the sedan coming into view from beyond the post office next door. The sedan had bullet holes in the hood and the windshield. The three figures—all of them men, Bessum now saw—fired as quickly as their rifles allowed them. Thankfully, this wasn't fast because two out of the three men had bolt-action hunting rifles while the third had a semi-auto.

Without thinking about anything other than the safety of the civilians in that vehicle, Bessum unlocked the door, stepped outside, and fired at the three men standing about forty yards away. One of the men flinched.

The sedan missed the driveway and jumped the curb, going a good forty miles an hour. Bessum hustled to his right so he wouldn't get hit and fired again. This shot dropped one of the men.

The car impacted a cruiser parked near the front door, the sound a great crash of metal and breaking glass.

Bessum knew better than to stop. He fired again, stepped forward two paces into the handicapped spot, and fired a fourth time. A second man dropped, blood spurting from his face and neck.

The last two shells took care of the third man, who wasn't dead, but soon would be.

As he turned to the sedan, he took the last three shells out of his pockets and loaded them into the shotgun. The sedan was a mess, and the inside was splashed with blood. Between that and the spider-webbed windows, he couldn't see inside. Before he could investigate further, he heard another car screaming down the street.

Turning, he pointed the shotgun as a beat-up Jaguar came tearing into the parking lot. The luxury car came rocking to a stop in the middle of the lot. A teenager jumped out of the front seat. He looked like he was about to say something when the crashed car caught his attention.

A moment later, Sammy Jobson jumped out of the driver's side, looking almost like a different person, thanks to the stress on her face. She, too, stared at the scene.

"Inside!" Bessum yelled, snapping them out of it. "Sharice! Come help me."

Sharice was looking out the front door, and she came out as soon as Bessum called.

The other two grabbed some items from their vehicle and ran into the police station.

Bessum got to the front passenger door of the crashed sedan and opened it. There was a dead woman sitting in the front seat, a bullet hole in her head. But there was a teenage girl and a toddler in the back, tucked into the footwell behind the front passenger seat. They were alive, hugging each other and sobbing.

"Let's get them inside," Bessum said. Sharice was already on it.

CHAPTER 24

"Please get on the radio and tell the Chief what's happening," Bessum said to Sharice.

They were in the bullpen, and they'd just plopped the two girls into one of the desk chairs in the back corner. The toddler, who was wearing pale pink pajamas decorated with cartoon unicorn heads, was bawling. Her sister—they were both blond and could've been twins if not for the age difference—held onto the younger girl but did nothing to quell the crying. She was staring into space.

Sammy and the teenage boy stood nearby, looking at Bessum with quiet expectancy. The kid had a lever-action Winchester rifle held to his chest, and he'd come in with a rifle case, which was sitting on top of a desk.

Bessum had no idea where to start. There were too many thoughts going through his mind. There was no clear path to take. No definite objective. As Sharice hustled out of the room, Bessum eyed the rifle and then the kid. Until he knew what was happening, he didn't feel comfortable with anyone else having a weapon in here. For all he knew, the moment he turned around, the kid would shoot him.

He just didn't know what the hell was going on. He was breathing heavily from the engagement outside. His senses were all keyed-up, and half of his auditory perception was still on the front door. It was locked, but it wouldn't take much for someone to break the glass and come on in.

He needed help. Backup. If the radio was somehow down, he didn't know what he'd do.

"Sammy," he said, speaking loudly over the crying toddler. "Are you okay? Where's Russell?"

She shook her head, gulping. "It killed him."

"It?"

She shook her head again. "We need to get out of here. Where is everyone else? Where are the other police officers?"

"Sharice is calling them right now," Bessum said. "What's your name?" he asked the teenage boy.

The kid looked up at Sammy. She nodded.

"Seth," he said. He had pale green eyes, sandy brown hair that was going shaggy, and the kind of skinny frame that was common among Olympic swimmers. He was probably an inch or two under six feet tall.

"Seth Granger?" Bessum asked.

The kid nodded.

When Bessum had done the interview with Mrs. Granger the day after Mr. Granger was found murdered, he had asked about the son. It was standard procedure. The kid's mother—Lidia—told him Seth was at camp and had been for much of the summer. Bessum had planned on interviewing the kid when he got back to town. And now here he was. Could that be a coincidence? It was a small town, but it wasn't *that* small, was it?

"I'm gonna need you to put the gun down, Seth," Bessum said.

Seth took a step forward and moved to put the rifle down. But then he stopped, brought it back up to his chest, and shook his head.

"You're with the police now. I'm a detective. You're safe. And I can't have you with a loaded gun in here."

"What if there's something wrong with you?" Seth said. "Something like what's wrong with my neighbors and those people out there?"

The kid had a point. "You're just going to have to trust me," Bessum said.

Seth shook his head again.

This time, Bessum shifted his gaze over to Sammy. He saw no support there.

"He's right," she said. "We're going to need all the guns we can get."

"What the hell are y'all doing?" Sharice yelled as she came back into the room, making a beeline for the crying child. She scooped the little girl out of her sister's arms and started rocking her and walking her around the room.

Seth stepped over to the teenager and put a hand on her shoulder. "Hey, Melanie? You okay?"

Melanie looked up into Seth's eyes. "They killed my mom, Seth." Tears spilled down her cheeks. "They shot her in the head."

Seth propped his Winchester against the desk and knelt in front of Melanie. As he embraced her, the floodgates opened. Pretty soon, it was the older sister balling while the younger one was finally getting calmed down.

"What's the word on the others?" Bessum asked Sharice.

"They're coming. And they got the county people with them."

Bessum knew that the county sheriff's office had only sent three people—a detective and two forensics experts. He doubted if the forensics team he'd met had firearms experience. But at least everyone else was getting back here. They could regroup and figure out just what the hell was going on. "Did you tell them what's happening?"

"I explained it the best I could," she said. "Told them we'd been fired on and that people in town seem to be going crazy."

"What about the . . . thing in the hallway?"

She shook her head. "They can see that for themselves when they get here. Oh, and Medina said he sent someone to check out the cell tower on Lookout Mountain. It's down, he said. Like someone damaged the anchor wires and made it fall."

Bessum nodded, not surprised. There were three towers around town, and he knew it wouldn't be too hard to take them down. That was why they didn't have cell service.

Sammy tapped Bessum on the shoulder, getting his attention. "There's something I need to show you."

"What you got?"

She stepped over to the rifle case Seth had brought in. "This was . . . sticking out of the ground, I think. In Seth's garage."

She unclipped the case and then opened it. There was a severed arm inside, half-rotten and pale everywhere except at the base of the arm, where the skin had gone black. And there was something else. Something that didn't belong.

Sticking out of the base of the arm were a half-dozen worm-like appendages that were about as black as the putrid flesh they stuck out of.

They were moving, twitching in the air like plucked spider legs.

CHAPTER 25

After Seth had done his best to get Melanie calmed down, he grabbed his father's rifle and limped to the front of the station with Sammy and the man she introduced as Oliver Bessum. Even now, he felt guilty for refusing Bessum's request to put the rifle down. He didn't know why he'd refused. Instinct, maybe. But it wasn't like he was a good shot or anything. He'd fired rifles before, with his friend Derek and Derek's dad. But it had been a while. He wasn't sure he had the nerve to fire at another person. In fact, he was pretty sure he didn't. Still, he clutched the rifle as though it were a lifeline, his mind seeming to teeter on the brink of total breakdown.

As they moved out of the bullpen, Sharice stayed back with Melanie and her sister Tessa.

Bessum arranged them in such a way that they could talk without being seen from outside, just in case someone wanted to take a shot at them. Bessum himself stood with his back to the wall next to the door so he could glance out every so often. This put both Sammy and Seth behind the front desk to the right of the door.

Sammy started off by telling her story. It began with Russell going to check on Mrs. Stein. Then, when it came to the point where they met up with Seth in the woods, it was Seth's turn to fill the detective in. His story started with following his mother down to the church.

For the rest of it, they took turns. Sammy broke down when she tried explaining exactly what had happened to Russell, so Seth had to take over. But he barely made it through without choking up. Not only because he was pretty sure his mom had suffered a similar fate, but also because he'd always liked Mr. Jobson.

They then went over what happened when running up the hill—how people had come out of their homes and started shooting at them. Finally, they ended with their escape and the arm that had grabbed Seth from under the car.

"The thing is," Sammy said. "I looked into the rearview mirror as we moved out of the garage. It was dark in there, but I would've seen someone lying under the car. There was no one there. But I think I did see a . . . hole or a divot or something. That's why I think it was sticking out of the ground."

Bessum's face betrayed no emotion. It was a face that immediately made Seth think of a World War II soldier in an old black-and-white movie. Maybe a general. He had that kind of craggy, serious face. And his high-and-tight haircut only added to the impression. Not to mention the salt-and-pepper five o'clock shadow on his jawline.

"I know this sounds crazy," Sammy said. "But it's all true. I don't know what's happening here, or why it's only affecting some people, but it's not good. We need serious help."

Bessum pressed his lips together, glanced out the front door again, and then turned back to them. "Come with me."

They followed him back into the station. Instead of going right toward the bullpen, they went left, moving through two offices before coming to a small room that was used as an armory. He grabbed several shotgun shells from a box, loading three into his shotgun and then stuffing his pockets with many more.

"Okay," he said. "This way."

They went back out of the armory and moved through an office door into a hallway. Bessum stood aside and gestured at the ground.

At first, Seth thought he was looking at roadkill that had been dragged inside. A deer, maybe, that had been run over by five or so semi-trucks. But as he looked closer at the mess littering the hallway, he recognized a human ear. There were some fingers there. A patch of skull with the scalp still attached.

"I arrested this kid earlier tonight," Bessum said. "He was acting real strange. His whole family was. His old man tried to kill us. Although it was strange . . . when I first came upon them, the old man seemed like he was mad at the kid for . . ." he trailed off, lost in thought. "Maybe he wasn't infected," Bessum said, talking to himself. "But he went nuts when he realized what had happened to his wife—and what was about to happen to his kids. Decided to go out in a hail of gunfire . . ."

Seth and Sammy looked at each other, confused.

"Anyway," Bessum said, looking back at Sammy. "I come back to check on the kid after finishing up at the crime scene, and he's got these . . . *tentacle* things coming out of his goddamn mouth. Next thing I know, he's breaking his skull so his head will fit through the bars. He got out of the cell, and then I blasted him with the shotgun."

"Who? Who was it?" Seth asked. He knew most of the kids in town, and he didn't relish the idea of one of his friends being spread all over the floor in the police station hallway.

"Grady Drummond."

Seth nodded somberly. He knew Grady. Everyone knew Grady. The kid was a piece of work. But Seth wasn't about to rejoice at his gruesome death. At the same time, he was glad it wasn't one of his friends.

The three of them stared at the mess for a long moment.

"Aliens, maybe?" Bessum asked suddenly.

Sammy shrugged. "I had the same thought. I mean, what else could it be? This is some John Carpenter stuff."

Seth wasn't sure who John Carpenter was, but he was right there with the two adults. He'd never been a huge fan of horror movies, but when he'd seen that thing rip Mr. Jobson apart back at the church, his mind could think of nothing else but aliens. Some kind of invasion, infecting the people of Seven Springs. And maybe even other places.

He figured the only reason he wasn't infected was the fact that he'd been at Camp Stillwater for nearly two months. But what about Bessum and Sammy and the other people? Why weren't they infected?

Maybe they were, he thought. They just weren't showing any signs yet. Or they were making it *seem* like they weren't infected until the time was right to kill Seth and anyone else who wasn't under alien control.

"What do we do?" Seth asked, pushing the distrustful thoughts away.

"We get the hell outta Dodge," Bessum said. "As soon as everyone else gets back, we'll formulate a plan and get gone."

"Wait," Sammy said. "Do you hear that?"

Seth listened, hearing faint popping sounds from outside. Gunshots.

"Maybe some people are fighting back," Bessum said.

Or maybe that's the sound of the infected killing the innocent, Seth thought, but didn't say.

From the bullpen, there was the low crackle of a radio. Even from the hallway, Seth could hear the frantic voice coming over the police radio, although he couldn't quite make out the words.

Bessum heard it too, and he moved down the hall, stepping into the bullpen. Sammy and Seth shared another look. This wasn't going to be good news.

"They got us pinned down!" the man on the radio said as Seth walked into the bullpen. "There's too damn many of them!"

"Where are they?" Bessum asked, holding his hand out for the portable radio.

"Town hall," Sharice said, handing the rover to the detective.

"Chief?" Bessum said. "Hang in there! I'm coming."

CHAPTER 26

"We're all going," Bessum said. "We need to get out of town, anyway. And the town hall's on the way. We'll take two cars and communicate by radio. One car will hang back while I go help Chief Medina and the others. Everyone okay with that?"

Seth nodded, praying he wouldn't be tapped to help the detective. He felt the sudden urge to pee, and his palms were sweaty against the smooth, processed wood of the Winchester.

Sammy and Sharice both nodded. Melanie and Tessa simply stared from where they sat, together again.

"I'll go with you to help Chief," Sharice said.

"Good," Bessum said. "Thank you. Let's get geared up." He turned to go, but stopped and turned back to Seth. "You fired that thing before?"

Seth looked down at the rifle. "Not this one," he said. "But it's loaded."

"Let's see it," Bessum said, stepping over and holding out his hand.

Seth's previous reluctance was gone. Half of him wanted nothing more than for Bessum to say that the gun was broken. That it wouldn't fire. That Seth was off the hook. He didn't have to carry a gun. He didn't have to fight anyone. So he handed the rifle over to the man.

Bessum inspected the rifle quickly. "Winchester Model 94," he said. "Looks like it's all steel. Probably made before 1964. Little beat up. Is this a family gun?"

"It was my dad's."

"And you never fired it with him?"

Seth shook his head.

"But you've fired a gun before?"

"Yes. A few times. Just not that one."

To Seth, the rifle looked like something out of an old western. Instead of a bolt, it featured a lever that you had to push forward and pull back to chamber a round. There was no scope on the rifle, only metal sights you had to line up. There was also no safety that he could find. On the way over to the police station, after he'd gotten the severed arm off his ankle, he opened the rifle case and took out the rifle. There was a box of bullets in the case, and he loaded the rifle through the injection port on the right side of the weapon. His pockets were currently heavy with bullets he'd shoved into them.

"You said it's loaded," Bessum said. "You have any more cartridges?"

"Cartridges?" Seth asked.

"Bullets. Do you have any more?"

"Yes."

"Can I see one?"

The teenager produced one from his pocket.

"That's a thirty-thirty round," Bessum said. "Packs a punch." Cartridge still in hand, he worked the lever, which pressed the hammer back, so it was ready to fire. Then he slid the cartridge into the injection port and held his hand out for another. Seth gave him one. Bessum tried to push it into the rifle, but it wouldn't go.

He handed the cartridge back. "I can't remember how many these things take. Six or seven, probably. Just be careful and don't aim it at any of us. It's ready to fire, so keep your finger off the trigger until you are, too. Got it?"

Seth's heart fell, but he nodded and took the proffered gun back from the detective.

"Good. Let's get moving."

Five minutes later, they were all wearing bulletproof vests and standing by the front door. Melanie held Tessa to her chest, one vest draped over them for some protection. Instead of the shotgun, Bessum had what looked to Seth like an assault rifle, whatever that was. He knew little about guns. It was the kind preferred by mass shooters, police, and military.

Sammy carried the shotgun in one hand. In the other, she had the rifle case with the severed arm in it. They were planning to give it to the authorities.

Sharice held a pistol, looking to Seth like she knew how to use it. She wasn't wearing a uniform, dressed in a white blouse and black slacks under her bulletproof vest. He wasn't sure if she was a cop or not, but she seemed confident. Or at least not terrified like Seth was.

Seth, Sammy, and the two girls were going to use the Jaguar again, while Bessum and Sharice were going to use Bessum's cruiser. But first, they had to get to them without getting attacked. The fact that they hadn't heard gunshots from outside for several minutes could either be a very good sign or a very bad one. They were about to find out.

Bessum glanced out the front door, then turned back to Sharice. "I don't see anyone. That doesn't mean they're not out there. Make sure you get to cover quickly. I'll call the rest of you out when it's clear."

Bessum counted down from three, and the two of them ran through the front door into the parking lot. There were no gunshots. A few moments later, Bessum yelled for them to come out.

Sammy went out first, followed closely by Melanie and Tessa, with Seth bringing up the rear, limping and wincing at the pain in his leg. He kept his finger off the trigger like Bessum had said. It was a good thing, too, because he was so busy looking around that he ran into Sammy just outside the Jaguar.

"Sorry," he mumbled, moving around the vehicle to the front passenger seat while Sammy put the shotgun and rifle case in the back seat. Melanie and Tessa got in next.

Bessum and Sharice were across the small parking lot, next to an unmarked police cruiser, looking around. They clearly hadn't seen anyone. Neither had Seth.

Once the Jaguar's engine came roaring to life, Bessum and Sharice got into the cruiser and fired it up. The Sedan with the girls' mom inside left no room for the cruiser to reverse, so Bessum simply hopped the curb and drove over the sidewalk into the street.

Sammy reversed and got turned around, then moved out through the driveway, turning left to follow Bessum. As they went, Seth glanced at the two dead bodies on the sidewalk across the street from the police station. There had been three men there when they pulled up. He wondered where the third had gone.

As they moved through the streets, toward the town hall just five blocks away, he wondered why the streets were now so quiet.

The radio had been silent the whole time they'd been getting ready. And now the humid summer night was just as quiet.

He figured it was either a good thing or an extremely bad thing for the people at the town hall.

The way tonight was going, he wasn't hopeful.

CHAPTER 27

"Oh my God," Sammy said, looking out the window. "You girls shut your eyes. You too, Seth."

It was too late. Seth had already seen the bodies. His gaze was fixed out the Jag's window, peering at the houses they passed.

A man and a woman lay on their front porch, their blood dripping down the stone steps. They'd each been shot in the head, the open front door providing enough illumination for Seth to see that clearly.

They passed three houses that looked normal enough. The doors were shut. There were no broken windows. No signs that anyone had been murdered in them. Then they came to a house with the front door open, a man lying in the doorway, unmoving.

By the time they were three blocks into the trip, Seth had counted at least a dozen bodies—and that was just on his side of the street.

It was as though someone had gone knocking on doors, and they just blew away whoever happened to open them. The thought of his friends from school and all the people he knew around town lying dead in their doorways made him slump down in his seat.

As they made a turn into the area of town with more businesses than homes, Seth forced his gaze out the windshield. The brake lights on the cruiser flared as the vehicle came to a stop. They were still a block away from the town hall, which was on the left side of the street. Seth couldn't see it because it was set back from the road and there was a two-story brick building in the way that housed a coffee shop.

Bessum jumped out of the cruiser, leaving the door open, and hustled back to the Jaguar. Sammy rolled the window down as he approached.

"Stay close," he said. "But if we take fire, back up quickly and get to cover."

"Is there anyone there?" Sammy asked. "Can you see anyone?"

"I didn't see any movement," Bessum said. "I can't see any cars there, either. So maybe they went somewhere else. But we still need to check it out."

"You haven't heard from them over the radio?" Seth asked.

Bessum looked grim. "No answer. We've been trying all the way over here."

Seth nodded. Tessa whimpered in the back, and her sister shushed her gently.

Bessum went back and got into the cruiser. A moment later, the brake lights flared again, and they moved off.

The town hall, although fairly small, sat in its own lot. Lawns flanked it on either side, along with a strip of grass at the front, bordering the parking lot with four rows of parking spots. There was a white and blue sign in that strip of grass that read Seven Springs Town Hall. Nearby, a flagpole with a limp American flag stood like a funeral attendant during a eulogy.

The building itself was rectangular and made of tan brick with a brownish-red roof. There were concrete steps leading up to the front doors, which were made of glass. Or had been, anyway. As they pulled into the parking lot, Seth saw that the glass panes had been broken. He also saw three bodies outside the front doors, one of which was sprawled on the steps.

The Jaguar's tires crunched over broken glass and shell casings in the parking lot. There had clearly been a firefight out here. And maybe in the building, too.

The two vehicles stopped. Seth turned in his seat to get a 360-degree view. He saw no one approaching. No movement. The businesses across the street were dark.

Again, Bessum jumped out of the cruiser. This time Sharice got out, too.

When the detective arrived at the Jaguar, he said, "I want you all to come inside with us. We need to stick together. I don't want you getting ambushed while we're inside."

"Couldn't I just drive off if that happens?" Sammy asked. "I mean, wouldn't the car protect us?"

Bessum shook his head. "Not likely. The only part of the car that will guaranteed stop a bullet is the engine block. It's not like the movies. They shoot into the car, you're likely to get hit."

"Okay," Sammy said. "That's all I need to hear."

They all got out of the Jaguar and moved toward the door, skirting the stairs by walking up the strips of lawn between the parking lot and the building.

"Just keep your eyes shut, Tess," Melanie said, still holding her sister to her chest.

Seth looked at the dead people on the stairs. It was two men and a woman. None of them wore police uniforms. And they all had guns close at hand. Given the wounds, it was clear they'd all been shot to death.

Bessum had the others stay back to the side of the front doors while he and Sharice moved inside. Seth scanned the parking lot, not out of any sense of duty or bravery, but because he was terrified of what would come out of the darkness. He knew he would run inside if he saw any movement. The only question seemed to be whether he would slow enough to hand his gun off to Sammy while he went.

He was saved from finding out when Bessum waved the rest of them inside after a moment. There were several lights on in the place. As he limped inside, Seth couldn't remember whether they'd been on when they pulled up or not. As the group walked past the reception area and down a hallway, they kicked shell casings on the tile floor. They tried their best to avoid drops and smears of blood here and there. Bessum ushered them past the reception area and down a short hallway into an office they'd already cleared.

"Stay here," Bessum said to everyone but Sharice. "I'm gonna shut the door. When I come back, I'll knock. Shave and a haircut, okay?" He turned to Seth. "If someone tries to come in here without knocking, you get ready to shoot, okay?"

"I can't," Seth said, finally breaking. "I can't do it." He tried to give the gun to Bessum, but the man's hands were already full with his own weapon. Instead, the detective looked over at Sammy, who nodded and came over.

"It's okay, Seth," she said, taking the Winchester from him. "It's okay."

"It's no easy thing," Bessum said. "It's not supposed to be easy. Nothing to be ashamed of. You got me?"

Seth nodded, clammy hands shaking as he jammed them into his pockets. He resisted the urge to look over at Melanie. It was crazy, but he wondered what she'd think of him. She would probably think he was a pussy. A beta male. And maybe he was. Maybe he just couldn't handle violence.

All he knew was that every dead body he saw widened a crack that had formed in his mind back at the church. He feared that if the crack widened enough, he would lose himself for good. He'd turn into a gibbering idiot. A walking vegetable. And he had a feeling that if he killed someone—with a rifle or any other kind of weapon—that crack would go so wide it would cease to be a crack altogether. It would be a chasm. A hole, down which he would disappear forever.

As much as he wanted to be the guy who stood guard with the gun, he couldn't do it. So he moved over to the corner of the office and fell to his knees behind a desk, trying not to weep too loudly.

CHAPTER 28

The blood and shell casings provided a trail Bessum and Sharice could easily follow. But as the detective stepped back into the hall, shutting the office door behind him, he patted the air in a "wait" signal. And he listened.

He could hear the older sister, Melanie, whispering to Tessa in the office. He could also hear the Granger kid weeping quietly. He didn't blame him. The kid was sixteen or seventeen, and this was a lot for anyone. Even Bessum had been teetering on the edge while driving over here. He'd just wanted to jam his foot on the gas and make a beeline for the fastest way out of this fucking town. This wasn't like dealing with some Podunk meth dealers or some mobbed-up drug dealers like back in Philly. This wasn't even the same sport. Not even the same fucking dimension.

But Sharice, who apparently played four-dimensional chess, had somehow known what he was thinking and had talked him down. There were people who needed their help. That was the important thing. That was what made this whole human race thing work—if it could be said to work in any way but dysfunctionally. Civilization wasn't just a mad scramble for self-preservation. It *was* that, but not *just* that.

And once she'd talked him down, the thoughts of running had seemed like someone else's. They seemed insane. *Of course* he couldn't just run. *Of course* he had to stop. There were people who needed their help.

But as he stood in the hallway, looking toward the meeting room near the back of the building, he wasn't so sure there was anyone left to help. Aside from the low sounds coming from the office behind him, the place was deathly silent. But there was, he thought, a faint dripping sound from up ahead.

He looked at Sharice and nodded once. They moved down the hall, stepping carefully to avoid kicking any brass casings. The place smelled strongly of gunpowder and sweat. When they came to the first office door on the right, Sharice opened the door while Bessum moved inside and cleared the room quickly. They repeated the process twice more for the next two closed offices. The door to the last one was open, and they didn't need to go inside to check it.

The wooden double doors with worn brass push handles that led to the meeting area were closed. There were no windows in the doors, either. They just had to go in and hope they weren't walking into a hail of gunfire.

For good measure, Bessum brought his rover out of his pocket and tried one more time to raise anyone. The only answer was static. Putting the radio back in his pocket, he got both hands back on his weapon, a Smith & Wesson M&P 15.

He gestured for Sharice to count it off. She did, mouthing the words as she counted down from three.

Using his hip, Bessum shoved the door open and swung it through its arc with his left shoulder while Sharice did similarly at the other door. He swept the room with his rifle, seeing nothing but dead friends and coworkers. The metallic smell of blood mixed with the semi-sweet scent of gunpowder and the sour, cloying stench of evacuated bowels.

He worked his way down the aisle between the two sections of seats and into the place where the town council would sit during a meeting, stepping over bodies as he went. Only when he was done sweeping the place did he stop and take stock of the scene.

Chief Medina was lying on the floor, his revolver in his right hand and several holes in his body. Paul Tulards was nearby, half his face missing. Ann Wesley's body was lying over the wooden partition between the seating area for citizens and the one for politicians. Jerry Spitz, the other Seven Springs detective who'd shown up at the Drummond house after finally being reached on his cell, was lying on his side in the fetal position amid a pool of blood. All the county employees were there, each of them just as dead as the others. Their brains and blood and, in some cases, eyes and teeth were scattered all over the room.

Sharice sat down heavily in one of the seats that wasn't splashed with blood. She put her free hand up to her face and sobbed.

Bessum moved over to her, his boots squelching on the thin, blood-soaked carpet. He rubbed her back with one hand while gazing around the room. It wasn't all that difficult to ascertain what had happened.

"They were all facing the inner doors, but they were hit from the back," Bessum said, speaking more to himself than to Sharice. "They were firing as they moved through the front doors and down the hall. Like they were being chased. But the only bodies are out front. I don't believe they would've fired so many shots in the hallway and not dropped anyone. That doesn't make any sense."

He stepped away from Sharice and moved back down into the rectangular area around the c-shaped seating area for the politicians.

There were two doors—one on either side of the seating area. He knew from experience that both doors led to rooms in the back where people like the mayor and other town officials would congregate before a meeting. He also knew there was an exterior door back there.

He surveyed the way all his friends and coworkers had fallen. And where the bits of them that had been blown away had landed. And he knew they'd all been gunned down from behind. Shot in the backs while all their attention was on the front doors.

But he also knew that Medina knew better. So did Tulards. They were good police, both of them. So why would they all be facing the same way when they knew about the back entrance?

"They were so scared of whatever was coming at them from the front, they didn't think about the back," he said. "And that let guys with guns come in through the back door and kill them all like they were nothing. Like they were fucking dogs in the street."

"Where's Penny?" Sharice asked suddenly, now up and peering at the dead bodies. "Where's Penny Wright?"

Ms. Wright was the only Seven Springs forensics expert. And Sharice was right. She wasn't here.

"Whoever did this took all their vehicles," Bessum said. "You saw outside. No cars at all. Maybe she got hit in one of them. Maybe she died in the parking lot."

"Or maybe she's still alive around here somewhere," Sharice said, her tone brokering no argument.

Bessum nodded. "Let's find out."

CHAPTER 29

S ammy stood at an angle to the office door, holding the Winchester to her shoulder with her finger pressed to the steel housing above the trigger. She'd fired a gun as a teenager a few times with her father, a couple of cousins, and her uncle. But she wasn't proficient with firearms by any means.

She really didn't want the responsibility of holding the weapon, but as the only adult in the room, she knew it was the right thing to do. And as she stood there, staring at the door, she was thankful she hadn't yet heard any gunshots or shouting from further in the building. Maybe they were really alone in here. She didn't want to think about what that would mean for the people who'd been here.

Out of the corner of her eye, she saw Melanie come up. Tessa had her head resting on her big sister's shoulder, eyes closed. Her arms were wrapped around Melanie's neck, but her legs hung limply from underneath the bulletproof vest still draped over them. Sammy thought the girl must've been getting tired of holding her sister. Her arms were probably screaming. But still she held her. And it didn't look like she'd be putting her down anytime soon.

"Mrs. Jobson?" the girl asked. "Can I tell you something?"

"Of course, Melanie." Sammy glanced at the girl, smiling as much as she could, before turning back to watch the door. "What is it?"

"I think something like this has happened before."

Sammy turned her gaze back to the girl. "What?"

"Last year, I did a report for Mr. Roebuck's history class," Melanie began. "It was supposed to be on local history. Most everyone else did something on the founding of the state or some portion in the capital's history. But I decided to do my report on the history of Seven Springs."

Sammy nodded for her to go on. She could see Seth over Melanie's shoulder, and the poor kid was looking their way, having clearly heard what they were talking about.

"Well, while I was doing my research, I found out that there was a massacre in this town just a few years after it was settled. It wasn't really even a town back then. Not officially. This was in 1788, when the massacre happened. I think it was 1788. Maybe 1789. Anyway, there were only about a hundred people living here then. And it's not real clear what happened, but I found an old newspaper article online from Victorville. It was a bigger town back then—I mean compared to Seven Springs—and they had a single newspaper."

Seth got up from his spot in the corner and came limping over, wiping his eyes. He stood nearby with most of his weight on his uninjured leg, listening intently as Melanie continued.

"The news article only said that the town had been massacred and many people dismembered while others were killed outright. They thought the Indians did it. That's what the guy who wrote the newspaper article thought, anyway."

Sammy was about to say that there were plenty of bloody massacres in the nation's history. But then Melanie said something that sent chills up her spine.

"But I saw the arm in that gun case you brought into the station. And I heard you tell Mr. Bessum about how the arm was sticking out of the ground. There was something similar in that newspaper article. The report said that they found some of the severed limbs planted in the ground around the settlement. They thought it was some kind of ritualistic thing. This was long before the Indians were killed or forced out of this region, and the people back then didn't really know much about them. So people from Victorville gathered together and killed any Indians living nearby.

"After that, there was no record of anyone living here for many years. People stayed away from this area for an entire generation. It was only after the memory of that strange massacre faded that anyone came back and started living here again. Not too long after that, the town was officially founded. Anyway, maybe the old-timey reporter was right. Maybe it was Indians. I just thought it sounded really similar."

"Was that the only article you found on it?" Sammy asked.

"Yeah. I looked for more, but I only found the one."

"Well, thank you for telling me. That could be helpful information."

Melanie nodded and went back to sit in the office chair she'd vacated. Her sister was still asleep. Sammy hoped she would stay that way until they got clear of town. She'd already seen too much. But she was young enough that she might not remember seeing her mother killed. One could hope.

Seth came close next, although he seemed hesitant to speak.

"How are you doing, Seth?" she asked.

"I'm sorry," he said. "For not . . . being better."

"Hey, there's nothing to be sorry about, okay? Absolutely nothing."

Seth gazed at the floor for a long moment before speaking again. "When I was at camp last night, I had a nightmare. I *thought* it was just a nightmare, you know? But now I think that something was trying to tell me . . . something."

"What was the nightmare?"

Seth told her about what he'd seen after falling asleep by the fire at camp last night. The cave. The dog that wasn't Dallas. The water and the blood and the arm.

Sammy listened, at first thinking it was nothing more than a teenager's nightmare. A coincidence. But when he got to the part about the severed arm floating to the surface of the blood-stained water, she could no longer shrug it off as happenstance.

What did that leave her with? Some notion that Seth had seen this coming through collective intelligence? Or that a deity had been trying to warn him?

None of it helped them in the here-and-now. So why did it matter?

It didn't. Not that she could tell.

"That's very interesting," she said to Seth. "But I'm not sure what to do with that, you know?"

"Yeah," Seth said. "Me either."

"If anything else happens that . . . lines up with your nightmare, let me know. How about that? Maybe there is something to it. You never know. Lots of unexplainable things happen every day."

"Yeah. I will."

Seth moved back to his corner. This time, he pulled out the desk chair and sat in it.

Sammy faced the door again and concentrated on listening for signs of Bessum and Sharice out there.

She hoped they'd found some or all of the people who'd been here.

CHAPTER 30

B essum and Sharice found one person. They found Penny Wright hiding in the maintenance closet attached to the men's bathroom. When Bessum wrenched open the door, she'd screamed and hit him with a mop stick on the left arm before realizing he wasn't about to kill her.

Bessum's arm stung from the hit, but not much. Penny Wright was a petite woman in her late twenties with a grown-out pixie haircut. She wore jeans, walking shoes, and a short-sleeved button-up turquoise shirt. She wasn't a trained police officer, and so didn't carry a weapon. Which was a good thing for Bessum. Otherwise, she might've shot him when he opened the door. Partly, that was his fault. He'd decided to not announce himself for fear that it would give him away if there was still a hostile hiding out in the building.

Sharice and Bessum listened to the woman's story, which wasn't very long or complicated. She'd been among the first people to run inside the town hall while a gunfight was still going on outside. She'd ducked into the men's room on a whim and found the maintenance closet, where she'd hid, listening to the screams and gunfire from outside.

"I panicked," she said, crying. "I was so scared, I just curled up into a ball and hid. I couldn't do anything else. I felt so useless."

"You lived," Sharice said, grabbing the other woman's hands. "That's what matters. You survived."

"What about the others?" Wright asked, not sounding hopeful. If she'd heard the gunfire from the meeting hall, which he was sure she had, then she probably had a good idea about what happened.

"They were ambushed," Bessum said. "They're dead. And we need to get out of here. We have some other survivors in an office down the hall."

"What the hell is going on?"

"I don't know," Bessum said. "Half the town has gone crazy. More than half. And we've seen some . . . unexplainable things. We need to get out and contact the authorities."

"When we were coming back into town from the Drummond house, we ran into a convoy going out," Penny said. "That's how this all started. There were probably ten vehicles. And two of the ones in front were trucks with people riding in the backs. Mostly men. And they were carrying guns. They looked at us as we passed. Then, Chief Medina turned around and flashed his lights to get them to pull over. That was when they started firing on us."

Bessum mulled that over. "They didn't do anything until Medina came up behind them?"

"That's right," Penny said.

"Where do you think they were going?"

"I don't know. I was wondering the same thing. It looked like they were going to war."

"What the fuck?" Bessum said softly. "So, what? They chased you here?"

"Yes. But when we were coming to the town hall, another group drove up and blocked the street. We had no choice but to pull into the parking lot. Then a bunch of us ran inside while the others laid down covering fire. Like I said, I was one of the first inside."

Bessum turned to Sharice. "Why would they take the cars?"

Sharice just shook her head.

"They took the cars?"

"There were no cars outside when we came up. The parking lot was empty."

"Maybe their goal is to spread out from town," Sharice said. "Whatever is wrong with those people, it's not anything anyone's ever heard of before. Maybe they're trying to spread it."

Bessum let that sink in. "We really need to go."

***

The shave and a haircut knock at the door prompted Seth to stand up. Sammy went stiff, pulling the rifle to her shoulder.

"It's Detective Bessum," came the voice from outside. "I'm opening the door. We have a new person with us."

"Okay," Sammy said, shifting her weight from foot to foot.

The door opened, and Bessum stepped inside. "We need to go. Now."

Sammy ushered the kids out and fell in line behind Seth as they followed the others out. Seth wasn't sure who the new woman was, but he didn't really know who many of the adults were in town, aside from his neighbors, his teachers, and a few friends' parents. The fact that there was only one of them got him curious about what had happened. Not that he was all that eager to find out. He just wanted to get out of town and find someone who would help figure all this out. And maybe find his mom and his dog. If they were still alive.

When they got to the front door, they did the same thing on leaving as they did when arriving. Bessum and Sharice went out first, making sure the coast was clear. Then they gave the go ahead.

The new woman got in the car with Bessum and Sharice, while the Jaguar seating was to be the same. As they reached the sedan, Sammy stopped Seth before he could go around. "I'm going to need you to hold this, Seth," she said, holding the rifle out.

Seth took the weapon, even though it was the last thing he wanted to do.

They moved out of the town hall parking lot and toward the edge of town, the cruiser in front and the Jag following behind. This time, Seth kept his gaze forward. He didn't want to see any more dead people lying in their doorways or on their porches. He couldn't bear to see another dead body. He thought he would break down if he did.

They were heading out of town on one of the back roads that was only used by locals instead of on the highway that passed within a mile of the opposite side of town. The road they were on—Mission Street—turned into State Route 64 on the outskirts of Seven Springs. It ran through the woods where there were a few cabins and some small farms until it reached a town called Blue Bluff fifteen miles away. Once they were out of town, Seth figured their phones would start working again. There was no way *all* the cell towers had been sabotaged. Was there?

One thing at a time, he told himself. *It'll be fine. We just need to get to safety. Of course the phones will work.*

Both cars drove with their lights off, going about forty-five. When they left the streetlights of town behind, it was very dark outside. The trees were tall and heavy with foliage. Some moonlight filtered down, but it wasn't much.

Seth got his phone out and checked for a signal. Still nothing. He put the device in his lap and resumed his front-facing gaze.

"Is he going to turn on his lights?" Sammy asked rhetorically, hunched over the steering wheel as she peered out into the darkness.

They rounded a bend in the road and the cruiser's brake lights came to life. The vehicle ahead came to a stop so fast that Sammy had to slam on the brakes. But the Jaguar wasn't stopping fast enough—maybe because Tim Granger had neglected the brake pads when fixing the car, or maybe because the cruiser needed to be able to stop on a dime. Sammy wrenched the wheel to the left, and the car finally came to a stop next to the cruiser.

Up ahead in the darkness were several cars arranged across the road. There were dark figures milling around the roadblock. There was a flash of light from one of these figures, and the simultaneous crack of a gunshot.

The bullet punched into the cruiser's windshield, and Detective Bessum rocked in his seat.

CHAPTER 31

The roadway was suddenly bright from spotlights and head-lights from the cars at the roadblock. Seth saw clearly into the adjacent cruiser as bullets from several guns slammed through the windshield and into the people inside. Blood spewed from wounds in Bessum's neck. A round caught him in the face, and the back of his head exploded onto the woman in the back seat, who was screaming and reaching for the door handle.

As Sammy reversed the Jaguar, Seth's angle changed, and he could see that Sharice had fared no better. The side of her head behind her badly damaged left eye was missing, and she was convulsing in her seat.

Tessa was awake now. And she was screaming. Melanie was crying.

Seth stared out the window, now looking at the woods beyond the cruiser. A man was there, running out of the woods toward them.

Bullets hit the side of the car as Sammy spun the wheel to get turned around. The man running out of the woods angled toward them. He was coming fast. He was wearing basketball shorts, a Tennessee Titans t-shirt, and socks with no shoes. His arms and face twitched violently as he ran.

As they got turned around, Seth twisted in his seat to see the woman from the back of the cruiser. She was running toward them, screaming for them to stop.

But as Seth watched, bloody flowers burst from her chest. She fell onto the road. The way her head hit the asphalt was all the indication he needed. She was dead. They were all dead.

The running man veered behind the Jag, blocking Seth's view of the woman. He was close. He leapt for the Jaguar's trunk, landing with a thud on the back. For a moment, it looked like he was going to slide off. His hands scrambled, unable to find purchase. Then his mouth opened, and four blackish-gray tentacles came rushing out as though shot from a cannon. They latched onto the car—two on the roof and one each on the two back windows—and kept the man from sliding off.

Now Sammy was screaming. Screaming at Seth.

At first, he didn't understand what she wanted. There was no way he could influence these events. Not him. Not Seth Granger, the sixteen-year-old kid from Seven Springs. This was a movie. And you couldn't influence the outcome of a movie, could you?

"Shoot him!" Sammy screamed, the words suddenly forming out of the din.

Still twisted in his seat, Seth looked down at the rifle he held, barrel pointed at the ceiling. Tessa and Melanie were clutching each other, Melanie's back pressed against the rear of Sammy's seat. She was screaming for Seth to shoot the man, too.

The guy got on his knees on the trunk. The tentacles were still affixed to the car as he brought a fist back to break the rear window. But before he could throw the punch, Sammy swerved. The man fell onto his side on the trunk, but he did not fall off. The tentacles held fast.

"Seth, please," Sammy cried. "Point and shoot."

Seth was still far away, feeling like a spectator. Or like he was in one of those dreams where it felt like you were moving through water and anything important you needed to do never happened because you could never quite get your body to cooperate with you.

The man raised up for another punch, and Sammy swerved again. This time, the two tentacles from the roof came down and attached to the rear window like suction cups. Seth could see that there were what looked like circles of little teeth inside the tendrils. As the man got back to his knees, the other two appendages attached themselves to the rear window next to the first two.

The things seemed to retract themselves back into the man's body, pulling his head swiftly down toward the back window. His head shattered the glass, busting a hole through. Blood welled from cuts on his face and head, but he didn't seem to mind. Whatever was controlling him either didn't feel his pain or could tolerate it with ease.

Seth's head rocked sideways as something struck him in the face. It took him a moment to realize that Sammy had backhanded him from the driver's seat.

"Shoot him, goddammit!" she screamed.

Seth raised the gun to his shoulder as the tentacles shot back out from the man's too-wide mouth, grabbing hold of Melanie and Tessa. There was no safety on the weapon, and it was still cocked from when Bessum had loaded a cartridge into the chamber. All he had to do was shoot. And it would be hard to miss from this distance. He got the barrel aimed at the man's head and pulled the trigger. The stock punched into his shoulder, and the sound of the gun was deafening in the enclosed space, but the lower-right portion of the man's jaw exploded. One of the tentacles was severed, and it began whipping around the car, its end still latched onto Melanie.

The rest of the tentacles were still working to pull the two girls out of the vehicle. Melanie had her feet against the back seat, her back jammed up against the driver's seat. She was still screaming, as was her sister, whose legs were both being pulled by two of the three still-functioning tentacles.

Seth jammed the rifle's lever down to load another cartridge into the chamber. The spent shell ejected directly into Sammy's lap, although Seth had no idea this had happened. He was busy lining up his second shot when Sammy screamed, swerving as the hot metal burned her through her light summer dress.

Seth accidentally pulled the trigger as he rocked with the movement of the vehicle. The bullet passed through the back window a foot to the right of the man's head.

As he worked the lever again, he had no idea it was a rifle shell that had made Sammy scream. But she'd apparently gotten whatever it was under control. When the second shell dumped into her lap, he didn't see her pick it up and toss it into the footwell with burning fingers.

But the missed shot and the wasted moment after the man had first smashed his head through the window added up to tragedy as the tentacles wrenched Tessa away from her sister by the legs, pulling the toddler out from under the draped bulletproof vest. Seth fired again just before the thing pulled the little girl toward the broken back window. The top of the man's head blasted apart, and he pulled back out of the window, dragging Tessa with him. The girl broke a larger hole in the back window as she flew out into the night, screaming and still reaching for her sister, who half-lunged through the broken window herself, cutting her arms up in an effort to save her baby sister.

But it was too late. Seth saw the way the girl bounced off the asphalt and rolled as the car sped away. The man who was no longer a man got to his feet as the tentacles flung Tessa's body aside. The tentacles retracted into his bloody mess of a head, and the man stood there in the road, a gruesome and impossible sight, watching them head back into Seven Springs.

CHAPTER 32

"Stop!" Melanie screamed, wrenching the severed tentacle off her arm and throwing it out the back window. It left a bloody circle on her arm, the skin torn. "We have to go back. We have to go back."

Seth could think of nothing to say. Sammy was also silent, driving as if on autopilot.

"Why aren't you listening to me?!" Melanie screamed, shoving herself into the space between the two front seats, prompting Seth to pull back with the rifle.

The teenage girl reached over Sammy's shoulder and grabbed the steering wheel. Sammy slammed on the brakes. The Jag came to a rocking stop in the road. They were no longer in sight of the monster who'd taken Tessa, having rounded a gentle curve in the road. But for all they knew, it could be following them.

"Melanie, please," Sammy said.

But now that the car was stopped, Melanie pulled herself into the back and opened the rear door, stepping out.

Seth got out of the vehicle with the rifle in hand and ran up to Melanie, who was walking back along the road. "She's gone," he said. "Please. She's gone."

Melanie whirled on him. "Fuck you!" she screamed, slapping Seth in the face. "Why didn't you just shoot him when you should've? It's your fault. It's your fucking fault, Seth!"

She hit him again and again. He winced under the blows, but he didn't move away. And he held the rifle down so it wouldn't be jostled by her strikes.

She was right. She was absolutely right. He'd had the chance to shoot the thing off the car, and he hadn't taken it. He'd been too scared. Catatonic with fear.

That crack in his mind opened even further. He seemed to be gazing into the dark depths within. Part of him wanted to take the leap. It was no more than he deserved.

Sammy came up and wrapped Melanie in a hug from behind and dragged her toward the car as the girl bawled and screamed.

"We need to get out of here," Sammy called. *And go where?* Seth thought, inner voice tinged with hysteria. There was nowhere to go. If they had a roadblock there, then they had roadblocks at the other two ways out of town. He was sure of it. They were trapped. Trapped until they were eventually killed or . . . infected. Taken over.

Seth walked back to the car, thinking once again about suicide. The dark thought was almost like an invader itself, squirming its way into his mind. A gunshot to the head from the Winchester would work. It was better than the alternative. The hot shame of his inaction filled him, making the deadly fantasy more attractive with each passing moment. He'd let a little girl get killed. He could've stopped it, but he didn't. Because he was too chickenshit scared.

He sat in the car, that surreal numbness coming back over him again. And as they drove into the outskirts of town, Melanie sobbing in the back seat and Sammy driving with silent determination, he thought about how best to do it. Or if he even *could* do it. Maybe he was too much of a coward, even for suicide.

Sammy made a left turn onto Blue Sky Road, which didn't lead out of town, but skirted the edge of town along a series of hills.

"If we can't drive out," Sammy said, "we can damn well walk out."

She sounded confident to Seth, but he doubted if even this was possible. They were trapped.

It was only a matter of time now.

***

They pulled up to a large house at the end of Blue Sky Road. Sammy said it was the closest they could get to a small road that led back to State Route 64 a good distance behind where the roadblock was. They would have to walk nearly two miles through the woods to the road, and then it was nearly twenty to the town of Blue Bluff. Really, they only needed to walk far enough to get a cell signal or to come across a house with inhabitants that hadn't been infected by whatever had taken over their town.

"The place looks dark," Sammy said, gesturing to the two-story house. It was a modern structure, and it looked expensive. It was all dark wood and rich stone veneers. They'd come up a long driveway and now sat about fifteen yards from the closed garage door. To the right of the connected garage, the dark house sat under tall trees filtering out the starlight.

"We can see if there are any supplies in there before we head out. We'll need water and food." She paused. "And weapons."

Melanie had been silent after being forced back into the car. She was still bleeding from the cuts on her arms, but none of them looked too bad, and she didn't pay them any mind. She stepped out of the vehicle and followed Sammy up to the front door. Seth got out and glanced down the paved driveway. There was no movement that he could see. No figures coming through the trees. No vehicles coming up the driveway. He worked the lever on the gun, ejecting the spent shell from his third shot and loading a fourth into the chamber.

As Sammy knocked on the front door, Seth limped up the stone steps and stopped well behind his two companions, as though he needed to be there in case something happened. But that was a joke. He'd already proved that he didn't have what it took to protect any of them. He didn't know what he was doing. Pretending. Going through the motions—the ones that didn't matter. Those were the easy ones.

He was a joke. And they all knew it.

As Sammy paused in her knocking, Seth listened for movement from inside the house. He heard none.

Sammy knocked again, louder this time.

Still nothing.

The woman tried the knob and found it was locked. "Seth, can you go around and try the back? We'll try the windows up here. Holler if you find a way in."

Melanie wouldn't meet Seth's gaze, and he didn't blame her. She kept her eyes fixed on Sammy.

Even so, he didn't think it was a mistake when he rounded the corner and heard Melanie say, "He's going to get us killed. You should take that gun away from him. He's fucking useless."

"Try those windows over there," Sammy said, choosing to ignore the outburst.

On the left side of the house, next to the garage, Seth leaned against the siding and fought off the urge to break down crying. Melanie was right, of course.

The memory of Tessa bouncing off the street played on repeat in his head. Again, he thought about using the gun on himself. But he quickly decided that there were so few bullets left, Sammy and Melanie would need them all when he was gone. So after he loaded the rifle to full from the cartridges in his pockets, he propped the gun against the side of the garage, where they would see it. He had three loose cartridges left, and those he set next to the rifle.

Then he limped around the back of the house. There was a small building about thirty yards distant, the two front windows dark. It looked like a workshop. He figured he could find something in there, some sharp implement, to cut his wrists with. That was one way people killed themselves, wasn't it? Cut deep and down the wrist to open up some veins there. Maybe even a major artery.

He moved up the path toward the workshop, past an area for cutting firewood that was missing an ax. The workshop looked to be about the size of the standalone garage at his house. Only it was sturdy and well-cared-for. There was a single wooden door in the middle, flanked by two square windows. He glanced in one window but saw nothing inside. It was too dark.

The door was unlocked. And as Seth stepped inside, his body stiffened. It took a moment for his conscious mind to catch up to his body, realizing that he was smelling blood—he'd smelled enough of it lately to know. There were also the rich smells of cut wood and varnish.

He slapped at the wall inside the doorway until he found a light switch. Two lights came on, bathing the place in orange illumination. The first thing he noticed was the bloody sheet of plastic on the floor in the middle of the three workbenches creating a U at the back of the structure. There were plenty of tools hanging on pegboards above the workbenches, but the two implements that kept Seth's focus were the hacksaw and ax sitting next to the plastic sheeting. Both were bloody.

The plastic sheet had been folded over something. It was a cloudy clear plastic, allowing him to see the blood staining much of it. As he looked around at the floor, he noticed even more blood that had soaked into the unfinished plywood. There were several trails of it leading to the door.

Seth moved to the plastic, bending down to pick it up and unfold it. Even though he had a pretty good idea what it was, he wanted to see what was underneath.

When all he saw was a pile of bloody clothes, he was slightly surprised. He'd expected to see a body part or two. But then he recognized the clothes. There was a pair of black jeans. A short-sleeved pink-and-black flannel shirt. And a pair of Converse All Star high tops. They were Kate Silver's clothes. She was the only girl at school who wore a pink-and-black flannel shirt.

Then the implications came rushing at him. He turned and looked through the open shop door, back down toward the house. And he saw lights on inside.

With a sudden twisting of his guts, he knew that someone was in that house. Someone infected. Someone dangerous.

Grabbing the ax on instinct, all thoughts of suicide momentarily pushed aside, he ran out the door and through the woods. He barely noticed the pain that shot up his injured leg with every stride. When he got to the side of the garage, the rifle was gone. So were the cartridges.

He ran around to the front and saw that one of the windows was open. There was light coming from inside. As he got closer, he heard Melanie's voice, pitched high with stress. She was pleading with someone.

"Let her go," she said. "Please, let her go. Don't do this."

Seth came up to the side of the window and peeked inside. He saw Melanie with her back to him, pointing the rifle at a tall old man with liver-spotted hands, entirely black eyes, and a shock of white hair on his head. He had his arms wrapped around Sammy's chest, pinning her to him. She squirmed and stomped his feet, but her captor held fast.

The old man's eyes bulged as he opened his mouth wide, jaw creaking. A moment later, four tentacles squirmed out and reached for Sammy's head.

CHAPTER 33

Seth lurched around to the back of the house, ax still in hand. He found a back door and tried the knob. He was about to use the ax on the door, which would've ruined the element of surprise, when he looked down and noticed a pet door. Using his foot, he tried to push it open but encountered a barrier.

Inside, Sammy started screaming. There was a gunshot, then a thud like someone's body hitting the floor. But Sammy continued screaming.

Seth dropped to his knees, setting the ax aside as he pulled the pet door's thick plastic flap toward him, revealing a piece of flat and sturdy plastic blocking the miniature door. He pressed both his palms against the plastic and pushed upward.

It moved.

He pushed it up enough to get his fingers in the gap at its base, and then pushed it up all the way, careful to not let it clatter to the floor. Setting it aside, he grabbed the ax and shoved his arms through. He had to angle his shoulders to fit through the door, but the rest was easy. Inside, he moved through a large kitchen just as Sammy's screaming died down to a muffled whimper. He went down a hallway lined with framed black-and-white pictures of buildings and plants until he came to the room where the conflict was happening.

Glancing around the corner and into the sitting room, he saw that Melanie was on the floor, seemingly unconscious. The Winchester lay nearby. The old man's back was toward him, and he still had Sammy clutched to him. Seth couldn't see what was happening, given the angle.

Melanie's words echoed in his head as he thought about how he would step out and strike the man in the head with the ax. *He's going to get us killed. He's fucking useless. He's going to get us killed. He's fucking useless.*

He couldn't even die right. Maybe if he'd helped them clear the house, he could've prevented this whole situation. Instead, he'd run off and left the weapon without even telling them where it was.

How long could he go on making terrible decisions?

I've got a chance to make this one right, he thought. *But if I don't do this—if I can't find the courage to do this—then she's right. I* am *useless. And it will be my fault when they die.*

He pivoted around the corner, raising the ax as he went. He swung the tool down, aiming for the circle of gray skin surrounded by thinning white hair. The blade bounced off the old man's head, splitting the skin with a wet crunch.

The man turned, still holding Sammy in front of him. Seth, raising the tool again, froze when he saw that the tentacles went from the man's mouth to Sammy's. Her eyes rolled and her hands grasped feebly at the old man's arms around her chest.

Seth faltered, shocked and no longer with a clear target. Now, he'd risk hitting Sammy if he swung. The first blow clearly hadn't affected the man enough to matter.

But Seth's eyes moved over to Melanie, who was grabbing for the Winchester as she got to her knees. The old man noticed this, and he turned to look at the girl with his black-as-night eyes.

The tentacles pulled out of Sammy's mouth, who sucked in a gasping breath. Two of the appendages zipped out toward Seth, and the other two toward Melanie. Seth slashed out with the ax and was rewarded with a glancing blow on one of them, while the other one dodged the ax and wrapped around his neck even as he backed up.

The one he'd struck with the ax was unharmed, and it joined the fray, grabbing for the tool still clutched in Seth's hands.

Meanwhile, the other two tentacles were fighting Melanie, one around her neck and the other around the gun.

As Seth realized he could no longer breathe, he flipped the ax around and tried to yank it toward the taut tentacle around his neck. He was hoping to cut it off, but the other one was incredibly strong, and it prevented him from moving the tool more than a few inches. It was all he could do to hang onto it.

Sammy, who was apparently coming back to her senses, shoved with her feet, pushing herself and the man backward until they hit the large bookshelf taking up much of the wall. This had little effect other than causing the man to redouble his grip on her with his arms.

So she tried something else. She slammed the back of her head up into the old man's jaw, making him clamp down on the tentacles. This caused the tentacles to spasm momentarily, as if flinching from brief pain. But that flinch was all Seth needed.

He yanked the ax up and out of the tentacle's grasp with shaking arms, sending the blade slicing into the tentacle that was choking him. Although it didn't cut clean through, it did the trick. The tentacle retracted from around his neck.

Sammy slammed her head into the man's chin again. This bought another precious second, and Seth lunged forward with the ax blade facing out again. Since the man was backed up against the bookshelf,

Seth used that to guide his blow. He aimed for the spot on the book-shelf just above the man's head, so even if he missed, he wouldn't hit Sammy.

The bottom corner of the blade jammed into the top of the old guy's skull while the top dented the wood of a shelf at an oblique angle.

The old man released Sammy and reached up to grab the ax out of his head, but before he could do that, Melanie fired the Winchester, blasting half his face away. The tentacles went crazy, flapping around. The one Seth had damaged sprayed syrupy black liquid everywhere. One of the tentacles went for Seth's neck again, but he flinched back and got an arm up. The appendage wrapped tightly around his arm and tried to pull him toward the man.

The man was still standing, just like the one Seth had shot in the face back on the road.

Melanie loaded another cartridge into the chamber and then fired at the man again. Only this time, she aimed for his chest.

The tentacles immediately retracted back down the old guy's gullet even as he fell to the floor, knocking the ax loose as he went.

"Again!" Sammy yelled. "In the chest again!"

Melanie worked the lever and then followed Sammy's advice, putting another 30-30 bullet into the guy's torso. He spasmed and flailed, but the tentacles didn't come back out. And when she put yet another bullet into him—this time in the stomach—he finally stopped moving.

The three of them stood a safe distance from the bloody man, breathing heavily.

"The head doesn't work," Sammy said. "The chest. The torso. That's where to hit them."

"Are you okay?" Seth asked her.

Sammy backed up and fell into one of the tan-colored armchairs. There were dirty water glasses and other dishes on the side table next to her. She looked up at Seth, then at Melanie. But when she spoke, she was looking at the old man on the floor. "I think it put something inside me."

CHAPTER 34

Seth stared at the old man lying in an expanding pool of black-tinged blood against the bookshelf. The sound of Sammy vomiting came from elsewhere in the house.

"What should we do?" Seth asked Melanie, who still held the gun pointed at the man.

"I don't know. I don't want to get close to him."

Seth darted forward and grabbed the ax up. The tool dripped blood from the blade, which had been in the expanding hemoglobin. The handle was dry.

"I think we should . . . tie him up or something," Seth said.

Both teenagers stared at the body. The one eye that was unharmed stood open, looking blankly into the corner of the room. The blackness was slowly fading from the eye as they watched. The other one—the right eye—had been blown away when Melanie shot him in the face. That whole side of his head was a bloody mess of floppy skin and exposed muscle.

"I think we should just leave," Melanie said. "We really need to get out of here."

"What if this is happening in other places?" Seth said. "What if it's not just our town?"

"Then why would they make a roadblock?"

That was a good point. And it gave Seth a minuscule slice of hope.

Sammy came walking into the room, carrying what looked like a filet knife. She wiped her mouth with her arm. "I don't think it came out," she said. "I think it's still in there."

She fell to her knees next to the body, her dress soaking up blood. She jammed the blade into the lower portion of the man's torso and started slicing up toward his rib cage.

"What are you doing?" Melanie asked, clearly appalled.

"I want to see it," Sammy said, still cutting. "I need to know."

Seth moved closer, his stomach clenching as he thought about what could've been put inside Mrs. Jobson. He wanted to be ready with the ax just in case whatever was inside the man was still alive. The gorge rose in his throat as he watched Sammy slit the man's abdomen open like a drunk surgeon in a hurry.

The smell that emanated from the body had Seth gagging and pulling the collar of his shirt over his nose.

Melanie rushed out of the room, one hand cupped over her mouth.

Seth didn't know if the smell was because the man had been shot in the intestines or if it had to do with the creature inside him. Either way, it was highly offensive to the nose.

But still he stayed, his curiosity and concern for Sammy trumping any urge to get away from the stench.

Sammy set the knife aside and pulled the man's skin apart with her blood-slick hands. Inside was a mess of organs that didn't look much of anything like the human anatomy illustrations Seth had seen in schoolbooks.

Sammy's focus was on the area directly under where the two portions of the man's rib cage met. She held the skin and muscle aside and whispered to herself as she looked in. "Liver," she said. "So that would be the stomach?"

She paused, and Seth looked on, waiting for a tentacle to shoot out and try to strangle his teacher.

"Oh my God," Sammy said.

"What? What is it?"

"His stomach," she said, reaching in with one hand and gently touching a gray-black organ.

"That's not normal?"

Sammy shook her head. "I'm not a doctor, but I know the stomach shouldn't be that color. And I'm pretty sure it's double the size of a normal stomach."

When it didn't react to her initial touch, Sammy poked it harder. Nothing happened. She pointed to a ragged hole in the organ. "That's where he was shot," she said.

Picking up the knife again, Sammy used the tip to widen the hole in the stomach. It was what Seth imagined cutting through a squid would look like.

When she'd cut along the length of the visible portion of the organ, she set the knife down and used that hand to separate the stomach lining. Two tentacles burst through the slit, causing both Sammy and Seth to jump. But they were clearly weak. They smacked Sammy in the face, but she batted them away before grabbing the knife and slashing at them. They tried to retreat into the stomach, but Sammy caught them both in her left hand and then sawed through them with the knife, tossing them aside when she was done. They smacked into one of the chairs and slid off onto the ground, writhing like a lizard's tail just separated from its body.

Sammy reached one hand into the stomach and pulled out two more tentacles. They wrapped ineffectually around her hand as she bunched it into a fist. She pulled on them, standing up as the things unspooled from inside the large stomach. When she finally reached across the room, the tentacles went taut and the stomach itself bulged out of the man's body as she pulled on them.

Once again, Seth gagged from the stench clearly wafting from the cut-open stomach.

"These are not the same as the ones that killed Russell," she said. "Those were much bigger. They couldn't fit inside a person. Not unless that person had a massive stomach."

Seth said nothing. He stared at the tentacles, which were a good ten feet long. Sammy was right. Russell had been killed by tentacles that were triple the width of these. And much longer.

"Cut them," Sammy said.

"Huh?"

She gestured with her chin toward the old man's body. "Cut them. We're taking them with us."

Seth stepped over, raising the ax. Then he stopped. He pulled out his phone and snapped several pictures of the man and the tentacles, trying to get close enough to show that they weren't just discolored intestines. That done, he pocketed his phone and got the ax up. Sammy let some of the slack out so both appendages were resting against the floor.

It took him three hacks each to cut them off.

"I'm going to find a bag for these. Then we need to gear up and go." Seth nodded.

"Go check on Melanie, please," she said.

Seth grimaced. "She doesn't want to see me. I let her sister get killed."

"So you better apologize," Sammy said.

"How do you apologize for something like that?"

Sammy shrugged. "I don't know. But I know you have to try. Even if she never forgives you, you have to try."

Seth watched Sammy head back toward the kitchen, her words clicking in his head. *You have to try.*

CHAPTER 35

Seth found Melanie in an upstairs office. She glanced over her shoulder as he came into the room.

"Look at this," she said, before he had a chance to start his apology. She picked up a notepad from one of the two desks in the room and held it out to Seth. It was a yellow legal pad open to a page about halfway down the stack. Seth took it from her with his free hand, his other still holding the ax. Handwriting filled most of the page. The writing at the top was neat, but it got much less so near the bottom. The last lines on the page were scribbled, the letters angling down and taking up two or three lines.

These largest words were the ones Seth read first: *I can't tell the difference anymore.*

He moved to the top of the page and read from the beginning. There was a date there from three weeks earlier.

Strange dreams again last night. I think my body is trying to tell me something. But I've been to see Doctor Richmond and he can't find anything wrong with me. Other than I'm old and my body is slowly falling apart. To be expected.

Sometimes I can't stop swallowing. Especially right after drinking a glass of water. Keep leaving water glasses around and not remembering.

Maybe Alzheimer's? Dementia?

Hard time working in the shop.

In my nightmares, I'm chopping a body apart.

Seth glanced up at Melanie after reading this excerpt. She nodded him on. The next one was dated five days after the first.

Five days without an entry. Not good. I only remember little things from the past days. Couldn't stop swallowing for an hour this morning. Made an appointment with Doctor Richmond, but Shandy said that I'd already made another appointment and missed it. Can't remember.

The well water tests have come back. They can find nothing wrong with my water. So much for that hypothesis. Spending my career in groundwater management has made me paranoid.

Had the nightmare again. Chopping a body up. This time it was a young girl. I used a hacksaw and my ax. Why did it seem so important?

The next entry was much sloppier than the first two. It was dated from a week and a half ago.

Something's inside me. I can feel it. It's taking over. Is this what dementia feels like, or is there something else wrong with me?

Then the last dated entry was from just three days ago.

I killed her. I did it. It was no nightmare. It was real.

She was at my door. Somehow, I knew she was there. We didn't even speak. I opened the door, and she walked in. Then she drank a glass of water and walked out the back door to the shop.

Something in the water? Something we don't know to test for?

I drank a glass of water and then got my hacksaw and my ax and I killed her. She smiled at me the whole time. Smiled at me while I chopped her arms off. She was dead when I moved to her legs. I took her limbs out and planted them. I put one of them in the cave. But it wasn't me who did it. It was someone else. Someone inside. Taking over. Or is it me?

I can't tell the difference anymore.

Seth looked into Melanie's face. "The water?"

"What about the water?" Sammy said from the office doorway.

Seth turned to her and held out the legal pad.

The woman stepped into the office, grocery bag bulging with severed tentacles hanging from her left hand. With her right, she took the paper.

While she read it, Seth stepped over to the wall. There were picture frames over two walls, but not all of them held pictures. One held a diploma. The one that Seth focused on held a newspaper clipping. There was a color photograph of a much younger version of the man lying dead downstairs. It was a waist-up shot of the man smiling. He held up a complicated-looking electronic device in one hand. Seth couldn't tell what it was by looking at it. But the headline told the story. *Victorville Man Revolutionizes Groundwater Testing.*

The article explained how the man, Payson Walther, had invented a way to improve upon groundwater testing devices, making the process cheaper and more efficient. Apparently, the device used electrodes to determine the pH levels in groundwater, along with salts, nutrients, and impurities. While the design had been around for many years, Walther had improved it after designing and testing his own version of the tool.

"It makes sense," Sammy said, pulling Seth's attention away from the article. "The water. It's in the water." She had set down the grocery bag and now tore the yellow paper from the pad as she spoke. She folded it and tucked it into a pocket.

Seth nodded blankly. "I've been away at camp for the summer. But what about you? What about everyone who wasn't infected? I mean, they wouldn't have killed all those people if they were infected too, would they?"

Melanie looked suddenly pale. "We get our water in five-gallon jugs delivered from a truck."

Sammy nodded. "So do we. Plus, Russell and I were on vacation. What about you? Does your mom drink tap water?"

Seth nodded again. "We have a well."

"Most houses around here have wells," Sammy said.

"How do you know that?" Melanie asked.

"Because there was an article about it in the news back in March, before spring break. I read the Victorville Herald for local news, and they had a big story about how Victorville had just opened a new water treatment plant and were getting their water from the Elk River, transitioning from the aquifer."

"What's an aquifer?" Seth asked.

"It's an area of permeable underground rock where water can move. It's where the wells in this whole area get their water. A well is essentially a hole drilled down to access water from the aquifer."

"So an aquifer is like a cave?"

"Not necessarily. Although there can be caves in the aquifer. Especially around here. There are all sorts of cave systems. But most aquifers are just made of layers of porous rock that hold water. But what I'm trying to tell you is that the story said the groundwater in this area would rise to its highest levels in over a hundred years. Because Victorville and the surrounding area would no longer be taking water from the aquifer." She paused and took a deep breath before finishing her thought. "And it said that the groundwater experts believed the aquifer would be fully recovered before summer started."

They were all silent for a long moment. Seth thought about how rainy it had been over the spring. They'd broken all kinds of rainfall records.

Seth broke the reverie. "That's why there were all those dirty water glasses around my house? And why I saw the same thing downstairs?"

"I saw something similar at my neighbor's house," Sammy said. "Mrs. Stein. She had dishes and water glasses everywhere, which isn't like her at all."

"What about the police officers? Why weren't they infected?" Melanie asked.

Sammy shrugged. "I saw a five-gallon water dispenser in the station. Maybe they all get their water like we do, even at home. Or maybe you have to drink enough infected water for it to . . . take hold. And do you remember what Bessum said about Grady Drummond's father? About how maybe he wasn't infected, but his family was?"

Seth nodded, not seeing the connection.

"Well," Sammy continued, "there's a rumor about him. I heard it from some teacher at school one day when we were talking about what a handful Grady Drummond was. The rumor is that Grady's father never drinks water—*drank*, I guess. That he only drank beer and soda. Never touched a glass of water. I thought it was just a dumb rumor, but maybe there's some truth to it."

The trio was silent. It seemed to make sense to Seth. At least *that* part of it. There was still plenty that didn't make sense to him.

"But what about the arm in the garage?" Seth asked. "What does that have to do with all this?"

Sammy shook her head. "I don't know. But the journal entry on that paper said that he *planted* the limbs he cut off the girl. Why would he plant a severed limb unless something was telling him to do it? He said he planted one in a cave." She paused for a moment, clearly lost in thought. "Mrs. Stein," she said. "Russell said he found something under her sink, but when I looked, there was nothing. I saw her out the back window of her house and she was clearly carrying something. Maybe it was a limb. Or a . . . head. Maybe they serve some kind of purpose for whatever the thing is that's infecting us."

The use of the word "us" gave Seth a jolt of fearful discomfort. Something was inside Sammy. Something planted by that thing that had been inside Walther. How long until she turned on them? How long until she tried to kill them, or to plant something inside *them*? Days? Hours? Minutes?

"We need to get out of here. We need to get you help," Melanie said.

Sammy nodded. "If the dates on the journal entries are any indication, I have some time until whatever is inside me . . . takes over."

Seth was surprised at how well she was taking this. She looked pale, and her eyes seemed to have shrunk back into her skull. Otherwise, she was holding it together well. And she was right. The dates on the piece of paper gave him hope. Right up until Melanie dashed it.

"We don't know that," the girl said. "If he—Walther—was infected by the water, it could've taken it weeks to form inside him. But what if he put something more advanced into you? Like an egg or something. A baby."

Seth had to swallow his rising gorge at the thought of a small, tentacled creature sitting inside Sammy's stomach, perhaps latching onto the organ's walls.

"You're right," Sammy said. "Which is why I'm not going to carry any weapons. And I'm going to walk ahead of you. Once we get to safety, I'll tell them to lock me up. I'll tell them what happened. That's why I'm bringing the paper and this." She raised the grocery bag.

But what if you can spread it? Seth thought. But that didn't really make sense. It wasn't like she was the only infected one around here. It seemed like most of the town was infected. So if they wanted to spread it, they wouldn't need Sammy to do it. Hell, they might already be doing it right now. So the best bet was still to get to someone who could study what was inside the grocery bag and inside Sammy to determine how to defeat the thing.

"Okay," Seth said. "Let's go."

CHAPTER 36

S eth carried the ax as he limped along next to Melanie, who carried the Winchester. Up ahead of them, carrying the grocery bag bulging with limp tentacles, walked Sammy. There were five bullets left—cartridges, as Bessum had called them. All five were loaded and ready to go. Seth had watched Melanie load the three loose cartridges she'd picked up when she found the rifle at the side of the garage. And he'd attempted his apology while she was momentarily occupied.

"I'm sorry," he had blurted. Despite himself, his voice cracked. Tears sprouted and rolled down cheeks that wouldn't see significant facial hair for at least another year yet—*if* he lived.

Melanie paused, one of the 30-30 cartridges halfway into the loading port. But she didn't raise her head to look at Seth. She just waited. Waited for him to apologize for something that could never be made right again.

Pulling himself together as best he could, Seth went on. "I was too scared. I couldn't do it. I'm sorry. I'm so sorry."

Melanie pushed the cartridge all the way into the port and then grabbed the last one from her lap. She held it in her hand, still looking down at the rifle. "The same thing happened to me," she said in a quiet voice. "When that thing had Sammy."

Seth shook his head. "But I heard you shoot when I was outside. And you were the one who killed him—it."

Melanie shook her head, sweat-stringy blond hair swaying. "I fired only on accident when one of the tentacles reached for me. I flinched back and fired as I tripped to the floor. It's a wonder I didn't hit Mrs. Jobson. Before that, I froze. I froze just like you did. It was only after you came in and hit him with the ax that I found the courage."

Finally, Melanie raised her head and looked at Seth. They shared the look for several long moments, neither of them saying a word. Seth knew that there *were* no words. She was trying to tell him that it was okay, but she could never say that. Because it wasn't okay. Her sister was dead. But she understood. Even if she didn't forgive him, she understood. And that's what she told him with the look. Forgiveness without forgiveness.

Now, as they walked through the woods side-by-side, there was a clear understanding between them. A sense of camaraderie that hadn't been there before. And although neither of them said it, they were united in their worry for their teacher.

The going was slow since they weren't using a flashlight. The last thing they wanted was to alert any possible sentinels to their presence. After all, they had the roads blocked. It would make sense to have guards around the outskirts of town if they were truly serious about keeping people inside the town limits.

As they moved down a gently sloping hill toward the bottom of a valley, the bark of a familiar dog erupted from ahead and to their right.

"Dallas!?" Seth whispered, peering through the onyx night toward the source of the sound.

"What?" Melanie asked. Up ahead, Sammy half-turned to see what the whispering was about.

"That was my dog," Seth said, no doubt in his mind.

"Are you sure?" Melanie whispered.

"Positive."

Sammy walked the few paces over to them. "We can't go looking for your dog, Seth. You know she's alive. That's enough for now. After we get help, you can come back for her."

Seth nodded. "I know." But knowing didn't make it any easier. He wanted to call out to her, but that was a bad idea.

Sammy turned back around and resumed walking toward the valley floor. Seth peered through the woods again, hoping to hear another bark. He held the ax in his right hand, and when he felt Melanie grab his left hand, he turned to face her.

"Let's go," she said, still gripping his hand, the rifle held in her left.

Seth nodded, and they started after Sammy, fingers intertwined and palms pressed together.

As they made it to the valley floor, Seth was able to see through a narrow clearing to a rock outcropping on their right. A dark oval in the pale rockface denoted either a cave or a divot in the rock.

Seth realized that he recognized it. Even through the darkness, he knew it was the mouth of a cave. And it looked just like the cave from his dream on the last night of camp. He stopped walking, and Melanie stopped soon after, their arms stretched taut.

"What is it?" Melanie asked, tightening her grip on him.

He pointed at the cave with the ax, searching for words that would make sense. "I dreamed about that cave. It's . . . important somehow."

Once again, Sammy had stopped and was looking back over her shoulder.

Melanie shook her head in disbelief. "So, what?" she said. "You're going to go in there because you dreamed of a cave that looked like this one?"

Before Seth could answer, another bark sounded. This time, its source was unmistakable. It had come from the cave. He looked from the dark oval and into Melanie's eyes. The draw of the cave was powerful. He couldn't explain it, but he knew he had to go there.

"You're fucking kidding me," Melanie said, jerking her hand away from his. "You're going to die in there. For a dog."

The words hit Seth hard, making him flinch.

"She's right," Sammy said, stepping closer. "Please don't do this, Seth. We're not far now. We can just keep going. We can get out of here and get help."

Seth felt like he was going insane. Not an hour ago, he'd gone searching for a sharp implement so he could slit his wrists. Now, he was ready to go off into a dark cave because . . . why? Why was he so ready to play at being a hero? He'd already proved he didn't have it in him to be courageous. What was it that made him think he could accomplish anything good by going into that cave?

"Please, Seth," Sammy said, swallowing hard. "Plea—" she swallowed again, interrupting her word even as she stepped forward, reaching out toward him with her free hand.

Seth stepped back as Sammy swallowed again and again, her eyes rolling up into the back of her head. Melanie stepped away, bringing the rifle up in both hands.

"What's wrong?" Seth asked. But he knew. He knew what was wrong.

The sounds of rustling erupted from both sides of the valley. Seth looked up to see people racing down toward them. Only they weren't exactly people anymore. There was something wrong with them. And Seth knew that whatever was inside Sammy had alerted the others to their presence.

Seth reached out and grabbed Melanie by the arm. "Run!" he yelled, yanking her away from Sammy and toward the cave. She came hesitantly at first, stumbling as she stared at Sammy.

Up ahead, Seth could see a figure running down the hill to block the cave mouth. It was a man, but his fingers seemed overly long, and his mouth was stretched open, tentacles whipping through the air around his head as he ran. The cave was their only means of escape—and it was where Seth was supposed to go. But they would never reach it safely at this rate.

Looking over his shoulder to yell at Melanie, Seth glanced at Sammy. All words deserted him when he saw his teacher.

Blood spewed from around Sammy's eyeballs as they were pushed out from inside her skull, both popping out in concert with a wet sucking sound. Two small tentacles emerged from the sockets, snaking around and jamming themselves into her ears. Her body cracked and convulsed, arms popping out of their sockets and twisting the wrong way. Two more tentacles emerged from inside her mouth and went immediately up her nostrils. Before Seth could make himself look away, the four tentacles reaching into Sammy's skull started yanking out her brains like they were so much stuffing inside a plush toy.

Melanie screamed, finally turning her full attention to running with Seth. They sprinted toward the cave mouth, jumping over roots and ducking under branches. But Seth could tell they were already too late. The figure he'd seen running to head them off was getting to the entrance, and they still had a good fifteen yards to go. The rest of the figures were closing in, the noose tightening. Even through the dark, Seth could tell that they didn't have guns. And he saw why. They were barely human anymore. Their bodies had been distorted from the inside out, and they moved in demented lurches.

Seth let go of Melanie's arm and put both hands low on the handle ax, raising it over his head as they came into the relatively clear area fronting the cave. The figure crouched there like a soccer goalie getting ready to defend the net. Now that they were closer, Seth could see what was wrong with his fingers. They had been split apart, making room for small-but-long tentacles that twitched and writhed.

Seth stutter-stepped and hurled the ax at the man, sending the tool flipping through the air. It moved fast, and Seth lost count of how many times it flipped, although he was sure it couldn't have been more than three. The blade hit the man in the face; it had been an impossibly perfect throw. One that he could've never hoped to replicate again. But it didn't stick in the man's face like it would have in some movie. Two tentacles reached out of his mouth to try to stop it, but the ax was moving too fast. It damaged the tendrils as it hit the man's face before careening off and clattering against the cave entrance. But that didn't make the damage to the man's face any less gruesome.

The blade, which had hit at a slight diagonal angle, caved in the man's nose and destroyed his left eye. He stumbled and fell, clearly dazed from the hit. But he didn't stay down. He was recovering as Seth and Melanie came to the cave.

Without hesitation, Melanie jammed the barrel of the gun into the man's gut and pulled the trigger. A chunk of the man's insides blew out his back, and he collapsed again, but this time, he wasn't so quick to get up. She worked the lever and shot him again, aiming slightly up from the previous wound. The man writhed on the ground, tentacles from mouth and fingers squirming like injured snakes.

Melanie hopped over the man and ran into the cave. Seth grabbed the ax and moved in after her, pulling out his phone and shaking it to turn on his flashlight.

Behind them, the sound of people crunching up to the cave mouth seemed impossibly loud.

Ahead of them, Dallas barked as if to show them the way.

CHAPTER 37

The leg sticking out of the cave floor twitched, sending a small cloud of flies into the air as Seth approached at a run. It was as though someone had been buried upside down in the floor with only one leg sticking out. That hadn't been part of his dream. While the cave entrance was identical to the one in his dream, the inside was not. Seth had no idea what that meant. His primary concern was escaping the people following him and Melanie.

He winced from the pain in his calf as he jumped over the leg, which looked to him like it had once belonged to a petite girl. Then he remembered the clothes he'd found in the workshop back on Payson Walther's property. Clothes that belonged to Kate Silver.

He had a moment to think about the arm that had grabbed him from under his father's Jaguar at his house. And about how, in Walther's journal entries, he said he'd *planted* a leg in a cave. This train of thought, which only occupied a couple of heartbeats, was set aside for more pressing matters as he looked up to see Melanie slowing ahead.

"Keep going!" he yelled. He could hear their pursuers gaining on them. They weren't shouting, like regular people would. Instead, the only indication that they were coming was the sound of their footsteps.

"I can't see!" Melanie yelled, just a second before the ground swallowed her up.

Seth slowed as he came to where she'd disappeared, seeing that the ground dropped away. Shining his flashlight down, he could see a steep slope made of bumpy rock. The sound of water splashing came to his ears as he moved the light to see Melanie some twenty yards down, thrashing around in a shallow pool of water at the bottom of the slope.

Knowing he had no choice, Seth stepped over the edge, hoping to run down the slope. But after taking only three steps, he lost his balance and fell backward, sliding painfully down the bumpy surface and tearing up the seat of his shorts while he went. He held the phone up as he hit the water, which was only knee deep.

"The gun!" Melanie called, still bent over and thrashing around in the dirty water, looking for the rifle.

Seth flashed the light up the slope, seeing that there was no time; several disfigured people were running down toward them, frenzied tentacles seeming to reach out for the two teenagers.

There were three potential exits from the area, striking Seth with a moment of indecision he could ill afford. Then a flash of black-and-white fur came from the narrow exit ahead and to his right. Dallas appeared there, barking once at him before turning back and disappearing into the waiting dark.

Seth grabbed Melanie and pulled her toward the exit. This time, she came without more than a brief note of hesitation. She still hadn't found the gun. They would have to do without it.

The opening in the stone wall where Dallas had emerged was little more than a curved slash in the rock, a few inches above the surface of the water. There was no way either teenager could fit through it without turning sideways. Which meant many of the figures behind them would have an even harder time navigating the gap.

Seth pushed Melanie ahead of him, and she moved with ease out of the water, slipping into the slash and moving quickly with hands braced against the leaning rock wall.

Seth, with the ax in one hand and his phone in the other, had no such luxury. He turned sideways, leading with his ax hand, moving his legs as fast as he could while pressing with the bottoms of his palms to keep him from falling into the tilted wall.

What had once been a fit-looking middle-aged man Seth knew as Lance Deiter, the owner of the Seven Springs hardware store, lurched up to the hole and slipped in sideways, tentacles reaching for Seth. A couple of the outstretched tendrils touched the back of Seth's left arm, but he yanked the limb away before they could grab him. But it was soon clear that Deiter could fit without much trouble in the irregular hole. He kept coming, and he moved fast.

The hole opened up around Seth, and he found that he could stand up straight now. Melanie was right there, yelling for him to do something.

"Get him!" she called. Dallas barked from behind her, seeming to support whatever Melanie was trying to tell Seth. The girl reached for his hand and yanked the phone away, pointing it at Deiter, who was only moments away from getting out of the tight space. Other figures were coming behind him.

Suddenly, Seth realized what Melanie wanted him to do, and why she'd freed up his other hand by taking the phone.

He brought the ax up, stepped up to the hole, and sent the blade sideways into the gap with both hands. Two tentacles from Deiter's mouth arrested the tool's motion before it could hit the man. They yanked the tool out of Seth's hands while two other tentacles flashed out, heading directly for Seth.

The teenager let go of the ax and threw himself back, falling to the ground as the two appendages swept through the air where his head had just been. Melanie reached down and helped him up, and they both turned to run deeper into the cave system. Dallas was up ahead at the edge of the flashlight's pool of illumination, leading the way.

Seth felt the last tentative remnants of hope slip away. He hadn't done anything to slow their pursuers down. All he'd done was lose the only weapon they had left.

Melanie still had the phone, which she shone down at the ground so they could avoid breaking an ankle or falling down another unseen slope. There were so many offshoots that Seth quickly became lost. He was sure he wouldn't be able to find his way out even if they did manage to escape the things still chasing them—which they seemed to be, at least momentarily.

Judging by the sounds, they were getting away from their pursuers. They were both smaller than most of the figures chasing them, and, it seemed, quicker. By following Dallas, they'd managed to take a seemingly random series of tunnels, which would, in theory, make them harder to find.

They slowed as they came to a wall of bulging stone. Seth fought off panic, thinking it was a dead end. But Dallas leaped up onto a rock outcropping and used it to leap up to another before disappearing behind a jutting wall about eight feet off the ground.

Melanie wasted no time. She moved forward and shone the light up. "There's a hole," she whispered, climbing up onto the first outcropping and then maneuvering onto the second, all while holding the phone.

Seth followed suit and found himself crawling on his hands and knees in a small tunnel that seemed to go slightly upward. They crawled like that for long enough to bloody their knees before coming out into a roughly circular cavern where they could stand up straight.

Dallas was in the middle of the cavern, growling and pulling at something there. Flies buzzed around in the moist air. Seth and Melanie moved closer, seeing that it was an arm, planted in the cave floor at the elbow. Dallas was trying to rip it out.

"Your dog has saved us once already," Melanie whispered. "I think we should do what she wants."

Seth nodded, moving over to pet Dallas. "I got it, girl," he said, keeping his voice low.

Dallas let the hand go and moved aside, looking at her human with her mismatched eyes. Seth crouched in front of the arm, gripping it at the wrist with both his hands. He braced his feet against the ground, flexed, and pulled.

It was like trying to pull a tree out of the ground with his bare hands. It didn't even seem to move an inch. Still, he tried, gritting his teeth and pulling with all he had.

When it was clear he wasn't making any progress, he stopped. The hand grabbed at him, and he had to pry its fingers off him to get it to let go.

"These are clearly important somehow," Melanie said, shining the light at the severed, planted limb.

"Yeah, but how?" Seth asked, breathing hard.

"I don't know. Maybe they're like . . . totems or something. Or amulets. Maybe they're necessary to give those things power."

Seth shook his head. "It seems powerful enough already. Why would it need severed limbs in the ground? What would that do?"

"Think about it," Melanie said. "Why else would someone go to the trouble to bring an arm all the way in here? They have to be important. There's no other explanation."

"If only we still had the ax. We could cut it out."

"Maybe it's how these things communicate. We have to assume that now that this arm knows we're here, the others do, too. They're all connected. Doesn't it seem that way?"

Seth nodded slowly. "I guess so."

"Remember what one of the old guy's journal entries said? He said that the girl just showed up—"

"Kate Silver," Seth said. "It was Kate Silver."

Shock swam over Melanie's face. "You sure?"

"I saw her clothes. No one else in town dresses like her."

"Man. When it's someone you know, it turns real."

"About as real as seeing your teacher's brains getting ripped out of her head through her nose," Seth said. The scene had been playing and replaying in the back of his mind since it had happened. There was something about it that bothered him. Something in addition to the sheer awfulness of it.

Both teenagers were silent for a long moment, staring down at the arm, the fingers of which twitched occasionally. Dallas sat nearby, panting and looking patiently up at the humans.

"He said in the entry," Melanie continued, "that Kate Silver showed up one day. Like she was presenting herself to him. He said she drank a glass of water—tainted water, we know now—and she just walked back out to his workshop. He said she was smiling even as he cut into her. Smiling until she died."

"So if she was infected—which I'm sure she was—something told her to go to the man. And something told the man to chop her up and take her limbs out into the woods. To plant them in the cave and elsewhere."

"Right," Melanie said. "That's what I'm saying. They're all connected. Something is pulling the strings. It's using human bodies to—I don't know—*expand* its area of control or something. Like laying down electric lines."

Seth nodded again. "And the limbs are like junction boxes. Or Wi-Fi routers."

"And if that's the case, then there's probably some main hub. Like a power station, right? If we can get to it, maybe we can stop it. Maybe we can shut off the power."

Dallas growled softly, drawing their attention. She huffed, standing up and wagging her tail.

"Okay," Seth said, stepping over and crouching next to the arm again. "See if you can find a sharp rock. We need to destroy this thing."

As Melanie headed to look for a rock, sounds of movement came from the tunnel they'd taken to get to the cavern.

CHAPTER 38

"Turn it off!" Seth said, still whispering.

Melanie went to unlock the phone to turn the flashlight off.

"Just shake it!" Seth said.

She did, and the light went off. They stood still, silent, listening. The sounds of movement continued—likely the *things* crawling in the tunnel. And they were getting louder.

Shit! Seth thought. *The arm!*

They'd just gotten done discussing the purpose the limbs served. If they were right, and the limb was in communication with the rest of the creatures, then their location was already known. They couldn't just wait around and hope the things bypassed the cavern.

Melanie seemed to be coming to the same conclusion. "We need to go," she said, moving over and grabbing Seth's arm.

"Which way?"

Melanie shook the phone again, turning the flashlight back on. They both looked at Dallas, who immediately darted down one of the tunnels leading from the cavern. Seth and Melanie moved after her, keeping the light on so they could see where they were stepping.

Dallas moved fast, and the two teenagers tried their best to keep up with her.

It seemed like they covered more than a mile of ground. Much of the time they were able to walk, often crouching thanks to the low ceilings. Other times, they had to get on all fours or crawl on their bellies through panic-inducing passageways that seemed to grow smaller as they moved through them.

When they went downhill, they often encountered water. Their route took them up and down, and they took turns with the phone when their arms got tired from holding it up or out of the sometimes chest-deep water they had to go through, walking behind a dog-paddling Dallas.

They saw several other limbs planted in the labyrinthine cave system, but they avoided them when they could. They didn't try to destroy any of them because Dallas never stopped for long enough to do so.

More than once Seth questioned the wisdom of following his dog. He loved Dallas, and she was smarter than many humans he'd seen, but he wasn't sure that she knew what was happening. Still, she seemed to know her way through the caves. And although some of the passages were very tight, she hadn't yet taken them through any that were too small for them.

"Did you know there were all these caves around Seven Springs?" Melanie asked when they were walking along a stretch of tunnel that was big enough for them to stand up. They were moving slowly, both of them approaching exhaustion.

"I knew there were caves around, yeah," Seth said. "But I didn't know they were like this."

"Did you ever explore any of them?"

"No way. My mom was very clear about that. She filled my head with horror stories of caves collapsing and killing people when I was a little kid. It worked. I never went more than a few feet into any cave. What about you?"

"No," Melanie said. "Exploring caves is kind of a boy thing."

"Or a tomboy thing," Seth said.

Melanie shrugged. "There are always exceptions. I just mean that none of my friends did much of that when I was growing up."

They moved on in silence. Up ahead, Dallas stopped and waited for them to catch up. She was having to do that more and more.

"Were you going to head to college?" Seth asked. He knew she was a year ahead of him. She was going into her last year of high school. Or she had been, before all this happened.

Melanie didn't answer at first. Finally, sniffling, she said, "I don't want to talk about that."

Seth dropped it. He was currently holding the phone, and he woke the screen to check the time and battery level. It was nearly midnight. And the phone battery was down to 6%. He still had no service.

"We don't have much battery left."

"Stop and I'll check my phone again," Melanie said. It had gotten wet when she fell down the slope and into the first pool of water. She'd made an effort to keep it dry since then, but as she tried to turn the power on, nothing happened. "It's toast."

"Yeah," Seth said, turning to follow Dallas again. He didn't see her in the tunnel ahead.

"Where'd she go?" Melanie asked.

Seth didn't answer. He hustled ahead, shining the light into every crack and crevasse he passed, looking for his dog. The tunnel took a curve ahead, and as he turned the corner, he saw Dallas racing down toward him, wagging her tail. Beyond her, fifteen yards down the tunnel, there was something different about the light. It wasn't as dark. As though there was some kind of light coming from above.

He glanced over his shoulder, seeing that Melanie had also noticed the difference. Dallas panted and turned back around, trotting toward the area, her tail swishing.

As Seth approached, he turned off his phone's flashlight. Sure enough, there was dull illumination coming down from overhead. There were bits of loose rock littering the tunnel floor. As though the stone had been broken away by someone or something.

Dallas stopped outside the pool of pale light, sitting and looking at the two teenagers.

Seth crept forward, craning his neck to look up. There was a roughly circular vertical passageway in the rock ceiling, about ten feet in diameter. It extended upward a good twenty feet before opening up into a structure with a roof. He could see the crossbeams under the A-frame roof.

Suddenly, he knew where they were.

"It's the church," he said, turning to look at Melanie. "The High Valley Methodist Church, right down the road from my house."

Melanie looked confused. "Why would she lead us here?"

"I don't know," Seth said. He looked beyond the pool of light coming from the church above—probably from a single lightbulb somewhere out of his field of view. The tunnel extended just a few feet beyond the pool of light before stopping at a sloping wall of loose boulders. It looked as if there'd been a cave-in. He stepped across, careful not to twist his ankle on any of the bits of broken rock on the tunnel floor. He climbed up some of the boulders, seeing dark holes at the top. They looked too small for him or Melanie to fit through.

Seth turned and looked at Dallas. She sat in the same place, looking at him. Then she turned her head and looked up toward the church.

"She wants us to go up there," he said, coming back over. "It doesn't look too hard to climb."

Melanie looked from Seth to his dog. "This is insane," she said. "But if it gets me out of these caves, I'm all for it."

"The thing is," Seth said, "this is where Mr. Jobson was killed earlier tonight. I don't know what's up there. But I've got to believe that Dallas wouldn't put us in danger if she could help it."

"Insane," Melanie said under her breath, shaking her head. "Let's go."

Seth put his phone in his mouth, not wanting to put it into one of his wet pockets. There wasn't much battery left, but they might need the 6%. He reached up and found a handhold, then did the same with his feet, starting the climb. Although he still walked with a limp, the pain in his leg was little more than a persistent throb now. Just one of many scrapes and bruises.

The stone was bumpy, and there was no shortage of divots all the way up. He made it to the top of the hole, seeing where much of the exposed stone was paler than the rest of it. It was where the people who'd been working inside the church earlier had broken through.

As he got his head up over the stone lip, the ground was mostly dirt, the sides of a hole surrounding stone bedrock. From here, he could see under the church, which had been built on a crawlspace foundation. A couple of feet overhead was the jagged hole in the wooden floor. He glanced around at the cobweb-shrouded crawl space, half expecting to see some tentacled creature rushing toward him. But there was no creature, tentacled or otherwise.

Seth reached up and gripped the edge of the hole in the wooden church floor, bringing his feet up onto the lip of the stone hole. He brought his head up into the church and looked around. The place was a wreck. The pews had been shoved aside, piled on each other to make room in the middle of the floor. There was a single light on over the stage area. The large wooden cross that had been affixed to the wall was gone, the light now shining on nothing but empty white wall.

When he was satisfied the coast was clear, he hefted himself up, rolling over and getting to his knees. When no one came out at him, he took his phone out of his mouth and looked down into the hole. "Come on," he said to Melanie, who stood below, looking up. Dallas was nearby, also looking up.

As Melanie started climbing, Seth realized he had no way to get Dallas out of the hole. "Wait!" he said. "How will we get Dallas out?"

Before Melanie could answer, the dog darted off down the tunnel below, heading toward the wall of boulders.

"Dallas!" Seth shouted.

"Shh!" Melanie said. "Don't yell!"

"Should we follow her?" Seth asked, getting ready to climb back down.

"No," Melanie said. "She's probably coming up to meet us. We couldn't fit through those gaps, anyway. But she can."

Seth suddenly remembered the ax thing. He'd thought that Dallas had been barking for him to attack Deiter, as Melanie had been urging him to do. "What if she's wrong? She was wrong about the ax thing."

"We're talking about a dog," Melanie said, resuming her climb. "Either she's just a dog or she's tapped into something . . . more, and she's trying to help us. Choose one and stick with it. She's got us this far, after all."

When she got to the edge of the hole, Seth reached down and helped her up. They stood for a moment in the middle of the church, looking around.

"Now what?" Seth asked.

Melanie shrugged. "Let's look around, I guess? Maybe there's some—"

"Shh!" Seth said, reaching a hand between them to silence her. He tilted his left ear down toward the hole. A moment later, the two teenagers shared a fearful look before backing away from the hole in the floor.

The sound of rushing footsteps was now unmistakable. Their pursuers had caught up with them.

They rushed toward the church's front door, knowing they had to get away from the building. They had to either keep running or find a place to hide. Seth was sure about one thing: they couldn't face those men—those things—and win.

He stepped to the set of double doors, opening the inward-swinging door for Melanie and moving aside so she could go through first. Melanie stepped outside, and Seth followed immediately behind her. But as he stepped out, he flinched backward—Melanie spun toward him, placed both hands on his chest, and shoved.

Seth tumbled back through the doorway, falling onto his back, confusion written on his face. Melanie lunged for him, shouting, trying to get back into the church. But before she could cross the threshold, a large and messy tentacle came out of nowhere and wrapped around her waist. She was lifted from her feet, legs kicking in the air and arms beating at the appendage around her abdomen.

Seth got his hands and feet moving, propelling him backward in a frenzied crab walk. As another large tentacle came thrusting through the door, Seth dropped himself onto his back, flattening out as the thing whipped around. He rolled as it slapped the floor where he'd just been. Then he was on his feet, running, sprinting for the hole in the floor.

The tentacle whipped toward him, dragging across the floor, aiming to snag his legs. He jumped and sailed toward the hole, clearing the slithery appendage and bringing into view the half dozen deformed people currently climbing up the stone sides of the hole.

CHAPTER 39

The gap between the church floor and the ground where the hole was couldn't have been more than two and a half feet. Seth aimed his feet for that gap as his momentum took him into the hole at a shallow angle. He reached out, aiming to grab the edge of the hole that had been sloppily smashed into the church floor. His plan—if a split-second decision could be considered a plan—was to swing his legs into the crawlspace area by controlling his momentum with his hands. Or at least using them to make sure he didn't smack face-first into the edge of the floor.

He certainly didn't want to fall back down into the cave system. Not only would the fall surely break some bones, but it would also leave him vulnerable to all the men climbing up the stone walls—and the creatures controlling them.

Seth managed to get his feet into the crawlspace area under the church, and he managed to catch hold of the edge of the hole, but things went sideways from there. He was moving too fast, and his angle was all wrong for his plan to work. His feet hit the relatively padded ground—whoever had dug the hole there to get to the stone had piled the dirt up around the hole. But he didn't slide smoothly into the crawlspace like he'd hoped. His knees buckled as he got his hands secured on the rough edge of the floor, trying to slow his momentum. His arms collapsed, and his chest slammed into his hands against the edge of the floor, sending bolts of pain through his hands and his chest and knocking his breath out.

He bounced off, his upper body going back and down, his arms extending out again as he teetered back over the hole. Despite the pain in his hands, Seth gripped the floor with all he had. His sweat-slick fingers slid along the wood. For one terrifying second, he was sure his hands were going to come off, and he was going to tumble backward into the hole.

But he didn't. His hands stopped their slide at the very edge of the lip, the tips of his fingers and thumbs holding fast and keeping him from falling. But they wouldn't hold for long.

Seth adjusted his grip and then swung his body into the crawlspace, looking over his shoulder to see the nearest figure about three feet down in the hole, tendrils reaching for him. Seth scrambled around as a quartet of snakelike tentacles emerged over the lip of the stone hole, slithering through the dirt, searching for him.

He crawled as fast as he could through the cobwebs toward the back of the church. He thought he could see an air vent there, which would allow him to break through the ancient stone foundation that encompassed the crawl space.

As he approached the vent, he threw himself forward, thrusting his hands out and churning his knees. His battered palms hit the wooden vent and the flimsy metal mesh that backed it. The wood was old—although not nearly as old as the foundation—and it cracked under the impact. Seth's upper body burst through the vent and out into the night. As he wriggled through the narrow gap, he heard something big coming around from the front of the church. Coming to get him like it had gotten Melanie.

There was a pile of discarded wood from the church fifteen yards away. It was the only place Seth could think of to get a weapon. He doubted he could hold them off for long with a two-by-four, but it was the only chance he had, his desperate and panicked mind grasping at straws.

He pulled his feet out of the vent hole and got up, bolting for the woodpile. He heard and sensed something massive rounding the back of the church. Unable to stop himself, he threw a frightened glance over his shoulder. But when he saw the thing that was bearing down on him, his glance turned into a terrified stare.

The monster loomed over ten feet tall and was nearly as wide. Its body was a mess of fused-together human parts with dozens of tentacles protruding here and there. Some of the alien appendages had their source in human mouths or eye sockets. Others seemed to protrude from the spaces between the bodies, where the flesh was dark red and bubbled as if from a severe burn. It moved much like an octopus, propelling itself forward on large tentacles while low to the ground. A few human legs stuck out from its underside at odd angles, and they would move to help the creature along when they had the opportunity.

The thing had no apparent head—it was simply a mass of flesh with no clear front or back. Those human heads that still had eyes stared out with the black orbs, blinking occasionally, faces frozen in sneers.

Seth could see no evidence of Melanie or his mother, but for all he knew, they'd both been subsumed by the creature. And there was no doubt in his mind that a similar fate was fast approaching for him.

His head still twisted over his shoulder and his legs still churning, he didn't notice how close he was to the pile of wood. He tripped over a floor joist, only whipping his head forward just before he crashed into the pile. A protruding nail sank into his left hand, and one stuck him in the thigh. Other sharp pieces of wood and metal gouged him as he crashed through the pile, coming to a rest in the middle of the discarded scraps.

Seth cried out in pain as he yanked his hand off the nail, which had skewered the appendage. He reached down and pulled the other nail and attached wood out of his leg. Blood streamed out of both wounds as he half-turned to look back at the approaching atrocity.

But it had stopped. It was ten yards away, moving back and forth in a shallow arc, like an excited dog at the end of its leash.

Seth didn't understand. He couldn't comprehend why the creature didn't come for him. He was helpless, wounded, defeated. But seconds passed, and the creature didn't move closer. It could've easily reached out with one of the messy-looking tentacles to grab him. But it didn't.

Seth looked behind him, at the trees standing darkly like mute witnesses to a crime. There was nothing there. No one. No reason why . . .

He looked down at the pile of wood he was slowly adding his blood to. And he saw it. Something down there, barely visible through layers of wood, was glowing. It was a pale, whitish-blue glow, but it was unmistakable.

"Come here, boy," a half-dozen voices, male and female, said all at once, causing Seth to jump. He looked toward the beast, unsure if what he heard had come from it.

When it spoke again, there was no mistaking it. "Come here. You can be with your mother again. You can be with your friends. Wouldn't you like that?"

Seth could see the human mouths moving in unison from their places fused into the beast. They all spoke with their own voices, the resulting sound just as disturbing as watching them speak. Those with eyes—black-coated eyes—looked at him. The tentacles undulated impatiently.

Seth looked back down at the source of the glow in the pile. He thought about Mrs. Jobson. Sammy. About how she'd died. It had been bothering him ever since. There had been meaning behind her murder. Up until that point, Seth had been ready to believe that whatever had been at work in their small town was acting on survival instinct. After all, parasites weren't inherently evil. Cancer didn't kill people because it hated them. Termites didn't invade houses because it had something against the people living there.

But what it—Seth was now certain it was an *it*, not a *them*—what it had done to Sammy was different.

Still looking down at the faint glow, Seth asked his question. "Why did you kill Sammy like that? You could've killed her in any other way, couldn't you? You didn't even have to kill her. You could've controlled her. But you decided to . . . torture her. Why did you do that?"

The beast was silent. Seth now saw the creatures who'd been climbing up the hole coming around the church. They stopped next to the beast, staring at him, apparently unwilling or unable to come any closer. Their tentacles—smaller versions of the ones protruding from the monster—writhed purposelessly.

"Was it because you wanted to scare us?" Seth asked. "Or was it because you enjoyed it?"

The creature was silent for a long moment. Then it said, "Come here, boy. So I can rip your limbs off like I did to your little girlfriend."

"That's what I thought," Seth said, barely able to contain the anger that came rushing into his chest. He shifted and reached down into the pile. As he grasped the glowing object, he realized it was wood. At first, this didn't make any sense to him. How could wood glow? But then he remembered the blank white wall in the church, where the big wooden cross had been.

He shifted and pulled on the piece of wood, bringing it out after a few seconds of struggle. It seemed to get brighter as he held it up between him and the creature. It was a rough stake that had been broken off the cross. And as he glanced down into the gap he'd just created in the pile, he saw other pieces glowing there. Other pieces of the smashed-apart cross.

Transferring the piece he held into his throbbing left hand, he went to reach for another piece. He wanted as many as he could get. After all, the cross seemed to be the only thing saving his life right now.

But as he plunged his hand down into the gap, he looked behind the pile at the dark woods, noticing two men walking toward him—men without tentacles protruding from their fingers or mouths. Figuring they would stop, he grabbed at the other piece, but found that it was much bigger than the one now in his hand.

The footsteps grew nearer, and Seth noticed that these two men seemed to be closer than the others behind him.

And they kept coming.

They both winced, scrunching their faces up as they approached the pile, now within five yards of it.

Seth's eyes widened. They weren't stopping. How?

Maybe they're newly infected, he thought even as he pulled his arm out of the gap, empty-handed. *Maybe only a week or two, whereas everyone else has been infected for longer.*

No matter the cause, it was clear they were coming for him.

As the grimacing men separated to flank him, Seth got to his feet. The wood shifted under him, but he kept his balance, slashing out with the glowing stake at one man and then the other. They flinched back as though he were waving a torch at them.

He moved to get off the precarious pile, but the men moved to prevent it. He had to keep spinning around, swiping at them in turn to keep them away from him. But he knew he couldn't keep it up for much longer. Blood soaked his leg and dripped steadily from his left hand. Fatigue was settling into his bones.

Behind him, the creature and the other men stood like spectators, waiting for him to grow tired. They knew just as well as he did that it was only a matter of time.

One of the men lunged forward, and Seth sunk the tip of the stake into his chest. The man screamed, a torrent of red-black liquid spewing out of the wound as Seth pulled the stake out. The injured man flailed, turning to run. Before Seth could spin around to face the second attacker, the uninjured man grabbed him from behind, pinning his arms to his sides.

Seth tried to do what Sammy had done, jerking his head back to hit the man in the face, but the man saw it coming and moved his head out of the way. He dragged Seth away from the woodpile—out of the sphere of its protection.

Like the flip of a switch, Seth's anger turned to panic. He kicked his legs and cried out, knowing that death was moments away. The prospect now terrified him, whereas mere hours earlier he had welcomed the thought.

Even in his current state, he realized there was a big difference in *how* you died. Maybe it was *all* the difference. And the fate he was now facing scared him senseless. Not because he was going to die, but because of *how* he was going to die. Because of the pain and panic and prolonged terror that would come with it.

But there was also a lingering thought in his mind that disturbed him even more. What if he wasn't going to die? What if he was about to be infected? That was a million times worse than death, in his mind.

In his thrashing panic, Seth tried to stab the man in the leg with the stake. In so doing, twisting the implement awkwardly in his hand and thrusting it backward, he struck it with his kicking leg, knocking the thing to the ground.

All hope left him. He stopped thrashing and went limp in the man's grip, staring down at the still-glowing stake as he was taken farther away from it. His throat constricted, and his thoughts turned to his mother and his dog. He'd failed to save his mother, but he hoped beyond all logic that Dallas would be okay.

So when he first saw the dog come bounding out of the woods to his right, he thought it was his imagination. He thought that whatever God was overseeing this whole show clearly didn't have the power or inclination to stop what was happening in Seven Springs. But He or She or It was conscientious enough to let a boy see his dog one last time before he left the world forever.

Dallas barked once as she came to a quick stop next to the stake. Only Seth realized it wasn't Dallas at all. Now that she was close, he could see that this dog had two brown eyes instead of the mismatched pair his dog had. In every other way she resembled Dallas, right down to her bark. She picked the stake up in her mouth and darted back the way she'd come, out into the woods beyond the neighborhood. Toward the spot in the woods that had looked so strange to Seth earlier, like there was a curious gap in the trees that hadn't been there before.

There was another familiar bark, this one coming from the road. It was followed by a frenzy of barking. Seth twisted his head around and looked beyond the spectators, now only five yards away, and saw a pack of dogs tearing around the church toward them. Dallas—the real Dallas—was leading the pack, but he recognized other dogs from the town. There were dozens of them. And they launched a frenzied attack without so much as slowing.

The creature whipped its tentacles out, hitting several of the dogs and sending them flying, yelping and whimpering as they hit the ground or slammed into the back of the church. Dallas leaped over one of these whipping appendages and ran full speed at Seth and his captor, who'd now spun around to use Seth as a shield.

Seth brought his legs up on instinct, using his core to hike his knees up toward his chin, clearing a path for Dallas. She didn't disappoint. Her teeth sank into the man's crotch. As soon as she latched on, she shook her whole body, the sound of ripping fabric and tearing flesh unmistakable. The man was still human enough to scream from the pain. He tried backpedaling but toppled backward after a few steps, Dallas still holding tight.

As they hit the ground, the man released Seth, who immediately rolled off and got to his feet. He knew what he had to do. He knew where he had to go.

He took off into the woods, ignoring the pain that flared in his leg with every step. He glanced over his shoulder to see the repulsive creature starting after him, tossing limp dog bodies from several of its tentacles. Dallas had let go of the man's crotch and was now attacking his throat, blackish blood spraying out as her teeth tore into him.

As the creature moved on its smoothly shifting appendages, it passed Dallas, grabbing her up with one tentacle even as several other dogs were still attacking it.

Seth stopped. "No!"

But it was too late. The creature threw his dog—his best friend. She hit a tree with a pained yelp, spinning from the impact and flying through the air to land behind some bushes on the ground.

Unable to help himself, Seth stared at those bushes, waiting to see Dallas dart out from behind them, knowing full well that the creature was bearing down on him. Tears slid down his cheeks, but he didn't blink. He stared at the bushes, hoping desperately for movement and seeing none.

The creature dodged around trees as it picked its way smoothly toward him, closing the distance.

Grimacing, Seth knew he couldn't wait any longer. He had to move. He had to *move*.

Finally, blinking, he darted away, going the same direction the Dallas lookalike dog had gone. The creature was close now, and he expected to feel a tentacle wrap around him any second. But its size was a hindrance in the woods. Seth picked a path that took him between close-growing trees, slowly pulling away from his gruesome pursuer.

He huffed as he ran limping up a sloping hill. Just ahead, over the hill's crest, he could see the tops of trees, some of them tilting badly. He knew the terrain well, and he knew that the hill had once extended upward much further. But when he came to the crest of the hill, he saw what had happened. It wasn't really a crest at all. He stood at the edge of a huge sinkhole, about a hundred yards in diameter. Some of the trees had managed to stay upright after the ground under them had given way. But many of them had fallen over or were leaning precipitously.

The sound of the creature approaching was getting louder. But he didn't know where to go. Not until he saw a faint bluish-white glow coming from the side of the sinkhole ahead and to his left. The dog with the glowing stake still in its mouth emerged from a cave there, stopping and looking at him for a moment before turning and heading back into the cave.

Seth jumped down into the sinkhole, rolling painfully as he landed. But he was up and running again before the creature reached the hole behind him.

CHAPTER 40

The sense of déjà vu made Seth feel like he was in a dream as he made his way through the cave, clambering over piles of fallen rocks and outcroppings. The wounds in his hand and leg throbbed, but there was a faraway sense to them. It was like he was playing a video game and the controller was vibrating while a ring of ragged red flashed on the screen, indicating that his character's health was getting low.

Even the strange roots that ran along the walls and ceiling added to the sense of unreality. The dark red tendrils were like no roots he'd ever seen before, and he knew they belonged to whatever creature was pulling the strings here. They weren't roots. Not anymore than the veins in a human body were roots. But Seth dared not touch them, afraid that if he did, they would pull themselves from the ground and rip him limb from limb.

So he avoided them as he moved deeper into the chill air of the cave. The dog was nowhere to be seen, and Seth used his phone to light his way. There wasn't much power left, but he hoped it would get him to where he needed to go.

And where's that? he asked himself. *Where am I going? And what am I supposed to do when I get there?*

A faint rustling sound came from behind him. He was still being pursued. He had no doubt about that. The giant creature couldn't possibly have fit into the cave, but the other human-creatures could be rushing after him. No choice but to keep going forward. Following the dog who wasn't Dallas. The dog carrying an impossible piece of glowing cross.

Seth had been doubting the existence of God for many years. Ever since his father's drinking had gotten really bad. Which was around the same time that he started comprehending the world as it really was, instead of how he wanted it to be. The bubble of his childhood had been slowly popping for many years—these kinds of things took time, he figured. There was no single moment of revelation. No epiphany that opened your eyes to the terror of the world. The injustice. The hate and derision.

At least there had been no such moment for him. In fact, he figured he was lucky to have lived in that childhood bubble at all. It was a luxury of growing up in a household where reasonably healthy food was readily available and the electricity didn't get shut off and there were no serious medical issues to drain the family bank accounts.

For years he'd been finding it hard to square what he'd heard at church camp and in the increasingly rare church visits with what he was learning about the world. He wanted to believe in God—any god, really. He recognized the comfort and the strength and the sense of community that came with it. But he also saw the hateful things people did in the name of their god or gods. And the cognitive dissonance had grown to the point where he oscillated between halfhearted belief and vehement nihilism.

He recalled the lesson on belief they'd been discussing on the last night at camp, shortly before he'd stuffed himself with sweets and fallen asleep. It was a lesson he'd heard many times before, always in different words. The crux of it was that humans possessed enough reasoning power to determine that there is a God, but not enough to know God's will. This had made sense to Seth as a child, but he could no longer square the circle.

It seemed to him that the whole premise of any religion rested on this central tenet: it's impossible to know God's will, so don't even try. Just know that He does everything for a reason.

It came down to faith. Because belief without faith was like a chair missing a leg. It would never be a solid platform.

But if Seth didn't believe in God—or if he lacked faith in God's plan—then why was he the one going into the cave now? Why was he the one still alive, and not his mother or Melanie or Sammy or Russell?

He couldn't believe that this was some lesson designed to get him to have faith in God again. If this was what it took to do that, Seth wanted no part of the God behind the scenes. So many were dead. So many had died horrible, violent deaths. Why hadn't God stepped in before tonight to prevent all the tragedy? Why did it always seem that He showed up only after some horrible thing happened to give strength to the survivors?

As Seth limped deeper into the cave, he knew he should be grateful for falling on the pile of wood outside the church. He knew he should be thankful that the dogs had saved him when it looked like he was about to be killed or invaded.

But he wasn't.

He was angry. His mother was gone. So was his dog. And his friends. Everyone he ever knew was now dead or close to it. There was not even a spark of thankfulness inside him. And he suddenly regretted not going through with the planned suicide back at the old man's house. If this was what awaited him in life, what was the point? He hadn't been able to make any difference at all. Sammy was dead. Melanie was dead. Dallas was dead. His continued presence in the world had done nothing but prolong the inevitable.

There is no plan, he thought with the clarity of bright-shining belief. There was nothing. Only human folly and the evil coursing through the roots along the tunnel walls and ceiling.

So what's the fucking point?

Up ahead, his flashlight beam picked out a drop. He slowed as he came to the edge, shining his light down at the pool of clear water below. The scene was similar to the one in his dream, but key details were different. The funnel of rock that held the water was lined with dark red tendrils. The hole at the bottom of the funnel, beyond which his light couldn't penetrate, seemed to be the source of them all. From there, they spread out, going in all directions. But the thicker roots seemed to point toward town. Some of them disappeared into the walls, while others led into dark crevasses or small tunnels only big enough for rodents. Then, of course, were the ones Seth had been following down the large tunnel.

There was a ledge on the opposite side of the pool, only a few feet above the water. And right on cue, the dog that wasn't Dallas appeared from the darkness, the stake still in her mouth. Her fur was wet—it hadn't been in the dream. And she didn't bark at him. She peered up at him and then padded to the edge, dropping the stake into the pool of water. Then she sat down and looked up at him again with her dark eyes.

From behind Seth came the sounds of movement, growing louder.

He looked at the pool, then at the ledge where the dog sat. It was clear that he was supposed to swim down into the hole with the stake. But he was done doing what he was *supposed* to do. He wasn't going to bat for a god that had taken away his friends—if there even *was* a god.

Still, he knew he had to do something. He wasn't about to stick around so he could be brutally murdered or infected and turned into one of them. He could get down there and continue through the tunnel on the other side. Maybe he could find a way out. Then he could get help—that had been the plan all along, after all. It wasn't like he could really do anything to stop the creature. Not Seth Granger, the painfully average small-town kid who, if given the chance, would probably grow up to be a hurtful alcoholic, just like his old man.

He sat down on the drop-off, legs dangling as he looked down at the craggy rock wall for footholds. If he jumped into the water, there was no way he could keep his phone dry. And he needed it to find his way out of here. Throwing it across would be the same thing as dropping it in the water. It might survive the throw, but he doubted it.

Putting the phone into his mouth, he flipped around and eased himself down, finding a foothold with the toes of his right foot. Then he found one with his left.

As he shifted back to look for his next move, the stone under his left foot gave way, the rock cracking and falling. Seth held on with his hands, biting into his phone from the pain emanating from the oozing wound in his left palm. He kicked his left foot around, looking for another place to put it. Desperate, he brought it over and tried to shove it into the hole his right foot was occupying. With the added weight, that foothold shifted under him. And then gave way altogether. Seth's hands slipped, and he fell backward into the pool of water with a splash.

He'd managed to hold his phone in his mouth, and as he came to the surface, he grabbed it with his right hand, extending it above his head and shaking it while he kicked his legs and left arm to swim to the side of the pool where the dog now stood. His flashlight was somehow still working, and he hoped it would continue to do so despite the phone getting wet.

As he got closer, the dog barked at him once. Then again. When he came to within a foot of the ledge, the dog was in full frenzy, barking and snarling and baring her teeth at him.

His flashlight flickered.

Oh no.

Seth reached out to grab the shelf of rock, pulling his hand back when the dog lunged for it, still barking and snarling.

"Let me up!" he shouted, looking at the dog. Then he saw something behind her as his flashlight flickered again. Something that made his stomach drop.

There was no tunnel. About five feet into the hole, the passage ended in a rock wall. There was no escape that way. And his pursuers would be upon him at any moment.

There was only one way to go. Down.

The flashlight on Seth's phone flickered again and then went out.

The only light in the cave came from the glowing wooden stake floating two feet away.

CHAPTER 41

S take in hand, Seth sucked in a deep breath and ducked under the water, muffling the sound of the barking dog. As he swam down, kicking into the dark funnel below, he heard a splash from above. A moment later, the shockwave rolled over him, shifting him slightly in the water. Glancing over his shoulder, he could just make out the shape of a man swimming down toward him.

Another muffled splash sounded, and another man was in the water.

Then a third.

He could not see tentacles coming from their mouths or fingers. Something about the cross. The more of the creature they had in them, the more pronounced its effects. But they didn't have to have tentacles to kill him. They could just use their bare hands.

A small splash came, and Seth could see that the dog was now in the water. And it seemed to be attacking one of the men. But the other two were coming for him.

Seth turned back around and swam as hard as he could, suddenly thankful for all the swimming he'd done at Camp Stillwater over the summer. Almost every day, he'd gotten into the water. He and some of the other kids had even competed to see who could hold their breath the longest and who could swim the fastest. Seth had never been at the top of either list, but he also hadn't been at the bottom.

Using the light from the stake to show him the way, he put all he had into swimming, his clothes and shoes hindering his efforts. He dared not glance back again, but he knew that the men were close behind. He could feel their effects on the water as they swam behind him.

The tunnel curved, and Seth followed it, no idea how far he would have to go before he could take another breath. The red-black roots closed together as the tunnel narrowed. And as Seth passed close to them with the stake in his hand, they seemed to shrivel, as though pulling away from the item.

His breath was running out fast, each kick of his legs and sweep of his arms pulling more oxygen from his lungs. But he could see no exit to the tunnel. The illumination only reached so far. Panic tightened his chest. Something touched his right foot. A hand. They were close.

Unable to help himself, he cried out in the water, sending more precious air from his lungs. He'd lost track of direction and could no longer tell if he was swimming up, down, or sideways.

He'd heard drowning was pleasant after the sheer panic and unadulterated fear of the lungs filling with water. It provided a small amount of solace. At least he wouldn't die at the hands of the creature.

His body wasn't yet ready to give up, though, even if his mind was. His legs kicked and arms swept as the burning in his chest ratcheted up.

He looked back again, seeing that the men were close. He'd pulled away somehow, but it wouldn't last. He was losing strength.

The back of his head and his shoulders broke through the surface first, and he automatically sucked in a huge breath, surprising himself. Before he knew quite what he was doing, he scrambled up a sloping shelf of rock out of the water. There were loose rocks here and there, the root-tendrils snaking around them as they led out of the water. Seth dropped the stake and grabbed a rock the size of a bowling ball, spinning around just as the first man's head emerged from the water.

Screaming, Seth threw the rock at the man's head with both hands. The stone hit the man in the forehead, collapsing his skull. Both rock and man went under the water, and the man's floating body came up a moment later, followed closely by the second man's thrashing body.

Spinning back around to find another rock, Seth noticed that the stake was sizzling through the two arm-sized roots he'd thrown it on. Like a piece of heated metal set on a block of ice.

He grabbed another stone, this one the size of a softball. As he turned around, the man lunged out of the water, tackling him to the ground.

Seth hit the ground hard, landing half on the strange root-veins and half on the rocky ground. The man gripped his face with one hand as he shifted on his knees, straddling Seth. His other hand came down toward the teenager's throat.

The man dug his fingers into Seth's eyes, trying to gouge them out. Seth screamed and lifted the stone, which he'd managed to hang onto. Unable to see, he whipped the stone up at the place where he'd last seen the man's head. There was a thump that resonated up his arm, and the man's hands came away, his weight coming off Seth's hips.

As Seth sat up, opening his eyes, he could just see the man through the swirling colors in his vision. He was now on his feet, holding the side of his bloody head. One of his eyes was looking off at an oblique angle. He looked afraid and confused.

Seth rushed toward him, raising the stone over his head. He smashed it into the man, bashing his face in. The man went down, falling with his ruined head in the water.

Seth looked at the pool for several long moments, waiting to see if anyone else would emerge. The moving surface slowed.

Dropping the stone, Seth turned around and grabbed the stake off the ground, where it had flattened and desiccated the root-veins there. He held it up so its light would shine into the cave. And he stepped back once, eyes going wide at what he saw.

The cave was a tunnel about fifteen feet across and seven feet tall at its widest point, where Seth now stood. It seemed to narrow as the ground went slightly uphill, coming to a point where it was only about six feet across and four feet tall. Beyond that, Seth could not see. But what he *could* see was enough.

The root-veins seemed to have their origin at the end of this cavern, through the hole up the sloping floor. There were hundreds of them. While many of them went down into the water, others took pathways through the rock. And while there were still gaps between them here, where the tunnel-like cavern was widest, this wasn't the case up where the cave narrowed. There, he could see in the light from the stake, the root-veins were so close together, they obscured the ground.

He knew instinctively that whatever had caused all the bloodshed and terror this night was just beyond that passageway. But it was a passageway covered with those root-veins.

Seth brought his attention down to his feet and prodded one of the reddish-black tendrils with the toe of his shoe. It wasn't like the tentacles that had nearly killed him more than once already. These were different. Harder. More robust. And they weren't trying to strangle him at the moment, which said a lot about their purpose.

Maybe they're attached to those limbs planted around town, Seth thought. *Maybe that's how it extends its reach. It infects people through the water. But once they're infected, they can only go so far away from whatever this thing is. So it has to plant infected limbs everywhere.*

It was only a guess, but he figured it was a pretty good one. It made sense to him.

He turned and looked up at the roughly circular passageway coated with bunched-up root-veins. And he started forward, forcing himself to take each step. Only now did he have a chance to contemplate the stench in the air. He'd been smelling it ever since emerging from the water, but he'd had larger concerns. Now, the malodorous reek was enough to twist his stomach into knots.

His entire body shook as he made his way forward. But not because he was wet in the relatively cool cave. He shook with fear.

Now that he wasn't being chased—now that he wasn't reacting defensively and instinctively to save his life—he had time to think about the absurdity of it all once again. And with each step closer to the dark passage, the thought that he was the wrong person for this only solidified itself. It was only a fluke that he was still alive. A fluke that wouldn't last much longer. Especially now that he had to face something so powerful it had killed an entire town.

His wet shoes squelched on the root-veins that gave slightly under his weight. The glow from the stake seemed to strengthen with every step.

As he came up to the passageway, which was about four feet in diameter, he held up the stake to let the light shine through. The stench was clearly coming from beyond the passage. But as he peered inside, he couldn't see what was causing it. All he could see was a large cavern not unlike the one he stood in. Only the ceiling was much higher—so high the glow from the stake couldn't reach it.

But there was something strange about the floor. The root-veins seemed to disappear into a glittering black substance just a few feet on the other side of the short passageway. The black substance seemed to cover large and small stones, like it was some kind of strange moss. And there was a resonant hum coming from in there, low but unmistakable.

As he looked closer, he thought he realized what he was seeing. But it didn't seem possible.

He moved back toward the water and the two men he'd killed. After selecting a golf-ball sized stone off the cave floor, he moved back up to the passageway. Holding the stake out with his left hand, he tossed the stone into the adjacent cavern. A great buzz filled the air, and the ground seemed to levitate where the stone hit. Then the floating ground broke up, revealing individual insects whirling around angrily in the air.

The ground wasn't coated in a strange moss. It was covered with flies.

Before the insects decided to settle back onto the cave floor, Seth saw what they'd been obscuring. The floor was coated in a carpet of rotting flesh. What Seth had thought was a stone of some kind was really a rotting human head sticking out of the flesh. Maggots writhed in the man's open mouth. But his eyelids came open, revealing black eyes that looked over at Seth.

Leaning through the passageway as far as he dared, Seth used the glowing stake to see as far into the cave as he could.

There had to be a billion flies there, coating what looked like a football field's worth of maggot-infested flesh that not only covered the floor, but the walls as well. And if every lump under the insects was a human head or limb, then a good portion of the town was there—at least parts of them.

Up toward the rear of the cave, Seth could just make out a large structure, about the size of a tall, round man. At a glance, it almost looked like a strange-colored rock. But as he peered at it, the thing moved. It opened up like a blooming flower briefly, strings of slime stretching between the six segments of its shell before they closed again.

Seth stared at it, eyes wide, holding his breath. After thirty seconds or so, it moved again, opening briefly and then closing. *Is it breathing?* Seth thought.

The flies he'd disturbed had settled again, obscuring the rotting head that had been staring at Seth. Still leaning through the passage, he swept the stake toward the ground, making sure the path was clear. It was a drop—the floors of the two caves weren't level—and the ground below was covered in about a foot of water. The liquid extended right up to where the fly-covered flesh started.

He didn't know what he was going to do with a single stake. But he knew he couldn't stay here. There was no telling when more people would come for him.

Seth crouched and stepped up into the passageway, which was only about two feet wide. The root-veins were slightly harder here, closer to their source in the rotting flesh.

He hopped down into the larger cave, feet splashing in the water. He expected something to happen, but nothing did. The flies remained where they were, milling about.

He peered up toward the strange creature, trying to see what was on its shell-like structure. It didn't take him long to recognize the grinning human skulls dotting its mottled shell segments. There were other bones, too, all belonging to humans. Hands. Feet. Legs. Ribcages. It had somehow used humans to create a shell around itself. They were fossilized, stuck together with a substance that looked from a distance like red coral.

Still shaking, Seth sloshed forward and stepped onto the flesh. A terrible screaming sound erupted from all around. Distant rumbles started in the ground, causing subtle vibrations. All the flies took flight, and Seth was suddenly blind as the insects flew at his face, into his mouth and nostrils. What he did manage to see, in little flashes between flies, were the limbs and heads the flies had been obscuring. They jerked and spasmed. Some of them were newer, the flesh not yet badly rotted, while others were older.

Raising his hands in a vain effort to keep the flies from his face, Seth stepped forward. He knew he had to get to the strange thing near the back of the cave. What he was going to do when he got there, he had no idea. But as he stepped forward again, a hand sticking out of the flesh grabbed his right ankle. It squeezed, and Seth was sure it would break the joint if he didn't do something.

He bent down and stabbed the limb with the stake, puncturing the skin. But it didn't let go. He stabbed it again and again, trying to yank his leg away. Finally, its grip loosened enough for Seth to free his leg with a jerk. He fell onto the disgusting mass, flies still attacking him. The distant rumbles grew closer, the vibrations more insistent. He felt a terrible pain in his left ear as one of the heads bit into him. Screaming, Seth scrambled up, yanking his head and coming away without a chunk of his ear.

As he tried to get to his feet, a hand grabbed his left arm at the wrist. It clamped down with a force no human had, and he felt the joint being crushed. Through the swirling cloud of flies, Seth stabbed the arm with the stake. He punctured the skin, and the grip loosened slightly. But when he went to yank his arm away, the hand redoubled its grip—this time around his four fingers.

Gritting his teeth, Seth stabbed the arm again, but it didn't let go. In his desperation, he tried to yank his hand away again. But as he did so, the arm yanked the other way. Seth felt an agonizing crunch as the four fingers of his left hand broke. He screamed again, but it was nothing compared to the screaming still coming from the creature, seeming to have its source everywhere and nowhere.

He stabbed the arm in a pain-driven frenzy. Finally, it let go. Seth cradled his left hand to his chest and stumbled back toward the passageway, spitting flies out of his mouth as he went. He clambered up and launched himself back to the other cave, rolling on the root-veins and coming to rest staring at his left hand and the fingers at odd angles to his palm.

As much as he wanted to lose himself in that pain, to forget the world around him and wallow in his suffering, he couldn't help but notice that the cave seemed to be collapsing. Underneath him, the root-veins were squirming. In the light of the stake still held in his right hand, he looked down toward the bloodstained water. And he saw what was happening.

The root-veins were retracting from the walls. They were pulling themselves back. And in so doing, they were changing the structural integrity of the cave. Seth realized that he must have triggered this when stepping upon the rotting mass in the adjacent cavern. It was the last line of defense. Maybe the root-veins were like giant tentacles, coming back to kill the intruder. Or maybe the creature knew that the cave would collapse. Maybe it knew that any human intruder wouldn't survive a cave-in. But *it* would survive. It surely would. That hard shell surrounding the thing would keep it from being crushed. He was sure of it.

Stones and boulders dropped from the ceiling as the root-veins slowly pulled themselves from the walls. Cracks spread across the walls and floors. Seth was safe where he was, given that he was completely surrounded by the strange appendages. But he wouldn't remain safe for long. He would soon be crushed by boulders or ripped apart by the retracting appendages.

And he welcomed the thought. He just wanted the pain to end. He wanted the despair to be gone.

He wanted oblivion.

Dropping the stake, Seth curled into a ball, hugging his legs with his right arm. The tears came easily, streaking down his cheeks as the pain in his hand and his ear and his leg became his whole world. The buzzing of the flies and the screeching from the adjacent cavern faded as the rumbling and vibrations grew louder and more violent.

"I can't," Seth whimpered as he rocked back and forth. "I can't."

The creature's defenses had worked. It had won and Seth had lost.

And that was the end of it.

CHAPTER 42

G iving up was a funny thing.

It was a kind of freedom Seth had never known. It was an end to the worrying he'd been perfecting since his father's drinking had gotten bad enough to pop his perfect bubble.

Or at least it would be once the end came.

But as he sat curled in a ball, waiting to die in the rumbling cave, he couldn't stop a bit of worry from seeping into his newly freed mind. Only it didn't start as worry. It started as a memory, vibrant and immense, like a vivid hallucination.

He was at camp again and it was still a week away from the last day. The melancholy was still several days off. And in the mind of a sixteen-year-old boy, several summer days might as well have been an eternity.

Seth, Darius, and a few other guys were walking through the woods after attending a small fellowship gathering. While the other guys joked or talked about girls, Seth was silent, his mind still back at the gathering. He was thinking about something the counselor said during the lesson. A verse from the book of Matthew, attributed to God: "I am with you always, even until the end of the world."

He knew it was supposed to be comforting to know that God was with you always, even in the worst of circumstances. But he wasn't comforted. As he thought about it, a flood of anger tensed his muscles.

He looked up at his friends. Darius and Elijah were talking about a movie that had come out while camp was in session. They were excited to watch it when they got back home. John ran to a tree and launched himself up, grabbing a branch with his hands. The thing snapped, and he fell to the ground with the piece of wood in his hands. Everyone but Seth, John included, burst out laughing.

For the first time in his young life, Seth comprehended the world at large—as much as any human can comprehend such a vast and unknowable thing.

His world had always been small. Seven Springs, relatively sheltered from the things that went on in larger towns or big cities, had been enough for him. Of course, he'd always known that the world was vast. He knew approximately how many billions of people were out there, living their lives. But he'd never really given it much serious thought. Thinking about the world had always been like looking at something through a haze, like the kind that sometimes filled the streets of Seven Springs in the early morning hours. The world was there, partially obscured. There was no doubt about that. But he could never see it clearly. Never truly comprehend it.

Not until that moment in the forest.

He was overcome with a sense of appreciation, which nearly brought him to tears right there in the woods with his friends. But the anger he'd been feeling lately was still there, under the surface. The two emotions mixed strangely as he thought about how awful it would be for the world to end. He observed his friends from the back of the group, thinking about how much comfort they would get from knowing that God was with them when the world ended. And he knew it didn't have to be the apocalypse. He knew that each death was a world dying. And that all his friends would one day have to die. He knew this not logically, as he had known it since learning about death as a child, but emotionally.

A thought came rushing into his mind, surprising him. *I wonder what it's like to kill yourself.*

The thought stopped him in his tracks. The other boys moved on without him.

Seth looked up at the sun shining through the trees, wondering why he would think such a thing. He'd been thinking about death, but suicide was . . . well it wasn't all that different, he realized. It had never seemed like something he could do, in those rare instances when he thought about it. But he *could* do it. Anyone could.

"Grange, you good?" Darius called from up ahead.

Seth looked at his friend and forced a smile. "Yeah," he said, hustling to keep up.

And as he caught up, he felt something change inside.

Was it a bad change? A good one?

He wasn't sure. He just felt the shift. And he did feel a little heavier.

He glanced at his friends as they walked toward the mess hall for lunch. Seth felt like he was seeing them clearly for the first time. Like he was seeing the world clearly for the first time.

No, not just seeing it. *Perceiving* it.

The memory suddenly faded away, replaced by the dark cave, the rumbling, and the crashing crunch of rocks falling. The root-veins were shifting faster underneath him.

But that worry stayed with him. That worry that he'd been experiencing ever since the change in the forest that day. The worry about his friends who lived in other towns. The worry about all the other people out there, living their lives.

It felt like his entire world had been destroyed tonight. But that was far from the case. His world had expanded in the woods that day. It was massive. So much larger than Seven Springs. It was *everything*.

He thought of Darius Lovett and his mother in Victorville. He thought of Jake Sullivan, Elijah Ryan, and Tricia Ulgard. He thought of John and Buster and the camp counselors and the eight billion other people living in the world.

While Seth Granger's world would end if he sat here and did nothing, what would happen to all those people? What would happen if he let the monster go on living? If he didn't at least try to stop it, despite his pain and his fear and his shaking body?

Maybe God *was* there for everyone at the end. Seth figured *something* was. But God wasn't enough, he realized with blinding clarity. Humans had to do their parts. *He* had to do *his* part. Otherwise, what was the point of any god?

It seemed so obvious now, like he should've known it a long time ago. Like some unconscious part of him had known it and had held it there for the rest of him to see when the time was right. He suddenly realized that the faith argument of every religion—the very foundation of religion as a concept—made sense when you thought about it in a certain light. Whether there was a god or not didn't really matter. What mattered was the belief, and what came along with it. The notion that a god would swoop down and keep bad things from happening took humans out of the equation altogether. It was a dangerous way to think.

Humans were the key. Without humans, there could be no gods. And if people didn't do whatever was in their power to stop things from happening, they were just as bad as an absentee god.

It made so much sense now. *It's not up to God*, Seth thought. *It's up to us. It's up to me. Because there is no one else. I'm the only one here. And I'm here for a reason.*

God or Universe or the spirit of all that is good, he'd been led here by something. And he had to finish it.

Now.

Seth lurched to his feet, stumbling on the shifting root-veins. He reached down to get the stake, which had flattened a portion of one of the root-veins. But that didn't stop the thing from moving with all the others.

Lifting the stake in his good hand, he glanced once more toward the water with the two bodies floating in it. As he did, his vision caught on something. It was a crack forming in the wall near the water. As the crack expanded, a chunk of stone broke off from it and tumbled down, followed by a pile of loose gravel and dirt. But something came out of the wall amid that loose gravel and dirt. Something cylindrical. Something man-made. Seth was sure of it.

Acting on an instinct deeper than anger or curiosity, Seth darted that way and grabbed the tip of the cylindrical object, managing to lift it up with the fingers of the same hand holding the stake. He dodged back, away from the moving root-veins, and looked at the item he held in his right hand.

It was an ancient stick of dynamite, whitish crystals stuck to its waxy tan paper. *Nitroglycerin.* The word floated in his mind like it had been crouching in its dark reaches, waiting to come forward. With it came the knowledge, probably gleaned from some movie or TV show, that old dynamite could be incredibly unstable. Especially if it was sweating nitroglycerin. A strong enough bump, and it could explode.

Seth turned around and faced the adjacent cave and the unseen creature therein. He transferred the stick of dynamite to his injured left hand, clamping it to his palm with his thumb. His four broken fingers were swollen and beginning to discolor. They throbbed with every heartbeat. He had to grit his teeth to hold the dynamite against his bloody palm, trying to ignore the pain it caused.

Gripping the stake in his right hand, he readied himself to do his part. As he stepped toward the hole, something wrapped around his left ankle and yanked him off his feet.

Acting more on an instinct to protect his damaged hand than one to keep the dynamite from being jarred, Seth twisted in the air and held his left hand up before hitting the ground. A smallish root-vein had worked its way all the way out of the stone and wrapped itself around him. It had a dozen or more smaller roots branching off from its tip, almost like a many-fingered hand. As he stabbed at it, the thing moved, jerking him further toward the portion of the cave that wasn't held together by other root veins. A rock crashed down nearby, narrowly missing his leg.

Instead of stabbing at the part of the root that was near his ankle, Seth shifted and stabbed at the portion that ran back into the other cavern, toward its source.

It didn't let go at first. Not until he stabbed it so much that it was almost severed did it finally unwrap itself from his leg. Getting to his feet, Seth ran toward the hole. Some of the other root-veins were coming fully out of the ground now. There was no more time. He had to do this now.

Climbing over the wriggling root-veins, he entered the other cave, looking up toward the dark thing near the top of the sloping cavern. At the edge of the fleshy substance coating the floor, beyond the reach of any of the limbs or heads, Seth stood for a moment. He was waiting for the shell-like structure to open again, like it had earlier.

But it didn't open. Seconds passed.

There was no more time to waste.

Knowing he had to get closer, Seth looked for a route through the limbs. It didn't look promising.

He could try throwing the stick of dynamite from where he stood, but he wasn't confident in his accuracy. This was the only chance he had. Anything but a direct hit wouldn't work. And even then, he wasn't sure it would do the trick. He wanted to throw the dynamite inside the thing. But if it was no longer opening and closing, he didn't know how he could manage it.

Either way, he had to get closer. He had to be sure.

He sensed movement from behind him and turned in time to see one of the many medium-sized root-veins whipping at him. He jumped out of the way as the thing flew past, wrapping itself around a leg sticking out of the glistening mass. A small cloud of flies launched into the air at the disturbance.

With no other choice and no more time, Seth jumped onto the mass before the root-tentacle could unwrap itself and try again. The awful screaming erupted again as the limbs and heads started their frenzied movements. Flies filled the air as he ran. He tried to stick to the route he'd planned but was unable to see more than two feet in front of him. The insects flew into his nose and bounced off his eyes, but Seth kept his mouth firmly shut.

He jumped over arms, dodged kicking legs, and stepped on top of heads. He moved swiftly, getting closer to the strange craggy thing that had to be this creature's version of a brain, encased in a protective skull made of long-dead people.

Halfway there, he slowed, bringing the stake up and clamping it in his left armpit. Then he grabbed the dynamite in his right hand and got ready to throw. Coming to a stop, he peered through the flies and made sure he was aiming at the right area.

He threw the dynamite, dropping to the ground just after releasing it. A hand reached out and grabbed his left arm. A nearby foot kicked him in the side.

The stick of explosives tumbled through the air, end over end, and struck the creature's craggy shell—and exploded.

The cave shook, the roar of the explosion sounding to Seth like the apocalypse. The brittle clatter of stones falling followed the blast. Debris rained down on Seth, who had his head covered with his free arm, the stake lying under his body. He expected the hand grabbing his left arm to go limp. He expected the foot kicking him to stop. And he expected the screaming and rumbling to cease. But none of it did.

The screaming got louder, the rumbling more insistent. Seth looked up to see that many of the flies had been decimated, allowing him to get a clear view of the creature. The thing was now surrounded by loose rocks that had apparently fallen from the ceiling overhead. Only the top couple of feet stuck out of the rock pile. Still, Seth could see enough to know that the dynamite had broken part of the shell that protected it, but apparently it hadn't done much else.

Knowing he wasn't done, he grabbed the stake and attacked the hand holding his upper left arm, stabbing it repeatedly until it let go. Screaming as he used his injured left hand to get up, Seth ran toward the creature, once again dodging the moving body parts as he ran.

He climbed atop the pile of rocks, angling toward the broken section of shell, which gave him a view inside the structure. As he came upon it, he could see a mass of large and hairy worms squirming inside. They were each about as large around as a good-sized garter snake, but they had stubby little hairs and they glistened as they writhed, dark pink in color.

As far as Seth could tell, there was no beginning or end to them. They simply looped down toward the bottom of the shell, creating a writhing mass about the size of a small child.

Fighting his revulsion, Seth stuck his arm into the shell and thrust the stake down into the writhing mass. He stabbed slightly off-center, the tip of the stake sinking down into the slimy flesh. The scream-ing—which Seth could now tell was coming from the creature he was now attacking—was so loud it drowned out the rumbling sound of the root-veins pulling out of the earth.

As he pulled the stake back up, the mass shifted, a hole opening in the center. Before Seth could react, a rush of rancid air came out of the newly formed hole, propelling thousands of little spores like black dandelion seeds. Seth inhaled many of them, which got him coughing and hacking even as he jammed the spike back down. He sunk it down into the hole, and the entire thing spasmed around his arm. But he pulled the appendage back out and resumed his frenzied stabbing.

The shell segment his chest was pressed up against moved, trying to throw him off. But Seth hunkered down and kept stabbing with the glowing stake, the rocks piled around the creature keeping it from opening the shell segments more than a few inches. Black liquid came out of the holes he produced with the sharp piece of wood. The strange worm-like things, which were really just part of one thing, all connected, writhed and tried to pull away. But they had nowhere to go. The creature's defenses had failed.

Seth kept stabbing.

He stabbed for a long time. The screaming continued, fluctuating with each thrust of the stake.

And when he finally realized that the thing was no longer moving, he found that it was no longer screaming, either. *He* was the one screaming.

Seth pulled the stake out of the pinkish-black mass of torn meat and looked over the rest of the structure. The limbs and heads were no longer moving. They were all limp. There was no more rumbling. The root-veins he could barely see in the glow from the stake were still.

Breathing heavily, he peered around, waiting for something else to happen.

Nothing did.

He was already half-sitting on the piled rocks, but now he slumped down, too exhausted to move off the uncomfortable stones.

A rush of emotions overwhelmed him, and he broke down, sobbing and laughing at the same time.

But he knew it wasn't over. The hardest part was yet to come.

Because he knew that going on with life after this would be so much harder than defeating the strange creature.

Still, for the first time since coming back from camp, Seth Granger felt an emotion he didn't think he'd ever feel again.

He felt hope.

CHAPTER 43

S eth made his way down across the spongy substance coating the ground. The limbs remained limp. It almost looked as if they had deflated slightly since he'd killed the creature in the shell. But the flies were still there, and they still buzzed erratically as Seth walked down toward the hole to the other cavern. He walked through the ankle-deep water and glanced through the passage, holding the stake up for illumination.

The root-veins in there were no longer moving. A few small rocks fell out of the ceiling here and there, but the rumbling had stopped now that the root-veins were no longer shifting. He could just see the pool of water he'd come through, the two bodies still floating in it. He didn't think he had it in him to swim back through there. He thought there was a better-than-good chance he'd drown. Even if he didn't, it would be hard to climb up that crumbly rock wall.

He stepped back from the hole and shone the light to his right, hoping to find a way out. He realized he hadn't been paying atten-tion to much of anything but the creature when he'd come into this chamber. Maybe there was a way out.

Seth felt his hope swell as the illumination from the stake uncovered what looked like a tunnel there. He walked along, feet splashing in water for a good ten yards before the rough and uneven but still large tunnel angled up out of the water. He followed it for what felt like a little over a hundred yards until he came to a wall of boulders. There were some small gaps at the top, none of them close to large enough for Seth to fit through.

Suddenly, he realized where he was. On the other side of the obstruction was the tunnel up to the church. He didn't have to look through one of the small gaps to know that. The implications came to him, and he pictured that awful creature who'd killed Melanie coming this way from where it had been made by the creature. Surely it had been the one to pile all the boulders here, to prevent easy access to the creature pulling the strings.

It meant this was also the way Dallas had come. He didn't think she would've been able to get up that steep wall where Seth had fallen into the pool, but there were so many smaller passageways that couldn't fit a human. He figured she'd used one of them to escape. To come and save Seth when he'd needed her most.

He peered around, hoping against hope that Dallas was still alive.

He needed to find a way out. Then he remembered the loose rocks that had fallen all around the creature after the dynamite exploded. They had to have come from the ceiling. Maybe they'd revealed a way out.

He made his way back along the tunnel and into the cave. He passed the limp limbs, ignoring the smell of rotting flesh and the flies constantly bouncing against him. Then he climbed up the rock pile once again. Holding the stake up, he could see that there was a passageway above the now-dead creature. He didn't know if it actually led to a way out, but it was his only shot.

He studied the wall and decided he could probably make it up the fifteen or so feet using only his legs and one hand.

He grasped the stake with left thumb against palm. And he started climbing.

His body felt heavy, and the going was tough, but he made it to a section of relatively flat ground that was littered with stones. Getting to his feet, he headed the only way he could.

His right foot kicked something metal, which bumped across the ground. He looked down, using the glowing stake to see. It was an old metal can. He could just make out a couple of the faded words on the lid: "Blasting Caps."

Seth straightened and continued along, hopeful that there was an exit up ahead.

He didn't have to go far before coming to a latticework of old, rotting wood. Peering between a couple of slats, he could see trees. A warm breeze kicked up and stirred his sweat-matted hair.

After kicking out a couple of slats, he got out of the cave, unsure exactly where he was. But he was out of the cave. He was out, and it was over.

He had to climb over a barbed wire fence and wander around for a little while before he recognized the area. He'd been on the other side of the hill from the church and the sinkhole. It was private property, which was why he hadn't recognized it.

He moved through the woods cautiously, heading toward where he'd last seen Dallas. He saw no sign of the huge creature that had chased him from the church grounds.

He found Dallas's body on the ground behind an irregular row of bushes. The injuries she'd suffered when thrown into the tree had been too much. A sob escaped his throat as he fell to his knees beside her body. He ran his right hand across her head and down her neck. Then collapsed next to her and put his head up under her chin, imitating their version of a hug—something they'd done for a decade. He recalled how they'd done their special greeting when he arrived home from camp with Mr. Winchell. He thought about how it had made him feel so much better. And about how calm she would always get when they did their version of a hug. But she was never calm like this. She'd never been lifeless like this.

He stayed like that for a long time, only pulling away when his stomach spasmed and he felt hot liquid racing up his throat. Scrambling away from Dallas, he got to his knees just before vomiting stringy black bile onto the ground. He remembered the strange spores the creature had shot out when he was stabbing it. He'd swallowed some, he was sure of it.

As he got shakily to his feet, he prayed they were all out of his body.

Silently promising to come back for Dallas's body, Seth limped away. He came upon the church from the side. As he got closer, he heard retching from nearby. Freezing, he peered around at the darkness. The retching continued. And it sounded like it was coming from inside the church.

Seth moved around to the front, holding the stake out, ready to use it. He opened the door with his good hand, then stepped inside. The single light was still on over the stage. And thanks to its illumination, he could see Melanie on the stage. She was on her knees, convulsing, a puddle of lumpy black vomit between her hands.

As he stepped further into the church, he saw several people slumped down in two of the pews that had been shoved to the sides of the building. They had drying streams of dark liquid coming out of their eyes, noses, and mouths. His heart sped up when he saw his mother sitting there. She was holding hands with the people on either side. And her eyes were open, staring blankly at the wall where the cross had once been.

He rushed up to her. "Mom?" he said, dropping the stake and

putting his hand on her arm. It was cold and clammy.

"Mom?!" he said, tears coming again. He shook her, and her head lolled, looking blankly past him at the only other living person in the building.

Melanie retched and spat.

Seth stood up and stared down at his mother for a long moment. Then he moved around the hole in the floor and looked down. The creature was there at the bottom of the hole, unmoving, all limp tentacles and blank, horrified faces. Seth spit into the hole, hitting the creature. It didn't move. He brought the stake up, seeing that its glow was fading. He held it out and let go of it. The stake bounced off the creature below and clattered to the tunnel floor, once again just another piece of wood. The creature didn't move.

Seth moved around the hole and approached Melanie. As he came near, she looked up at him.

He knelt beside her and put his right hand on her back. She was warm. Alive. Human.

She sat up after a long moment, apparently done expelling whatever the creature had put inside her. He put his arm around her back. She returned the gesture. They leaned their heads together and sat in silence.

Outside the church, not far away, came the familiar bark of a dog.

EPILOGUE

The sky in the east was lightening with the promise of dawn. In the faint but growing illumination, Seth and Melanie could see the roadblock. Although not the same one they'd encountered with Bessum and Sharice, the vehicles were arrayed much the same.

The big difference was the bodies.

Some of them were inside the vehicles, barely visible as dark, unmoving shapes. Some lay slumped over truck beds or across hoods. Others lay on the ground, dropped weapons nearby.

Some of them were deformed, limp tentacles sprouting from stretched mouths, fingers split by messy tendrils.

Seth and Melanie moved toward the gathered vehicles, arms still around each other. They leaned heavily on one another, both physically and emotionally. Up ahead, beyond the roadblock, a police cruiser crested a hill. It was coming fast, lights on, but no siren.

As the two teenagers squeezed between a truck and an SUV, the bark of a dog sounded from the woods. Seth turned that way to see the dog that didn't quite look like Dallas come running out from the trees.

"Hey there," Seth said, getting painfully down to one knee as the dog approached.

The police car came to a screeching stop some twenty yards away.

Seth rubbed the dog with his right hand, mangled left hand still swollen and painful. He moved to get up, but the dog put her paw on his forearm.

"What in God's name happened here?" the police officer said, getting out of his squad car and looking at the bodies.

Melanie said nothing. Seth just glanced at the officer and then turned back to the dog. Acting on some instinct that came flooding into him, he ducked his head down toward the dog's nose. A moment later, he felt the dog settle her chin on his head.

They stayed like that for a long moment, Seth's eyes squeezed shut against welling tears.

The officer's boots crunched along the asphalt toward them as Seth and the dog separated.

It's not Dallas, Seth thought. *But it is. How is that possible?*

He stood up and turned toward the officer. He was a county sheriff with a young, plump face and a flattop haircut. He swallowed loudly, one hand on his gun as he surveyed the scene in the burgeoning morning light. Finally, after a long moment of looking at the bodies, he turned his gaze to Seth and Melanie. He swallowed again.

"Are you kids okay?"

As he said the words, a darkness fell across his eyes. Like two curtains of black liquid coming across. Like oil spilling into clean water.

Seth stiffened, unsure whether his imagination was playing tricks on him.

Next to him, the dog who wasn't Dallas started growling.

***

THE END

***

Thanks so much for reading Hole. If you enjoyed the story, you could make this indie author very happy by leaving a review. Reviews tell the Almighty Amazon Algorithm that people enjoy the book, which can help get the work in front of other people who will enjoy it.

Also, don't forget to head over to MatthewDoggettAuthor.com/Horror to get five free short horror stories!

Also by Matthew Doggett

The Undead Trilogy

A zombie apocalypse series with a dash of humor and a whole lot of blood. All three books are available on Amazon and free on Kindle Unlimited.

Praise for Undead Annihilation

"A 'Must Read' for end-of-the-world, we're-all-gonna-die, zombie apocalypse story lovers!" -Reedsy Reviewer

"A work of genius. I've read hundreds of zombie books and this is now in my top 2." -Amazon Reviewer

"This book is a MUST!"

"Not to be missed."

"Undead Annihilation starts off fast and just keeps on going."

***

Horror Short Story Collections

3 Volumes with 20 spine-tingling tales each. Available on Amazon.

***

Hole: A Small-Town Horror Novel

A teenage boy and his dog face a gruesome evil in this coming-of-age horror novel.

***

The Trouble Series – Gritty Action Thrillers You Can Read in Any Order

Too Much Trouble

When a robbery gone wrong lands him in the middle of a cartel war, Trouble starts running out of options fast. And when these operatives cross the line and go after Trouble's friends, only death will stop him from righting the wrongs and making the cartels pay for what they've done. Available on Amazon and free on Kindle Unlimited.

The Death Dealers

When he prevents a murder, Trouble is thrown into a twisted conspiracy that points to the most dangerous gang in Los Angeles. Available on Amazon and free on Kindle Unlimited.

The Deadly Divine

Trouble's a one-man wrecking crew. When he crosses paths with a

charismatic lunatic, can he blow away the murderous brainwashing?
Available on Amazon and free on Kindle Unlimited.

Dead Man's Hatch

Trouble works alone, busting heads and bashing bullies. But when he
joins a crew of trained professionals, he becomes a target in a deadly
revenge plot. Available on Amazon and free on Kindle Unlimited.

Kill Squad

Trouble infiltrates a domestic terrorist ring, posing as a white su-
premacist. The clock is ticking as he races to thwart their plot to
destroy America.

Trouble

When Trouble stands up for what's right, he finds himself in the
crosshairs of an insane small-town sheriff with one goal: kill Trouble.
Available for free when you sign up for my email list at MatthewDo
ggettAuthor.com/Trouble